STICKS & STONES

STICKS & STONES

ERIC PETE

www.urbanbooks.com

Urban Books
1199 Straight Path
West Babylon, NY 11704

ISBN- 13: 978-1-60162-146-7
ISBN- 10: 1-60162-146-9

First Printing February 2009
Printed in the United States of America

10 9 8 7 6 5 4 3 2 1

Distributed by Kensington Publishing Corp.
Submit Wholesale Orders to:
Kensington Publishing Corp.
C/O Penguin Group (USA) Inc.
Attention: Order Processing
405 Murray Hill Parkway
East Rutherford, NJ 07073-2316
Phone: 1-800-526-0275
Fax: 1-800-227-9604

To my Uncle,

Percy Bushnell
1924-2008

A quiet, humble man whose inner strength
was deafening.

You touched so many of us.

Acknowledgments

Tomorrow's never promised, so I give thanks to God for letting me type these words today.

As I write this, I reflect on all the changes that life brings. Both the highs and lows of this past year, I am grateful for. I've been up, I've been down, I've been tested, I've been uplifted, I've been saddened, I've been loved, and maybe even hated on by a few. But in the end, I persevere.

In a past interview of mine (Google it if you want. Thanks Silver Fox!), I mentioned there being a story on the back burner that was, in my opinion, "too tasty a dish to let sit." Well, you're now holding that dish, so grab a fork, a big-ass napkin, and dig in. It's hot and ready to digest. I just hope you got a big appetite.

As writers, we get our inspiration from a variety of sources. This case is no different. Years ago, I saw the movie *Romy and Michelle's High School Reunion*. Did you see it? Funny stuff . . . Post-it notes. Heh. Well, this story is just like that. Not really. But it does have a reunion. And that's just enough to get a brother thinking.

And thoughts can be dangerous. Welcome to *Sticks & Stones*.

To my wife Marsha and my Starlette Chelsea: I couldn't ask for a more wonderful family. You make the long days and nights worth it, for I want nothing but the best for you. Thanks for having my back. Luv ya, mom. Virginia, thank you.

To my people, both by blood and the bonds of friendship, you know who you are and how I feel about you. We go back like babies and pacifiers, Ol' Dirt Dog no liar.

To my ghost readers over the years, Shontea, Jackie, Jacqueline, Carmel, Jamie, Natalie, Bob, Shelia; thank you for allowing me to share in the insanity.

To my agent, Portia Cannon: You da shit! Your tireless dedication is appreciated. Thank you for helping me continue to do what I do.

Dwayne S. Joseph, a fantastic author who deserves much props—Thank you for being such a great friend, bro. Dude, we hit it off from Jump Street and I appreciate all you've done.

Carl Weber, Martha Weber, Candace K, Natalie Weber and the whole Urban Books/Kensington team—Feels good to be part of this Urban Renaissance. A change is in the wind, indeed. Can you feel it?

To a few of my author friends, who've been there whenever stuff gets rough, thank you:

Kim Roby, Kendra Norman Bellamy, Victor McGlothin, Nancy Gilliam, Mary "Honey B" Morrison, Zane, Jacqueline Scott, Reshonda Tate Billingsley, Lolita Files, Dionne Character, Karen E. Quinones Miller, Electa Rome Parks, Pat Tucker, Naleighna Kai, JL Woodson, Brenda L. Thomas, Earl Sewell, Gloria Mallette, William Fredrick Cooper, Donna Hill, Vanessa Johnson, Kim Robinson and Evelyn Palfrey.

To all the readers and book clubs who've been there with me through *Real for Me*, *Someone's In the Kitchen*, *Gets No Love*, *Don't Get It Twisted*, *Lady Sings the Cruels*, and *Blow Your Mind*; thank you for allowing me to entertain you, thank you for allowing me into your hearts and minds. You have given me longevity in this business. Hope you stick around. To my readers in the U.K., the Netherlands, and in the Armed Forces abroad, thanks for the feedback. I love hearing from you and hope to see you on tour one day.

Special shout-out to Divas Read 2 for the awesome reception in Dallas, Mitchie's Gallery in Austin for the incredible crowd, and UCAAB and Marcus Books in Cali for such a memorable start to my last tour.

To all reviewers and those in the media, thank you for taking the time out of your busy schedules to share your thoughts of my works and/or for allowing me to share my thoughts also, be it in print, on the net, or on the air.

I'm going to wrap this up, so I can get to work on the next one . . . and so you can get on with this book. If I missed someone, I'm getting old. *About to collect Social Security, y'know?* Chalk it up to my head, not my heart.

If you need to holler at me, just visit: *www.ericpete.com* (Thanks to Cross The Network for keeping my site tight.) or *www.myspace.com/authorericpete* (Thanks to . . . uh . . . Tom for all those warnings about phishing, spammers and system maintenance).

I'm Eric Pete . . . and I approve this message like a mutha.

Can't stop. Won't stop. Believe that.

STICKS & STONES

It starts with 1 . . .

"Shhh," he said, caressing my leg. My thigh trembled beneath the stretch material of my navy gym shorts. My name, written in marker on the white stripe, had faded from a year's worth of washings.

"I don't know about this. Maybe we shouldn't." The squeak-squeak of shoes on the gymnasium floor outside his office gave me pause. It seemed they were getting closer and closer, but I knew they weren't. It was simply a game being played beyond the door by young, immature little boys. They weren't like Coach Taylor. He was a man.

Coach Taylor didn't make fun of me like they did and on more than one occasion even made the boys run extra laps for their fat jokes in PE class. Until now, he had been gentle and understanding. He was still the same person who would allow me to sit in his office and share with him all my dreams. He made me feel good about myself and would never try to take advantage of me. That's what I thought and I would have argued you down if you said otherwise. I was such a fool.

"It's all right, Trayce. They're not coming in without knocking." Pausing, he squinted at the door. "They know better."

"It's not that. This doesn't feel right."

"Trayce, I would never do anything to hurt you. You know that, right?"

I didn't answer. I tried awkwardly to move off the desk, but Coach Taylor's powerful arms on both sides had me corralled. He had slid his chair closer to where he was positioned between my legs.

He raised his calloused hand and placed it softly against my face. Embarrassed, I tried not to look into his eyes. He repeated himself. "You know that, right?" In that instant, I saw what I wanted to see. Genuine affection.

"I guess," I answered shyly.

"Good."

I felt his lips on mine, closed my eyes and kissed him back. Coach Taylor stood up from his seat and reeled me in like a prized fish. I felt his teeth nipping at my ear lobes and the warmth of his breath in my ear made me shiver.

"You're very special," he said as his breathing became heavy and labored. He had reached down into his sweat pants. I could see his bulge growing as he stroked it and it scared the hell out of me. Forcefully, he pushed me onto my back with his free hand. The stapler and pencils from his desk went tumbling to the floor.

"No, no. Stop," I said to the wind.

"Relax."

I heard the squeak-squeak again as a loose basketball bounced off the door.

"Just relax, Trayce. It's going to be all right." In one fell swoop, my PE shirt and bra were slid up together over my large breasts. I wasn't a small girl by any means, but this man, who had been a friend and confidant, was imposing himself at will . . . and against mine.

"Coach, stop. Get off me."

"You know you want it. You just didn't know how to ask," he chided, tugging on my shorts for emphasis. "Now, just be quiet and relax."

Tears streamed down my face as I felt his penis ramming inside me. It hurt so bad that I wanted to scream. All my tightened throat could squeeze out was an indiscernible whimper. *Why doesn't somebody come into the office and why was he doing this to me,* I wondered as I tried to block out Coach Taylor's grunts.

When finished, he hurriedly assisted me with putting my clothes back on and grabbed a tissue for my eyes. A switch had been flipped and the person I only wanted to be my friend had returned. "I wasn't too rough, huh?" he asked.

"No," I lied. I couldn't look him in the eye. I just wanted to get out of there and never come back.

"Good. I wouldn't want to hurt you . . . just show you how to be a woman." He was talking but distracted as he fumbled in his desk drawer for a can of Lysol spray.

"How? By being less than a man?" I asked as a surge of strength overcame me. It wasn't my voice then, but as if my future self was being channeled through me.

"What did you say?" His eyes showed he was nervous, but he hadn't heard a word. He had only picked up on my tone.

"Nothing. I have to go."

I was almost to the door when he darted in front of me. That familiar smile of his was lodged in place again. "Look," he said as he gathered his thoughts. "You're not going to tell anyone about our special friendship, right?"

"No. I—"

He continued, "'Cause I wouldn't want the faculty to

take things the wrong way. You're doing so well in school and all and I wouldn't want them misunderstanding."

A grown man was resorting to threatening a teenager, but he got his point across. In my state, I even fell for it.

I stared at him blankly for a solid minute. "I have to change for next period."

Walking out into the gym, I stayed along the wall to avoid the boys whose basketball game had just been whistled to a halt by the assistant coach, Mr. Sutton. The other girls were lining up to head to the locker room, so I tried to walk as "normal" as possible and fell in behind them. They were whispering and giggling as most girls my age did, so I tried to ignore it and hoped it wasn't about me.

"How come you didn't participate today?" Donna, our student council president and all-around gossip asked. Oh. She was also on the school newspaper.

"Didn't feel well," I answered. "I was resting in the office."

"With Coach?"

"He was in there," I answered, looking back at her to make sure she wasn't accusing me of anything. "I think he was working on the football team's roster or something."

"Oh. He's always letting you get away without participating."

I had turned around, so Donna didn't see me close my eyes and take a deep breath. I felt unclean. I just wanted to make it to the locker room shower. Then I was going to do everything in my power to never return to PE.

The boys were being lined up opposite us by Coach Taylor, who was complimenting them on "good hustle," whatever that was, even though he had missed almost the entire class. There was one boy sitting atop the bleachers—

the strange one. He didn't say much nor participate much and probably had straight Fs in PE. All he seemed to do was watch people. At this particular moment, he was watching me intently. With each stunted step forward I took in line, his eyes would follow. He did this until Mr. Sutton screamed for him to get off the bleachers and fall in. I looked away and breathed a sigh of relief as I made it to the safety of the girls' locker room. The sting of his gaze was felt long after though.

2 Trayce

It was a beautiful day. I looked out upon the never-ending expanse of Lake Michigan before me and wished I were sailing on it, or at least jogging up Lake Shore Drive. The magnificent office view I was afforded in exchange for allowing the buy-out of my small company offered some consolation though. When I first started out as a dirt-poor entrepreneur, I had dreams but never of this scope.

I looked admiringly upon my reflection in the window. It was like gazing upon a total stranger. It felt odd not getting my usual relaxer, but the hours I'd spent in the chair the night before with the African hair braider were relatively pain-free and very rewarding. She told me she was new to this country and a little shaky with her English skills, but was already off to a great start with her business. I had taken several of her business cards, planning to hand them out at the next First Fridays event. Her shop was located on the Southside, near the Evergreen Mall in Beverly. Actually, the locals referred to it as Ever*black* Mall due to most of its patrons being of my persuasion.

"Miss Hedgecomb," my assistant Rosalina said, interrupting my self-admiration.

"What'd I tell you about that?"

"Oh. Sorry, Trayce. I'll get used to it."

"You'd better," I smiled. "First names only with me, mami."

Laughing at my fake accent, the svelte Dominican woman several dress sizes smaller than me replied. "I gotcha, mami. Ooo. Somebody got their hair done."

"Do you like it?"

Rosalina approached me curiously and held one of the strands. "Yeah. Shit is tight. Have the white boys over in systems seen it yet?"

"No. You know they ask too many questions," I laughed. "Anything *ethnic* freaks them out."

"Yep. When friggin' Sammy Sosa got caught with a corked bat and they wanted to know my friggin' *perspective* on it. And I loathe baseball. I'm still waiting for a good Bulls team," she huffed. Focusing back on what she came for, she held out something for me. "This was in your P.O. box."

"Aww, you didn't have to do that right now. Thanks though."

"Hey, if you don't want me to do something, you gotta tell me, y'know!"

"I know now." In the six months since I'd come aboard to oversee my own Internet company, Rosalina had been my right-hand woman, there to help with the transition. After the big dot.com bust, I was fortunate to create a company worth something and that others were willing to pay handsomely to acquire; like those guys who sold YouTube to Google. I liked being my own boss, but preferred the stability plus benefits I had now. Okay, the extra money was a big plus too.

Being new to Chicago from the west coast, where I'd

attended Pepperdine, I was a little dry and restrained at first. But I was really beginning to feel at home in the Windy City. Of course, I was saying all this without having lived through a full winter yet.

Going through the mail handed to me, I scanned the yellow labels signifying which stuff had been forwarded— the typical music clubs offering twelve free CDs in exchange for your soul and eternal damnation, an offer from *Black Expressions*, and a cell phone bill run up by my ex that I was withholding from paying on principle. A colorful envelope with too many stamps and way too much tape on it caught my eye. I smiled; knowing who it was from already. I hadn't talked to her in a few days so I excused Rosalina and made the call.

My mother was an hour ahead of me, so I knew she would be playing chess or having her afternoon coffee with my aunt. My mother, when selecting a retirement home, had moved one town over, but was still near my aunt, who would visit her every day. I had asked her to move in with me, but she would never leave the South. Every other place was either too cold or too weird— sometimes both—in her eyes.

I waited to be connected to her room.

"What'd you send me this time?"

"Hello to you too, baby," she said in her usual drawl. "Ready to come home?"

Since high school, I'd learned to move far, far away and this was no different. California was too far the first time and this was only a *little* better in her eyes. It would almost be humorous if it weren't so sad. My mother had no idea how things really were for me when I attended Marion High. Those four years, she thought her daughter was one of the most popular kids there and I did nothing to tell her otherwise. Having a sick, manipulative teacher force himself on me was a low point I kept to myself, but that was only the beginning of the deep pain that my transcripts wouldn't reveal.

"No, I like it here in Chicago. Why don't you come visit? I have plenty of space. I could show you the sights. You could shop the Magnificent Mile. Maybe see Oprah's show."

"Nah, baby. You know I don't fly since September 11 and all that screening. But maybe what I sent you will change your mind."

"What is it? A Greyhound ticket?" I laughed.

"Open it."

"Momma, you know you shouldn't put all this tape on your envelopes," I said, trying to work my letter opener into a seam that wasn't covered by her handiwork.

"Just don't want anybody tryin' to steal your stuff."

"It must be something valuable," I said facetiously.

My mother paused, as if waiting for me to be let in on her secret. I knew she was smiling on the other end of the phone.

"Oh."

"Trayce, what's wrong? Did you open it?"

I wasn't expecting to see the familiar eagle crest on the linen envelope I had pulled out of hers.

"I don't see what the big deal is," Rosalina said as she surveyed the wine menu. We had left work late and decided to have dinner together at Bianci's near Washington Square. We were waiting on one other guest so we could order.

"It is a big deal."

"It's just an invitation," she shrugged as she fished a fresh breadstick from the basket. I hated her ability to eat anything and everything and not gain a pound. "You don't want to go to your high school reunion?"

"No."

"Why not? You're successful as all hell, making a boat-
load of money. Y'know," she said, pausing to chew and
swallow, "you should rent a big-ass limo and a couple of
male escorts. That would show them all up."

"I don't want to show anyone up, mami."

"But that's the fun part, mami," she shot back with the
thick accent she could turn off and on at will. "Make 'em
lick your boots. Yeah. I like the sound of that."

"You are too crazy," I chuckled.

Across the semi-filled restaurant, I noticed the waiter
escorting the final party to our table. A Jewish blonde in
her early forties with shoulder-length hair and eye-
glasses was being escorted over. Her red business attire
screamed she was a late worker too.

"Hey, Trayce. Hey, baby," she said, acknowledging us.
Rosalina wiped her mouth with the napkin and stood
up.

"Hey, baby," Rosalina replied as she planted a sensuous
kiss on her girlfriend's lips. Knowing how her partner Alison felt about public displays of affection, Rosalina took
her thumb and wiped the lipstick smudge from her lips.
Alison frowned from behind her glasses, but as she
looked into her partner's eyes, she couldn't sustain it.

"Get a room, you two," I said, interrupting the lovers'
gaze. "I'm ready to order." Alison, feeling a bit of embar-
rassment, composed herself and took a seat.

Alison was a segment producer at the local super sta-
tion; she had gotten her start with my idol and role
model, Oprah. From what Rosalina tells me, it was during a taping of Oprah's show that they first met. Alison
lived in Skokie at the time. The two of them shared a
condo in Hyde Park, but were looking to buy a home in
Northbrook. To me, Alison seemed a bit conservative for
Rosalina's tastes and fiery streak, but her fall to Rosalina's spring had a certain synergy.

Into our second bottle of wine, Rosalina felt safe enough to broach the subject of my reunion again. I tried unsuccessfully to shush her as she mentioned it to Alison to get her thoughts. Alison had removed her glasses and rubbed her brow, trying no doubt to dispel the remainder of the day's stress.

She looked at me quizzically while pondering whether to pour herself another glass of Chianti.

"Hated high school too, huh?"

"How could you tell?"

"Trayce, I still make that same face when my mother brings up chorus."

"But you sing beautifully," Rosalina said.

"It didn't mean that I liked being forced into chorus in high school though," Alison countered. "So, Trayce," she continued. "Was your mother pushy as well?"

"No," I answered as I thought back. "She just didn't have a clue."

3 Solomon

"Look, I'm not going to talk about this at work." She kept talking in that wild, frenzied pace she knew worked on my nerves.

"No. The twins are my children too and I have a right to see them whenever I want," I stressed while trying to keep my voice low.

In spite of my objections, she was succeeding in drawing me in. Our divorce was final, but the custody battle was going to be the tough one.

"Linda, I honestly don't care what your attorney says," I huffed. Over the intercom came a call, interrupting my argument. One of my new employees needed assistance with a return at her register. I had been transferred to manage the Walgreens on Floyd Baker Boulevard because of its high turnover and was trying to be patient. I was always bounced around to trouble spots and this was more of the same.

I prayed someone else would assist her and continued, in vain, my pleas over the phone to get my ex-wife to see my point of view. As she droned on, I lowered my head and sighed.

On my desk before me was my copy of *Black Enterprise*. I had brought it in with my mail from the day before and had yet to finish it. It was opened to an article on successful entrepreneurs. I smirked, thinking of my dashed dreams of being featured alongside them. My meeting Linda right out of high school, then getting her pregnant had seen to that. Don't get me wrong. I was grateful to have such wonderful, healthy kids but I still had so much unfinished business. Dreams deferred as some might choose to think. I mindlessly scanned over the pictures until one of them caught my attention. The person lived way in Chicago, but the name seemed familiar. It couldn't be anybody from our small town, I thought. A faint image skipped across my brain and I began searching for a lost memory.

I moved the receiver away from my ear and looked at it curiously. I could still hear Linda's voice, although squeaky and diminished. Her voice became faint just before I hung up on her. We would continue right where we left off. We always did.

The intercom squawked once again and I knew my assistance was needed. My name was being called specifically now. I hurriedly read the profile beneath the name in the magazine then flipped the pages shut. In my garbage can was a discarded letter, which I had left unopened. I quickly snatched it out from among the granola bar wrappers and wiped it off. There it was, just below the mighty eagle that was our mascot, was my first name misspelled.

SOLEMN.

It was either a stupid twist of fate or some cruel joke. Either way it was accurate. Imagine how it is upon graduation for your name to be called and to hear nothing. Or even worse, have nobody know or care who you are. That's what I was in high school, a short little enigma nobody cared to know or find out anything about. I simply existed within the locker-lined hallways, but never truly lived. I lived through others. Others I watched, snatching up bits of their lives or whatever emotions their hormones coughed up during those four years.

I picked up the phone and answered the intercom page. "I'll be right up," I said to the now-frantic cashier. I put my blue manager's vest back on and stood up. I had decided to open it, but the envelope would have to wait just a little while longer.

4 Janet

"So, I'll see you again?"

"You bet," he stuttered as his excitement overcame him. "Godiva, you're incredible."

"And this chocolate is all for you, baby."

I counted the wad of hundreds I had just been handed. Not as profitable as NBA All-Star Weekend, but nothing to scoff at. I didn't know which was going to be harder for the man—explaining the light wallet to his wife or the large cum stain on his pants. Either way, it wasn't my problem. "Jim," as he called himself, was another in a long line of satisfied customers. I was more than happy to take their money and fulfill their feeble little fantasies. I never used my real name in the profession. This was Las Vegas after all, where everybody came to reinvent themselves or maybe to just forget. Everything was an illusion or mirage in this desert town. Some of them were just more convincing than others though.

As I left the room, I handed some of my earnings to the club's security, Kevin, who ensured "Jim" wouldn't lay a hand on me and who also allowed me to do the extra stuff that made for good pay.

Making sure my breasts were nestled securely back inside my top, I put on my game face and sashayed back into the loud, public area of the club. At center stage was a veteran by the name of Misty. Her blond extensions flowed past her shoulders, parting for her new implants, while she sensuously worked her pelvis to the rhythms of Sean Paul's "Temperature" for the patrons. Sliding her plump derriere toward the edge of the stage, she glanced in my general direction and smiled as her thick legs slid open with a sensual, fluid motion. She playfully raised one breast to her snake-like tongue and tickled the nipple with her tongue stud. My eyebrow went up as the throngs of twenties, fifties, and a few hundreds popped up readily in the hopes of a closer look at Misty's twists and turns in a private session later.

The two of us were the top earners from last year and she was putting forth the effort to reestablish herself as the sole queen of the place. I was due to be off my shift in the next half hour so I could've just returned to the dressing room backstage and counted how well my night had been. I wasn't that easy these days.

I chose to take the long route through the club. I adjusted the sheer scarf that served as my modest covering as well as toy and walked past Misty's gentlemen. Making eye contact with several, I discretely ran my fingers through my flawless weave and gave them that modest, subservient stare that made men eager to be my teacher. That was all I had to do. Sometimes, less was best.

Marty, the manager and part owner of The Standard, was talking to the deejay and saw me coming over.

"Marty, I want to do one more number," I demanded over the noise.

"G, you're through for the night. Misty has one more and then I have Peaches set to go."

"Now Marty," I said as I moved into his personal space, "you know I bring in three times as much as Peaches." Marty was a balding former pro ball player whose body was just giving into the *roundness* of middle age. With The Standard, he found that he could make more selling fantasies than the used cars he pushed following his forced retirement from the NFL for violating its substance abuse policies one too many times.

Marty adjusted his posture. "Now G, how is Peaches ever going to work her way to your level if I let you and Misty hog all the time? I gotta work her in. Go home."

It was supposed to be a secret, but everyone in the club from the bartenders to the valet parking attendants knew Peaches was Marty's big-chested niece from tiny Tazewell, Georgia. He had promised his sister to look after "Peaches" and figured the best way to keep an eye on her in Vegas was to have her right in front of him at all times.

Ignoring Marty, I asserted myself and spoke to the deejay instead. He still owed me for a lap dance anyway. "I'm going on next," I dictated. "You know what song."

Marty glared at me, but bit his tongue. I could easily move on to another club.

Knowing what he was thinking, I played diplomat. "Peaches can go on right after me. She can watch. Might learn something too."

A few hours later, I was off work. I turned up Whitney Houston's "Saving All My Love For You" and sang along as my XLR whizzed down I-515 to my place in town. I had pushed the button on the console and the Cadillac's hardtop had just stowed itself automatically. Earlier in the night, while I was *shakin' my thang*, a thunderstorm had passed over and the desert air smelled so fresh and alive now. As alive as I wanted to be.

Back at my apartment complex, everyone was asleep, anticipating their normal workdays that would begin in a few hours. As my garage door slowly rose, my thoughts were of getting under the covers and cuddling. My old Taurus was parked in its usual spot inside. It was my first car out of school and it had gotten me all the way to Las Vegas without incident. I kept it around as a reminder and was now letting my boyfriend use it for transportation. Seeing it parked there let me know he was home and not out carousing in the casinos or clubs with money he didn't have. In the early days of our relationship, Gerald used to come by The Standard. I did say *used to*. Gerald's jealous streak and my choice of occupation didn't make for good performances and really messed with my money, so that had to end. Now, he was content to stay up for me and sulk instead.

Once my money was secure, I grabbed my .25 from the glove compartment and made sure the safety was off. When I first started as an exotic dancer, there was one girl who was followed home by a customer. Bad stuff. Of course, I was more concerned about my money.

Once upon a time, money was the least of my concerns. In high school, my boyfriend at the time, Shaw, was voted "most likely to succeed." I was head cheerleader and homecoming queen my senior year at Marion. The running joke was that I was voted "most likely to marry someone to succeed." My classmates had me dead to rights. My plan was flawless, until Shaw dumped me right after graduation with no explanation. To say I had mild resentment would be an understatement.

Rather than stay home and be the constant butt of jokes, I cleaned out my savings, bought a car, and headed here where I quickly found a way to make the most with what I had. Janet had arrived in town, but it took Godiva to discover the brains that lurked behind all this beauty. I was no longer waiting for a man to give something to me or provide for me. I was going to take what I wanted while I had the means to do it.

"Honey, I'm home," I said as I came through the door. I slipped the safety back on and dropped the pistol into my handbag. My answering machine on the kitchen counter showed "0" on it, so I knew Gerald had played my messages. I always had messages.

I slipped out of my Manolo Blahnik slides and put my keys on the hook. From the living room, I heard voices. It was a man and a woman.

He better not have some bitch up in here, I thought, my hand slipping back into my handbag.

Gerald had fallen asleep and left the TV on Cinemax. He lay asleep in my recliner with the remote in his hand and a cereal bowl in his lap. On the floor beside him was an open box of Crispix and plastic bottle of milk. In the air, I could smell the remnants of a dime bag. I hated when he did that.

I released my grip on the .25 and smacked Gerald upside his head to wake him up.

"Huh? Whazzat?" he asked, startled and dazed.

"I told you about blazin' up in here, boy!"

"Nah, nah," he groggily protested. "I was just watchin' some movies and . . ."

"And eatin' all the Crispix!" I yelled. "You know you only eat that when you're high. Put up your bowl 'n shit. I'm too tired to be cleaning up behind your ass. And don't do that shit in here again. You know I can't stand that smell!"

Walking to my bedroom in disgust, I unzipped my True Religions, working them off my hips until they dropped onto the hardwood floor. I then grasped them with my toes and used my leg to flip them up to my open hand. Behind me, I heard Gerald banging around the kitchen as he put things away.

Gerald wasn't what women would call a prime choice, but he suited my needs. He was one of those temperamental artist types who sought that balance between his art and earning a buck. Translation: He spent more time between jobs than actually working. He was my baby though—as faithful as one could expect of a man and a master with his tongue. I think I was in love.

"Are you coming to bed? Or are you still watching movies?" I asked, feeling my desire to spoon return in spite of his unflattering hobby.

"I'm coming," he replied, speeding to catch up with me down the hall. As he got closer, I playfully began running. He quickly overtook me, grasping the back of my thong to yank me back.

"Hey! Careful," I pouted. "Don't stretch the thong. It's a Cosabella."

Gerald now barred my path to the bedroom. His worn, faded T-shirt of Che Guevera was discarded, revealing his hairy chest. He really looked like a young Teddy Pendergrass.

"Anything else you need?" he asked, his sinewy arms pulling me toward him. The irritating residue of marijuana was still there, but his manly odor overrode all else before my senses.

"Make a deposit at the bank for me?" I asked, holding my deposit bag up.

"Money isn't everything," he said as he took the bag from me. He unzipped it and let the various bills and denominations rain on us before taking their place on the floor. "Anything else you need?"

"Not a need," I said coyly. "But maybe a *want*." I put

my index finger in my mouth and sucked on it. Pressing through his jeans, his thickness longed to get at my kitty. His top and my bottoms were missing as if we were a mismatched pair of twins. We each helped the other remove what was left and slowly sank onto the currency-littered floor amidst a barrage of wild, reckless kisses.

5 Karim

The tune coming from my pants pocket startled her. "What is that playing?"

"Mozart."

The statuesque beauty went back to what she was doing, then paused. Looking up at me with a perplexed stare on her face, she asked, "Didn't he sign with Def Jam?"

I just shook my head—the one she wasn't sucking on. "Nah. Mozart. The classical composer," I volunteered.

Not knowing how to respond, she simply let out an "Oh." While she went back to giving me brain like a champ, I leaned over to snatch my Blackberry from my jeans, which had been hastily discarded on the side of my bed.

I chuckled upon reading the message that had been sent to me. It was from On-Phire Records, this record label down south. Jason North, the label head, had stepped to me during a party for the Essence Music Festival's return to New Orleans. Following Katrina, it looked like On-Phire had finally joined the big boys, inking a mega-distribution deal which meant they could now afford my services.

"Am I doing something wrong? You seem distracted." My friend, whose name escaped me at the moment, had met me during the casting call for my newest video. She claimed she had ideas to share and had followed me back to my Manhattan studio. I'm still not sure what she was expecting out of me, but I was open to listening to her *proposal.*

"No. You were fine . . . great," I casually replied. "Um, why don't you stop?"

I slowly sat up, careful to do it while she was on the upstroke, fearful of pissing her off with my dick in her mouth—never a good thing, mind you.

Concepts flowing through my brain because of the text message drove me at the moment. Without uttering a word, I left the befuddled dancer in my bed and briskly walked over to my computer. I don't know how long I was sitting there composing my thoughts, but my appetite had returned. A box of Lo Mein that had been sent up earlier in the night was nearby. Rolling my chair out from the desk, I picked it up along with the chopsticks and began helping myself from the box.

I was scrolling down a screen with the mouse while slurping up the cold noodles. I still couldn't remember her name, but she wrapped a sheet around herself and strutted across the floor with more attitude than most runway models.

"Let me get this straight. You left *me* nude in your bed to come sit in front of the computer?"

"Want some?" I asked, holding up a piece of chicken and some noodles in between the sticks without so much as a glance. "It's still good."

She knocked the chopstick from my hand and stood there with hand on hip waiting for me to react. I wasn't going to give her the satisfaction. One of the skinny noodles had landed in my hair. Fishing it out of my red mane, I chuckled before flicking it in her direction.

"You're a rude, arrogant son of a bitch."

"Yeah. I can be that at times, love," I said, swiveling my chair to look her in her eye. "But you have to go now. I need to think and can't do it with pussy on my mind."

"Is that all I am to you?"

"Well . . . yeah," I shrugged. "But you knew that when you came over. Do you want me to call a cab?"

"Go to hell!" she shouted, fuming as she cast off my sheet. I broke my concentration for a while to enjoy how beautiful her body looked as she stormed off in search of her clothes. She had one of those perfect asses on her. Like Beyoncé Lopez. Yeah, I said it. Don't try to steal it, either.

"Speaking of hell," I said, making light of the situation and probably because I felt a stirring in my loins again, "don't you have a flight out of Jersey in the morning?"

A pair of hazel eyes rolled as she gave me the middle finger, signaling she was my Number 1 fan.

"Hey, it's nothing personal. Maybe we can get together next time you're in town."

With her shoes in hand, she stormed past me on her way out the door. "I doubt it," she replied.

Giving up on any future liaisons or remembering her name, I went back to my brainstorming on the Apple. I wouldn't get off that easy—she did have some parting advice for me.

Stepping into my elevator, she slid her slender little feet into her shoes, adding another few inches to her height. "I hope you don't always treat your women this rude," she huffed. "Oh. And by the way . . . your videos absolutely SUCK!"

I looked out onto the street below and made sure she

was safely in her cab before trying to get some work done again. The ideas that were flowing so smoothly were now locked up. I kept starting a sentence about a concept, but couldn't get past the first few words. I pounded my fist on the keyboard in frustration.

I took offense to her talking smack about my craft, but she was dead-on about my relationships with women. Quite simply, I had had women, but never what I would call a relationship with one. I guess I was still holding out.

I was worlds away from that red-headed, freckle-faced kid who constantly got his ass kicked after school, but still clung to my fascination, or infatuation if you prefer, with that one particular woman.

Being new to town, I hadn't the benefit of having any established friendships when I transferred to Marion High my freshman year. Being a gangly, smart kid didn't endear me to a lot of the cliques that had carved out their little kingdoms. Who am I kidding? It didn't endear me to *any* of them. If red headed white boys catch hell, then my odd features for a black boy just made some kids want to pound on me more.

I was getting punched, pushed, or shoved on the regular. The "beat up the new kid" show would start mornings before school on the parking lot, but I did say I was smart. I simply began walking more slowly to school. Yeah. Better to be tardy and conserve my strength for running in the afternoon.

Even with the bad shit, there was a bright spot—someone who risked her rep and ignored the taunts hurled in my direction by her clique, "The Crew." This girl was a beautiful angel, and she still soared in my dreams.

Police sirens outside snapped me out of my pity session. The same scant words greeted me on the monitor. I obviously wasn't going to get any work accomplished. A pile of mail sat in my in tray and I fished my hand in the middle of it, pulling out a single white envelope. I played with it, holding it up to the light and flipping it over and over between my fingers before setting it down again.

I sighed deeply and ran my fingers through my curly hair. Looking back at the monitor, I saved what little notes and thoughts I had typed and began surfing travel sites on the Internet.

In the name of love . . .

"Hell yeah," he shouted, imitating Dr. Dre as the album *The Chronic* blared from room number 237. As our door closed behind us, he staggered sideways causing me to almost fall.

"Hey!"

"Get down," he mumbled. "You know I'm buzzin', girl."

My prom dress was hiked up to my thighs as my legs dangled around Shaw. One of my shoes slipped off and bounced on the cheap dark green carpet as he twirled around. I playfully laughed as he dumped me onto the bed.

"What?" he asked, as I smiled and got caught up in his brown eyes. Even reeking of alcohol, he looked so handsome in his white tux.

"Next year is ours, baby," I insisted. "Next year is ours."

"Yeah," he chuckled as he took a gulp of gin & juice from his cup. "We're going to run things at Marion. The Crew!"

We were only juniors, but we were already the shit at school. Everybody wanted to hang with us and be like us, but they couldn't. We looked the best, we dressed the best, and, most importantly, we threw the best parties. We thought we ruled the world and would have called you crazy if you said otherwise. I was the luckiest of all The Crew. I had Shaw.

"Make sure the door's locked." I spoke softly, but with an air of urgency. Outside, the party continued three rooms over as I heard Shaw's drunken teammates calling out for him. The world could have him, Mr. Football and Track, later. Tonight was going to be our special night.

"Janet, you want something else to drink?" he asked, motioning toward the door with his thumb. I knew he heard their calls. "I think I need another cup."

"No, you're through for the night. You want to pass out on me? *On our prom night?*" I tried to strike as seductive a pose as I could. Sitting on the edge of the bed, I slid my legs open and leaned forward to give him a view of the tops of my breasts. I didn't really know what I was doing, but I had seen the pose before in one of my dad's dirty magazines. It worked in computer class with Mr. Anderson, who gave me straight A's, so I knew I was on to something with it.

Shaw just laughed and brought his tall, muscular frame over. Something about the way he walked made me hot just watching. Okay, maybe it was my teenage hormones 'cause he didn't have to do much to make me hot.

"You make me so happy," I said.

"Yeah. Today was a good day," he said, his voice mimicking the rapper Ice Cube.

"Boy, you know you ain't no gangster."

"Girl, you don't know me."

"I know enough to know you're not a gangster," I laughed. "Now come here."

I put my hands in his; felt the calluses from the football he commanded so expertly. Even though they were rough, there was a tenderness about them. Being a jock, he still maintained flawless manicures. His teammates teased him about it, but a star athlete was allowed such eccentricities.

"Your hands. They're trembling. What's wrong?"

"Nothin'," he shrugged. Instinctively, he withdrew his hands and snatched his cup from the table. He downed the rest of his drink in one final gulp.

"Something wrong, baby?" I asked. I walked behind him and grasped his broad shoulders. With my shoes off, I had to stand on my tiptoes to whisper in his ear. "This is our night. Just me . . . and you."

Shaw continued to stare at the motel curtain and the twinkle of light that escaped from outside at its edges whenever the breeze from the air conditioner would hit it. My hands drifted around to his lapels to remove his jacket. He said nothing, but lowered his arms and let me take it off. We swayed to our imaginary music, my body ingrained firmly against his, as I worked the buttons to his vest then yanked his shirt free of his pants.

"Careful, I gotta return this in one piece."

"Maybe you should take it off yourself." I slowly grazed his abs and chest with the tips of my nails. "Now. Take me. Tonight."

Tired of waiting, I began unfastening his belt then his pants. When I got to his zipper, he yanked my hands away. Twirling around quickly, he startled me further. Before I had a chance to react or take a breath, Shaw kissed me deeply. My lips quickly submitted to his passion and allowed themselves to be tasted and sucked at his leisure. I felt a tug at my zipper, then the cool air at my back. Goosebumps would've formed, but Shaw was there, his warm hands caressing my skin and sifting through my muscles. He undid my bra then tenderly, attentively brought my chest against his. I could feel our hearts beating in unison.

"I love you."

Everything came grinding to a halt at the utterance of those three words. I had seen this before. Shaw would just "nut up" when I expressed my feelings, but I had to say it this night. It wasn't something I tried to hide. Besides, I knew he loved me too, but like most guys he had a hard time with *those words*.

"I love you too," he said.

"What?"

"I love you," he said softly this time, as if embarrassed. "Don't make me say it again."

In the dim light, my eyes twinkled like distant stars. I smiled and so did he. I knew this night was going to be magical.

Scooping me up in his arms, Shaw carried me to the bed. He pulled the multi-colored bed spread back before lowering me onto the semi-white sheets. I scooted over to give him room, then slid my panties off under the covers.

Shaw smiled eagerly then finished taking off his clothes. His white boxers remained, breaking up his chocolate outline. Under the covers, he joined me where we continued our wild kisses. He moved down my neck then to my breasts. His fingers worked between my legs, a little rough at first, then my natural juices assisted him. I was so wet for him, wanting to feel as special as I'd dreamed. I began sliding off his boxers.

"Make love to me, Shaw. I can't take this. I want to feel you. Put it in."

"Uh."

"What?" My hands reached for his dick, but he stopped me.

"I can't." He got off me and pulled his boxers back up.

"Why not?" I demanded, frustrated as all hell. "Did one of those freshmen hoes give you something? I saw them tryin' to rap to you after the game. If so, I will kick a bitch ass!"

He sat at the edge of the bed with his back to me and just shook his head. He chuckled. "Nah. You know I ain't fucked nobody else."

"Hell, you ain't fucked me either."

"You know what I mean. You're my girl."

"Then what's wrong? I'm not pretty enough? Did I do something? Was it something I said?"

"Nothin' like that." He was looking at the curtain again. It was as if he wanted desperately to escape. The party was still going strong outside. "You're perfect."

"Thank you," I snorted confidently. "So are you."

"I just don't want to do this now. I want to wait."

I almost choked. "You mean until we're married?"

"Yeah. That's it. I need to be true to the Lord . . . and myself."

"Oh." That spirituality stuff again.

"I still love you though."

"Alright. Since we're going to be together forever maybe we could . . ."

"No." His head lowered and he still refused to look at me. "I hope you understand."

This wasn't the first time Shaw had hit me with something like this, but tonight . . . tonight was our prom night. Blowjobs weren't cutting it anymore. I didn't have such hang-ups about sex, especially the way I felt about him. I was about to burst and wanted to cry from the frustration I felt.

"I understand," I answered. I had no choice. I loved him. I gathered the covers around me and turned over. Balled up in a fetal position, I tried to will myself to sleep. Shaw slid back under the covers and spooned with me the rest of the night. It ended on a real tender note with me feeling rather foolish. I was rushing to have something I would have the rest of my life. Our wedding night was going to be even more special because of this, I told myself as I drifted off to sleep.

That morning, we would check out and have breakfast at the Waffle House with the rest of The Crew. Shaw would give all the guys high-fives and drop subtle hints about how wild our night had been. I would be a little more discrete, but would nod approvingly to my girl-friends. I wasn't about to let another girl think I wasn't satisfying my man.

7 Trayce

Sulking wasn't my style. I decided I wasn't going to go home, but wanted to at least call my mother and apologize for being so gruff with her. *She doesn't know and wouldn't understand,* I told myself. I always told myself that. It was my credo that I lived by.

Saturday, I knew she would be returning from church. My mother was a Seventh Day Adventist and had been limited since she no longer drove, but she assisted at Sabbath school whenever she could. I was raised one too, but was still finding myself in the world. My mother hated hearing that. *A soul cast adrift without a rudder on the sea known as salvation,* she would probably say.

I was watching Rosalina and Alison's dog, a hyper Great Dane by the name of Brutus, for the weekend and had just returned from a jog with him. Having him yank me around town had shaved a few minutes off my best time and had me gasping for air. Maybe I'd lost a few pounds in the process too. Once I tied him up and composed myself, I made the call.

"Did you go to church today?" she asked.

"No, momma. I'll try to go tomorrow."

"Try? I'll bet you ain't even found a church. Girl, you know I didn't raise you like that."

"True enough," was my only reply. Fishing to the back of the fridge, I found my last bottled water.

"Pastor Frye asked about you today."

"Is he still parading his woman around the church in front of his wife?"

"Trayce!"

"Momma, you know it's true. I remember him hitting on you at that picnic."

"Girl, you know that's not true. He was just complimenting me on my legs."

"Only because he wanted to get between them," I spat out with a slew of bitterness before my brain kicked in.

The silence on the phone was deafening. I hoped we had lost our connection. Then my mother spoke. "Shame, shame, shame. Who taught you such stuff? Lord knows I didn't."

"I'm sorry, momma." I really wasn't. I had meant what I said. "I didn't call to argue. I just wanted to talk to you. Forgive me?"

Using the moment to her full advantage, she pressed. "If you come home."

"Momma, I already told you—"

"Just to visit. Don't get all worked up, girl."

I sighed heavily, then nudged the bottle of spring water against my forehead. Cold beads dripped down to combine with the sweat on my chest. "I'll see. I need to check things at work."

"Baby?"

"Yeah, momma?"

"Why don't you want to go to your reunion? You really should go."

"Why? I got my diploma."

"Maybe they'll give you some kind of special award. You were always so involved. My baby, the class valedictorian," she puffed proudly.

"Momma."

"Yeah, baby?"

"I wasn't valedictorian."

"Oh that's right," she muttered lowly. "That *high-yella* boy with the funny hair."

"Karim. His name was Karim."

"*Hmph.* Whatever. You know you were smarter than him. Now you know the only thing that gave you a lower average was your PE grades. Coach Taylor coulda' done you better."

"I . . . I don't want to talk about that anymore. I'm through with Marion. I have absolutely no interest in reliving any high school memories." I was reliving them every night. My therapy bills proved it.

"You know it's being torn down."

"Huh?"

"Yeah. It made the news. Marion closed last year. A big fence is around it. They're gonna build one of them factory outlet malls on the site."

A smile crossed my face for the first time. "Good."

"You don't care?"

"Not really."

"That's the problem with you these days, daughter of mine. You don't seem to care about anything."

"That's a lie. Look at my career."

"Your career's not your life."

"It is these days."

"What about me?"

"You know what I meant, momma. You know I love you."

I thought there was silence again, but my mother was sniffling. "It's always the same. People ask me where you

at and when you coming to visit. I can't answer them be-
cause I have no idea. You never come around, Trayce.
You act like you're ashamed of your town . . . your roots.
Are you ashamed of us? *Of me?*"

Did you ever think that it's maybe me that I'm ashamed of?
"No, momma. I'm just always so busy. Trying to be a success."

"You are a success and I am so proud of you. Look, I
know I can be pushy at times, but I just want everybody
else to see how well my child is doing."

"I love you, momma."

"I love you too, daughter of mine."

"Look. I'll call you later. I'm watching a dog and I just
heard something crash."

Brutus barked loudly from my porch. Everything was
still in its place. He obediently wagged his tail with a
thump, thump on the wooden deck. I slid the door open
and looked at him.

"Thanks," I said.

8 Solomon

"I.T., how may I help you?"

"Is Trayce Hedgecomb in?"

"Please hold."

I wasn't quite sure why I was calling. Directory assistance had easily provided me with the number and offered to connect me for free. I was already driving, so I just went along for the ride. This hot summer day, my air conditioning wasn't up to par. I wanted to turn the air up, but wanted to be able to still hear. My pockets weren't swollen enough for one of those Bluetooths.

"Ms. Hedgecomb's office. Rosalina speaking. How may I help you?"

"Yes, may I speak to Ms. Hedgecomb?"

There was a pause as if she were checking something. "I'm sorry. She's currently on the phone assisting someone. Would you like to leave a message? Or I can transfer you to her voicemail."

"No. That's alright. Thanks." I flipped the magazine on the passenger seat shut.

Off Turner Lane was our dream home. The white frame

single-story with the matching picket fence was going to be the first house we owned. Our family was to live there. Only my children and my ex, Linda, made it. When everything went south for us, she had her boyfriend buy it for her instead. That's when I learned the true level of Linda's contempt for me.

Under the shade tree was her new Nissan Murano, its temporary license plate taped to the back window. Another present from her man. I shamed it with the arrival of my dirty, old-in-the-tooth Sunbird. At least mine was paid for with legal money.

I touched one of the posts on the front porch, remembering the day the real estate agent first showed us the place. It was smaller than we'd liked, but it was something within our means and we had fallen in love with it. Too bad we weren't in love with each other.

The front door was open. Inside, I could hear Linda hollering for my daughter, Justine, to hurry up and get ready. If I was right, Jordan would be sitting in front of the TV playing the X-Box 360 I had bought for him.

I tapped on the door before entering. I always felt so uncomfortable stepping foot inside, but it didn't really matter. I'd walk over hot coals for my kids.

Linda wore red this evening, her favorite color. The designer dress announced she had plans. Her blonde hair was up. That was one of the first things to change about her, her hair color. "You're late," she screeched, smirking at my manager's vest I still wore before shifting her attention back to the hallway. "Justine, your daddy's here. Finally. Hurry up."

Jordan was where I expected, in front of the TV, but the video game was off. He was watching 106 & Park on BET. The guest host was Natalia, a beautiful talented young singer who could dance her ass off, but was way too small and bony for my tastes. I liked my women with more substance, a little extra to hold . . . I guess like Linda. I didn't comment on the expensive basketball jersey he was wearing.

"Hey, man," I said to my son. "Ready to go?"

"Uh huh." He motioned toward his packed bags positioned by the door. He was the introvert of our two children. Like father like son, damn it. It was so hard to pull Jordan out of his music videos. I had taken to watching them myself just to share a common bond. Funny. My son took after Linda in terms of build, while Justine, my daughter, shared my slightness. The school counselors referred to Jordan as "borderline obese." Those same people are going to be cheering him when he's ripping the heads off quarterbacks in college.

"Going out tonight?" I asked Linda just to make small talk.

"I don't know who in the fuck you think you are hanging up on me yesterday," she said in one breath. I was used to her ignoring my questions. "You're lucky I'm letting you take them for the weekend."

She was the lucky one in that she didn't have to pay a babysitter. I knew Bo was on his way over, ready to whisk Linda off to some club where they would sit in the VIP section until the wee hours of the morning. I knew she had been seeing him before our breakup, I just didn't know how long. It probably started when I was working graveyard at our first 24-hour location. Linda always liked to party beyond my means. Bo claimed he was a barber, but everyone as far as two counties away knew he was cutting something other than heads at his establishment.

"Have fun with Bozo."

"You know that ain't his name. You're just mad 'cause he's successful and you ain't shit."

"We both know what kind of money paid for this stuff.

You can throw your life away for all I care. Just keep my kids away from him."

Linda knew I was dead serious about that. Bo kept his distance somewhat and never spent the night as long as my kids were home . . . far as I knew. Linda had been bought and paid for with the jewelry, the house, the new car, but the twins were off limits.

"They're *our* kids, Solomon. Don't forget that. Besides, I don't know what you're talking about. Bo's a legit businessman," she said, full of delusions.

"If you believe that, you're not as smart as I *thought* you were."

"I knew well enough to leave your underachieving ass."

"Hurt me some more why don't you," I mumbled. "Justine, hurry up! I've gone over my five-minute time limit. Your mother is starting to get on my nerves."

I heard my daughter laugh. I normally didn't say things like that about Linda to them, but Justine knew it was true. Of my two kids, she's the one who took it in stride. I think Jordan still harbored hope for us.

"Ready, Dad." She cheerfully strolled from her room, with a duffle bag draped over her shoulder. Justine was nearly nine, but tall for her age. I don't know whose side of the family she got that from. She wore a Hollister tee, denim shorts, and matching flip-flops, her favorite things to put on her feet these days. Linda had put her first relaxer in last week and Justine was still adjusting to hair falling in her face.

Jordan fidgeted for a second, debating on whether to watch one more video or not, then stood up. He adjusted his jersey then clicked the large flat screen off with the remote. He joined his sister by the front door.

"Give your mother a kiss," I told both of them before letting them run to the car. They obeyed and headed outside in step. I watched Justine whisper something to Jordan, probably a joke, as he let a sheepish grin cross his face in response.

"They're good kids," Linda said as she saw it too. This was rare in that we hadn't shared a moment in years. She then went back to thinking of herself and looked at her watch.

"Need anything before we go?" I asked.

"Nope. Just don't call me and I will see them Sunday night when you bring them home."

"Just like that, huh?"

"Has it ever been any other way?" she asked, an incredulous sneer detracting from her pretty face.

"Yeah. Once."

Linda held up her hand, signaling me she wasn't going there. She went into the kitchen to get her pack of cigarettes. It was time for me to go anyway. Outside, Bo's red Land Rover was pulling up to the curb. Jordan and Justine watched intently from my car as he turned his music down and honked twice.

"I'm out. Have fun tonight," I shouted in Linda's general direction.

I hated the large man who walked across the lawn toward me. This guy had been sleeping with Linda while we were still married. They never admitted it, but I knew. For some reason, I hadn't seen it coming. I guess I was tired of seeing everything, all the patterns and ways of the world, and decided to put blinders on.

I saw Bo squat down—probably to tie his shoe—and walked past him without speaking.

"Put your seatbelts on," I said to my kids. Justine, situated in the back seat, rolled her eyes. Jordan simply complied.

Walking over to Jordan's window that was down, Bo flipped something into the car. It landed on my lap. "You dropped your nametag, Mr. Manager," he said with a laugh. He ran his hand across the top of Jordan's cornrows.

"Like that, huh?" he asked of Jordan about the jersey Linda had bought with his money. "If you ask me, they should've stayed the Bullets. 'Wizards' sounds so soft." With a tisk, tisk, he scrutinized Jordan's head once again. He looked at me, all smiles, and spoke. "When that boy of yours is ready for a cut, just send him over."

"I'd rather take him to Super Cuts than bring him to you."

Bo scoffed. "Whatever, man. That's probably all you can afford. Don't worry. I'll do it for free since he's Linda's boy. Anything for Linda."

I wanted to say something, to curse him out and dare to trade blows with a man twice my size and weight, but there wasn't going to be a circus today in front of my kids. I stared at Bo like he was crazy, then took my leave. Shaking his head, he whistled as he turned around and continued toward the house. Linda, lit cigarette in hand, was holding the front door open for him.

"Y'all hungry? Want me to stop at KFC?" I asked, driving up Miller Avenue with the windows still down to release the stifling heat.

"Can we eat somewhere else, Dad?" It was Justine. "You always take us to KFC."

"Dad? Dad? What happened to 'Daddy', baby girl?" I chided in an effort to add some levity to the hot car.

"Dad, I'm almost a teenager."

"Oh. I see. I must have missed something . . . like a few years. So, you're not calling me 'Daddy' anymore?"

"Nope," she said with a smile.

"Not even when you want me to buy you something in the mall and I don't want to?"

She giggled, that sound of innocence. "That's different."

"Just for that, we're letting Jordan pick this time. He never picks."

"Only his nose," Justine giggled.

"Justine!" It was funny, but I tried to conceal my smile. "Jordan, where are we eating? It's on you, my man."

"I don't care," he said, lost in his own world. "KFC's fine."

"See! Jordan likes KFC!"

"Unh-uh. Jordan hates KFC. He told me."

After Justine's remark, I eyed my son until he finally decided to look back. "Can we go to Macaroni Grill instead?" he asked politely, a smile now gracing his face.

It was going to be a week before I had some Macaroni Grill money. I switched lanes and made a quick U-turn. "If that's what you want then that's where we're going," I answered, thinking about which bill I would juggle this month.

I turned up the radio and let the kids unwind to some sing-songy rap out of Atlanta.

"Daddy, Justine's doing that dance." Jordan was hurriedly pointing to his sister in the backseat who, following the song's instructions, was doing wild gyrations as if having a seizure. I laughed out loud and shook my head.

A few verses into the song, I said, "I like the remix with Trina better."

"Dang, you know about the remix?"

"Yep," I proclaimed proudly, "even saw the video for it."

Justine couldn't resist. "Ooooo, Dad just likes to look at Trina."

"Maybe just a little," I guiltily agreed while tapping my hand on the steering wheel.

"I'm'ma tell momma," Jordan teased.

"He's not with momma no more, stupid," Justine answered for me in her own unfettered way.

I didn't respond, but continued tapping to the music as if nothing were wrong. My wedding band was still on that ring finger. Tap. Tap. Tap.

9 Janet

Gerald ran his hands across the small of my back then slowly upward. His fingertips dug into my skin, breaking through the knots of tension I didn't know existed. When he woke me up like this, it usually meant he wanted to go another round. This time he just wanted to talk.

"You asleep?"

"I was," I said, groaning to emphasize my disapproval.

"Oh. I thought you were awake."

I was sleepy as hell, but I tried to play along. "What's up?"

"Just thinking about work."

"That's good."

"Ever thought about moving?"

I turned over in the bed and opened one eye. "No. Where?"

"Out west . . . to LA. I've been thinking about it," Gerald saw he had my attention, all too briefly, so he made the most of it. "I got a cousin out there. Smitty."

"Smitty? Tell me that's not his real name."

Gerald sat up in bed. "Worse. His real name's Wallace, but that's beside the point."

"What is the point?" I groaned. Dreamland was pulling me back. I valued my days off.

"I might as well admit it. I can't make any money out here. Not doing what I do. I think the move would do us good. Smitty says he's doing well and knows some people. I could sell some of my work down at Venice."

"Venice?" I hissed. "Baby, Vegas is where it's at. Why do you think so many people from LA are flooding here? That place isn't affordable. I couldn't come close to having a place like this or make this kind of money. Speaking of money, *what am I gonna do out there*?"

"You wouldn't have to work. I'll take care of you." The look on his face told me he truly believed that. Loving fool.

As if in a bad dream, I coolly replied. "Yeah. Right. No man is going to take care of me. I gave up on that pipe dream years ago. Besides, I am the shit here." I turned back over and drifted off. "The mother fuckin' shit."

Have you ever had a time when you said something without thinking? I know you have, so don't lie and say you haven't. I didn't remember everything, but was feeling bad when I awoke in the afternoon. Gerald knew better than to try to have a legit conversation after our lovemaking. Perhaps he was trying to catch me in a weakened state, manipulate me. Perhaps not. Whatever the case was, he didn't answer when I called out to him. I could hear the TV in the living room, but no other sounds.

"Gerald? Honey, you in there?"

Nothing.

A glance at my alarm clock told me I should be up anyway. From the bed, I saw Gerald had picked our clothes up off the hallway floor. If I knew him right, and I did, the stuff would probably be washed and in the dryer already. After brushing my teeth and putting on a robe, I sashayed toward the sound of Judge Judy chastising someone she had already judged incompetent from the second they walked into her court. I don't know how Gerald put up with those shows.

"Where are you?" I asked, scoping the brightly lit area for a sight of him. The remote was sticking out of the space between sofa cushions and I picked it up.

"Take that," I said, aiming the remote like a six-shooter and pulling the trigger. Her cantankerous image was replaced with the more pleasing sound of smooth jazz from my digital cable channel. I blew on the tip of my "gun" and pretended to replace it in its holster.

Realizing Gerald wasn't home, I resigned myself to some of my favorite coffee. Two new packs of Gevalia had arrived and I had been dying to try the flavors. The smell of hazelnut spread throughout the kitchen, sparking my senses to attention. My earnings from the night before sat neatly stacked on the counter.

"Hmm," I pondered while counting the money. It was wrong of me, but I stuck to my habits. It was all there. A slip of paper lay beside it—a note from Gerald. I read it as I went to pour myself a steaming cup of pick-me-up. Gerald was out interviewing for jobs. He made a point to let me know he didn't take my Taurus and that he wouldn't want to impair my "being the shit." From its tone, I could tell I had royally pissed him off. I wanted to call him and make up, but knew he was the type who needed to cool off alone. *Who knows . . . he may even come home with a J-O-B.*

At my job, I was so used to men needing to feel they were in control even if they weren't that I thought I knew everything about them. I then had this peculiar habit of checking all that knowledge at the front door to my own home. Stupid move on my part because I wound up alienating the good one I had. I wasn't going to change, but I could've at least put forth some effort and consideration before I just blurted out shit.

Finishing my second cup of coffee and a leftover pastry, I saw my garbage was overflowing. I crammed my coffee grounds and filter on top of the heap, then put on some clothes to take out the trash.

Not halfway to the dumpster, the overstuffed plastic bag gave. All over the parking lot, its contents spilled out of the tear in the side causing me to curse to high heaven and everywhere in between. I hated touching garbage. I ran to the dumpster and threw away what I had, then came back to pick up the rest.

As I picked up the leftovers, I saw an unopened white envelope. It was damp and covered in brown stains, but I knew I hadn't thrown it away. *Probably junk mail*, I thought as I gingerly turned it over, trying not to get anything on my nails.

"What the—"

10 Karim

"*K*rispy Kremes! You brought me Krispy Kremes? Yeah, *that's what I'm talkin' 'bout, dawg!*"

"*Just a small token of our appreciation for working with us, Special K,*" he said. "*You're the man when it comes to videos and I just wanted you to know we do our research.*"

"Much love, Jason," I said as I gave him dap. I could feel the warmth through the box. I didn't eat the donuts if they were cold. I wasn't a prima donna like some directors in this business, but I still had some demands. "This relationship is off to a beautiful start," I said as I sniffed loudly for laughs.

Being from down south myself, I could appreciate these brothers making money, but I got bad vibes off this Jason North. He had a smarmy nature about him that wasn't concealed by his snakelike charm. With the money his label was paying me, it didn't matter. I had accepted green from worse, I kept telling myself.

On-Phire Records had a new singing group that had scored with a hot single in the clubs throughout the

South and up the east coast. It was time for them to strike and no better way than a hot video to go with their next single. That was where I came in. I had juggled my schedule, after a certain figure was guaranteed, and was at this warehouse in Brooklyn to work my magic this morning. It was early, but sound and lighting had been here before day setting up monitors, speakers and green screens. Later, we were going to shoot the outdoor scenes at a nearby basketball park. Four air-conditioned trailers were present to cater to all the stars' needs. I checked my Blackberry for messages, then grabbed a donut before handing the box off to my assistant.

"Dancers ready, Brady?"

"Yep. The choreographer's going over some last-minute changes with them."

"Last-minute changes?" My eyebrow went up instinctively.

"No biggie. Traneesha became *inspired*." Brady waved his arms around imitating one of the most sought-after choreographer's mannerisms.

"Long as her inspiration doesn't cost us any time, then its cool." I moved down my mental checklist. "Did we land that girl from Diddy's last video?"

"The one in the white thong?"

"That's the one," I said with a grin.

"She's sick. Bad case of the flu."

"What's she need? Some Nyquil? I would've had it sent over in a limo."

"I'll make a note of it for next time," he said as he walked off laughing. He had a million things to check on that, in the end, made me look like a genius.

I saw a large gathering by the trailers. I always made a point to meet with the artists I was going to be working with and get to know them, so I walked over. In the middle of the bodyguards, handlers, caterers, and a crowd of groupies, there they were. The quartet's name was Saint Roch, supposedly after the street where they grew up singing. Cute story, but that was probably all it was. Like most of these groups, they were auditioned and thrown together, told what to wear, what to say, and how to say it. They had their formula down pat—the babyface, the deep-voiced smooth one, the white guy for some Justin Timberlake flavor, and the bad boy, who was missing at the moment.

One of their bodyguards tried to earn his money before the babyface told him I was the director. He then lowered his sunglasses for a better look before a smile of recognition crossed his face as well. The three group members seemed pretty straight-up, but had been coached about me also. The smooth one began reciting my resume back to my very first video straight out of college. Jason North didn't leave anything to chance.

A few of the groupies seemed irritated by my robbing them of their time with the fellas. Looking in the direction of the most vocal ones, I saw what appeared to be four young ladies barely legal. One of them I think I recognized from another video shoot. Some girls in this town were professionals, who because of low self-esteem or maybe just straight-up greed, would camp out wherever people in this biz were known to hang. I can't front and say that I didn't partake of this element, but I had some limits I didn't cross.

Looking at the time, I had some technical details to work out, but wanted to say "Hi" to the final member before I went into dictator mode later.

The bad boy of the group was inside the trailer near us.

"He kinda busy, but he'll be calling us soon," the white

guy said in a tone filled with hidden meaning the other two picked up on. They all laughed and touched fists. He continued, "You might want to check him out now. Get yours first, y'know."

The kind of stuff he's hinting at can wait until after the video, I thought. I remembered the last blowup on the set. The shit set us back a week while the cops investigated assault charges filed by a dismissed "fan." I wasn't up for that again.

I confirmed the trailer then walked up the stairs to the door. I knocked once, then waited. Nothing. I knocked a little harder the next time.

"*Who the fuck is it?*" I heard muffled by the trailer's insulation. I had found our bad boy.

I grabbed the door handle and walked in before some of the On-Phire security or his boys could decide to stop me.

"Your director," I answered to the question he didn't really expect an answer to.

"Oh," he replied, absent any enthusiasm. A brother larger than I imagined sat alone on the couch. An open bottle of vodka danced back and forth between his hands. "What's up, bruh?" he asked.

I heard him but didn't answer. His guest had my attention. Lying at his feet was a young girl, who had been dancing for him. She had stripped down to her panties and an A-cup bra. Her pink designer jogging suit rested in a bundle next to him. The girl wore enough makeup to make her appear older . . . maybe eighteen.

"How old are you?"

"Twenty-one," she said softly. *Why did they always say that*? Rather than go for something kinda realistic, the kiddies always went for twenty-one.

"She about to show me what she's workin' with, bruh,"

he squealed like a little kid himself, making a thrusting motion with his pelvis. "You down?"

I strode over to the couch and threw her clothes at her. "Get outta here," I said.

"Huh?" they said in unison. I still ignored him.

She wasn't dressing quickly enough and looked past me, waiting for word from him. I got up in her face, ignoring his cursing. "How old are you?" I asked.

"Twenty-one," she repeated, a lot of attitude in her now.

"Thirteen? Fourteen?" I spoke more than I asked. She blinked and tried to look away.

"Get out of here. Don't let me catch you around my set again." I gave shorty another second to get her clothes on before shoving her out the door. I was going to leave right behind her, but felt a shove. The Armadale vodka had the bad boy feeling jumpy. I closed the door, so no one could see what was going on. I was still a businessman.

"You direct," he barked, jabbing his finger into my chest. "Got it? You don't tell me another mother-fuckin' thing. I pay your mother fuckin' bills!"

He said a lot more, but to tell you the truth, I didn't hear it. A grown-ass woman could make her own decisions, but this was a child, no matter what she thought. This was not a good business in which to cast judgment, but I had done just that and found that I didn't particularly like this jerk. I waited for him to thump his finger in my chest . . . one . . . more . . . time.

"Ow!" he screamed. He found himself with his face to the floor before he could get a coherent thought to form. I applied a little more pressure to the wristlock I held him in.

"You crazy, man! You crazy!"

"Let's get one thing straight, my friend," I said in a low, even tone. "I don't care if you pay my cable bill. You don't put your hands on me. Ever. Got it?"

Tears rolled down his face, but he put the words together. "Yeah, bruh."

"And while you're on my set, don't challeng●e. Can you live with that?"

"Yeah. Whatever."

I waited for his breathing to slow and lessened my grip. I helped him up to his feet and did my best to reassure him none of this was personal. We all had our egos and I wasn't trying to destroy his, just keep his dumb ass from winding up in jail on a statutory charge. I then left the trailer, allowing him to compose himself before we shot.

Outside, I ignored the blank stares that were trying to piece together what had just happened in the trailer and calmly walked off. My days of getting my ass kicked had ended way before I earned my black belt in Brazilian Jiujitsu on Fifth Avenue, right here in Brooklyn.

Brady had quietly stood to the back of the gathering crowd. We met up and I just shook my head. He was inquisitive, but knew not to pry too much.

"Traneesha has her girls whipped into shape. She wants you to see the walkthrough before they interact with *them*," he said, an accusing eye cast at the four members of Saint Roch who were huddled up as the bad boy tried to downplay what happened. "Are you alright, brotherman?"

"Yeah, never felt better," I shot off. "Tell you what though. When I'm finished with this job, I'm taking some time off." The dancers, who were all dime pieces, were working on their moves in front of the green screen, where backgrounds and special effects would be digitally filled in later. Their cheerleading outfits got me thinking. Back. Back to another place, another time, another Karim. "Y'know, Brady," I said, folding my arms. "I need to re-assess a few things in my life."

A few stolen moments . . .

"**O**ooh, I'll never get this stuff!"

She always pitched a fit like this. I did what I always did. Smiled and waited patiently for her to calm down. Her tantrums gave me more time with her anyway. Beggars couldn't be choosers and I was definitely begging. Begging for her attention, a minute of her time, her smile . . . but she didn't know. Too self-absorbed and fixated on another. Someone she felt worthy. Shaw.

"What'd y'all do this weekend?" I tried to look nonchalant as I took a bite of my *high school surprise*, the stuff that's not quite chili-mac or spaghetti, but tastes a little like both. They'd shovel it and we'd eat it. Besides, I was on the free lunch program.

Janet's whole disposition changed with that question. For one, it gave her a chance to take her mind off the geometry she wasn't getting. For another, it gave her a chance to talk about something she enjoyed. I watched her reposition herself in her chair and move her leg out from under her. There was going to be a pep rally that afternoon, so she wore her hair pulled back in a ponytail.

She always did this when she was in her cheerleader outfit.

"We went bowling. You'd think he'd want to make
things up to me, but I wind up sitting at the damn bowling alley. Did I tell you I was dressed up? *Hmph.* Lookin'
good too." She shifted the geometry book around, then
muttered softly to herself, "A bowling alley."

"Y'all got problems?" I asked, hoping.

"No," she paused. A frown came across her face. "I just
heard some stuff."

"Oh." I had been playing my Walkman at a low vol-
ume, like I usually did over lunch. My *Lords of the Underground* cassette was being worn out. I turned it off and
hung my headphones around my neck.

"I shouldn't be telling you this, but you're such a good
friend." Friend. The curse every boy in school hates to
hear from a beautiful girl. Makes you want to spit from
the bad taste.

"What?"

"My girl Shauna told me some stuff. She heard Shaw
'n' 'em had a little too much fun with that fat ho Trayce
after the game last week."

"We beat Spartanburg, right?" I never went to our
games and always prayed our team would get the snot
knocked out of them. That usually left them in no mood.
to mess with me on Monday. When they came off a win-
ning high, they were usually cockier.

"You didn't go?"

"Busy." I had just blown all my money on my first CD
player and was wrapping myself up in music I didn't
have to rewind or fast-forward to get to my favorite
tracks.

"Oh. You missed these bomb-ass cheers we did at half-
time."

"I'm sorry I missed that, too." My usual cool demeanor came unglued as I let Janet see the lust I had for her. She blinked as if startled, not knowing what to make of my crossing the dreaded *friend* line. She then regained her composure and batted those eyelashes, not one to let a compliment go wasted.

"Ooo, Karim you're so sweet." Sweet. Another dreaded word. Sweet meant *you have no chance with me, but thanks for letting me know you like me . . . sucker.*

"Sweet?" He laughed. Shaw's best friend Michael. One of my worst tormentors. "Yeah, you a sweet one. Huh, Carrot Top? Ain't that right, yella boy?" He stood behind me with some of his teammates, junior members of The Crew, and wafted his hand through my plume. My mind debated whether I was up for another ass kicking while my stomach simply curled up in knots.

"Leave him alone," Janet scolded. "Don't you have something better to do?"

Michael thought for a second. "Nah," he said to a chorus of laughs from the two ogres in letterman jackets at his side. "Why aren't you wearing my boy's jacket?"

"Because I don't want to," she answered. "Why are you so concerned? You're his girlfriend now, Mike?"

He hated being ridiculed, but knew better than to overstep his boundaries with Shaw's girl and say something stupid. He and his clowns found somebody else in the lunchroom with which to pick a fight and decided to take their leave. "Shaw's lookin' for ya," was all he said.

"Good. He knows where to find me." Her index finger rested on her temple. She was irate with Shaw and I loved it. Every jab she took at him made my heart beat faster. Crazy, irrational stuff like that got me through the day back then. An imagination fueled.

I decided to egg things on. "Is that why you're mad at him? You think he did something with Trayce?"

"Yeah. No," she said, sifting through conflicting thoughts. "I don't know."

"Then why do you stay with him?"

"It's complicated. Look, I think I'll work on this geometry tonight." A lie. She would be bugging me in class tomorrow. "Thanks for your help, baby." She gathered her stuff from the table and scampered off. The only thing left warm at the table was the spot where she'd been sitting. Looking over my shoulder at her, I saw Janet had joined Shaw. He had been leaning against the railing outside the cafeteria the whole time, watching. I never knew what to make of him. If Janet were my girl, I would've bent over backwards to make her happy. I guess that's why I was on the outside looking in. It was always the other guy who had it easy.

12 Trayce

I paused, waiting for Rosalina to leave after putting some reports on my desk.

"Trayce?"

"Yes. I'm still here."

"Do you want to continue?"

"Yes."

"You know," she said as she prepared to lecture me, "it might be easier for you to find a therapist there in Chicago."

I rocked back in my chair. "You might be right. I just don't have the time."

"That was your excuse when we first began our visits." Visits. I liked how she made everything seem so informal. It was a huge coincidence how I began seeing her. Her office was on the same floor as mine back in California and late one night we shared an elevator ride to the parking garage. She seemed nice enough that I felt comfortable asking a few questions. Those questions led her to invite me over for a "visit." That was two years ago. "What do you want to talk about today?" she asked.

"Home."

"California?"

"No. My real home." She knew what I meant. She just wanted me to acknowledge it. Most of our "visits" hinged around those years—a time I wanted to forget, but couldn't. She was helping me to live with it and move on.

"Are you going back to visit?" I knew a silent *finally* was tacked on.

"I'm considering it."

"You don't have to be so business-like with your answers, Trayce. Remember. You have to let your guard down sometime."

"I know, I know. It's a habit."

"We've made so much progress. Let's not waste it. You're going see your mother?"

"Yeah, I think. She wants me to go down there for my reunion."

"Your high school reunion?"

I bit my bottom lip. "Yeah."

"Oh. Do you plan on telling her?"

"No. She's so proud of me. I can't."

"I see. Are you ready to confront those memories? Those people?"

I didn't answer.

"Trayce?"

"I'm here," I answered. I caught a case of nerves and ignored her question. "You know," I paused, "I checked into it and some of the proceeds from the reunion go toward a literacy fund for underprivileged children."

"Sounds like a good cause, Trayce."

"I believe so."

"Sounds like you've already made up your mind."

"Yes."

"If you need to call me, for any reason, don't hesitate. You're going to get through this, Trayce."

"Thank you. Just send me your bill."

"The call's free this time. Congratulations on the *Black Enterprise* piece, by the way."

"You read it?"

"Yes. You took a fine picture."

"My hair's different now. I have braids. Maybe lost a pound or two since that picture. I've been jogging."

"Chicago's been a breath of fresh air for you, hasn't it?"

"I think so. Well, I'd love to stay on the phone since it's free this time, but I have work to get back to."

She laughed. "Me too."

Shortly after I hung up, Rosalina returned to my office. From her desk, she could monitor whether or not my phone was off the hook. She was my friend, but some things in my personal life were off limits. This was a business and there always was someone ready to step up and capitalize on your shortcomings.

"Any calls?"

"Two," she answered. "Here's the message from one. The other didn't leave a message and didn't want me to put him through to your voicemail. He sounded sexy in a nerdy kind of way. *Secret admirer*?"

"Please. If I had an admirer, it wouldn't be secret," I said as I gestured at the framed pictures adorning my desk. With the exception of my mother, the photos were of places and things. Not people.

"Don't sell yourself short, mami. He probably just wants to speak with you *personally*." Rosalina didn't let up as she did a terrible imitation of Marilyn Monroe. "When you need *the Trayce Hedgecombe*, a message just won't do."

"Oh, cut it out." I began thumbing through the company productivity reports, scanning for the parts that were pertinent to our division. Rosalina was dashing away, when I called out. "Hey."

"What?"

"I'll be taking a few days off shortly. I'll give you the dates to mark on your calendar."

"Must be big. You never take off."

"I'm going."

"Where?" A shit-eating grin appeared as it dawned on her. "Oooooh! The reunion!" Rosalina ran around the desk and began vigorously shaking me.

"Yeah. You don't have to act so excited."

"But I am. You know what this means, right?"

"No."

"Shopping! We gotta get you some clothes, mami. First, we'll start down on Michigan Avenue then we'll take a drive out to Woodfield Mall in Schaumburg, just for a little something different—"

"Excuse me?" I said, cutting off Rosalina's rant. "What's wrong with my clothes?"

"Nothing. It's just that you tech-heads can be *just a little* stale," she said as she put her thumb and index finger together for emphasis. "We're gonna take care of that though," she said smugly with a wink. "They won't know what hit 'em."

13 Solomon

"Dad?"

"Huh?"

"How come somebody just walked in front of the screen?"

"I must've missed that, Justine."

I'd surprised my kids with a movie on DVD that was still in the theatres, a movie they had been dying to see. I should've known that anything I bought from "hustle-man," the local black-market entrepreneur, would be questionable in its quality, but wanted to impress Jordan and Justine. Jordan didn't seem to mind the camcorder view of the screen, but Justine was going to have a fit if the sound of someone's cell phone or a crying baby were heard next.

The microwave beeped and I went to get our popcorn from the kitchen. It was my last night together with the kids this month. In the morning, the kids were going back to Linda's and my apartment was going to seem that much smaller.

As I tore open the steaming paper bag and poured the

buttery corn into the bowl, I watched Justine shove Jordan, then Jordan shove her back. I wanted so bad to be there for simple stuff like this. This is what I was missing. How much had I missed already? What more could I have done! I asked myself as I did every other day.

While handing the bowl of buttered popcorn to the kids, my cell phone rang out. Recognizing the number on the caller ID, I let out an inaudible groan. I ran into my bedroom to take it. No need for Jordan and Justine to overhear what was sure to be another confrontation.

"Hello."

"Took you long enough to answer it," she remarked.

"I have them 'til morning," I said, anticipating her usual tirade.

"I'm not calling you about that."

"Oh?" I pulled the phone closer to my ear, suddenly curious.

"I need you to keep them over there an extra day."

"Linda, you know I'd like nothing more, but I'm scheduled for work already. What's going on?"

"Why can't you just say, 'Yes'? Always asking too many questions."

"When it concerns you, I have to ask questions."

"I'm not your concern, Solomon."

"I meant the kids. You're their mother. You knew what I meant." I paused to listen for noises coming from the living room. The movie was still playing. "Now . . . what's up? You need some more time alone with Bo?"

"No, I just need you to keep the kids." She was hiding something.

"I'm already skating on thin ice at work from the last time you did this. You really know how to put me in tough situations. I'll have to go by and pick up some extra clothes for them."

"No," she blurted out. "I'll bring them over. Just tell

me what you need." Linda never came around. She claimed my place was depressing and Bo, with some seriously misguided thoughts, didn't want her near me alone. He gave her everything she wanted and I had nothing.

"Don't bullshit me. What's really going on?"

"The house is messed up."

"I don't care how messy things are."

"No . . . it's messed up. They ransacked it. Tore up stuff. They even broke Jordan's X-Box 360 you bought."

"What? Who?" I asked, equally enraged and confused.

"The sheriff. They came crashing in all in black with flashlights and masks. They were looking for stuff."

Images ran through my mind. I frantically paced around before pushing the bedroom door shut. "Are you keeping drugs in there? *With my kids*?" I yelled.

"No. You know I don't do that stuff. It was a big misunderstanding."

"Bullshit. You know nothing involving Bo is a misunderstanding. Where's he at anyway? I hope he's helping you put your house back together."

"He's in jail."

"This shit just gets better and better."

"They didn't find anything on him . . . or in the house, so they made up stuff. Some old traffic tickets. When Bo calls me, I gotta go downtown and bail him out."

"You need to wise up and leave him locked up."

"Stop with the hating, Solomon. You're way too jealous of Bo."

"Let's get one damn thing straight, Linda. I don't want you and could care less about the country kingpin. I don't want my kids in that unsafe environment you have over there."

Linda sounded as if she were at her wits' end, like she was holding back tears. "If you're threatening to take my babies again, I'll fight you every step of the way," she said.

I knew she would too. Judges around here didn't favor a father in this sort of matter, as I'd found out during our divorce. I was barely holding on to my job because of shit like this and, unlike Linda, didn't have a lawyer in my family to help me for free. Things needed to change for me for the better soon.

"Calm down. I'm not threatening that," I said, not up for this battle yet. "I don't want the kids to see their house like that either. Just bring their clothes by once you get things in order."

Linda agreed and said she would call first.

When I hung up, I was more determined than ever to do something about this situation. I knew I had the brains to put things together and just needed the right opportunity. On my bed, lay that magazine again. It had a way of following me around—like a sign. No more standing on the sidelines watching life pass me by, I thought to myself. For my kids, I was going to take action.

14 Janet

*"*T*o the wiiiiiiiiiiiindow to the wall,"* the Yin Yang Twins chanted on Lil' Jon & The Eastside Boyz' song "Get Low."

I moved my nude body from behind the pole and gyrated across the stage, following the instructions of the song as the three drunken frat boys right of stage sang along. Turning my back to everyone, I spread my legs and bent over giving me an upside down view of the patrons. Even from this vantage point, the lust streaming from their eyes told me they wanted me as usual, but my mind wasn't there. It was as if I were going through the motions, giving them just enough of myself that they didn't realize they were farther away from their feeble fantasies than usual. I felt the beat of the music, but didn't hear it.

I only heard the raised voices of Gerald and me.

"What's the big deal?" He asked with a shrug. I had been waiting for him to step through the door all day.

"What's the big deal?" I repeated, mimicking his shrug. "How'd you like it if I threw your shit away? Huh?"

Gerald simply walked away. He dropped his house keys on the kitchen counter then went toward the fridge in search of something to drink. "Honestly, I didn't think much of it. I thought you put all that shit behind you," he said, pretending it was an afterthought.

"When you start off something with 'honestly,' then I know you're lying," I yelled.

"Oh, some more of your stripper psychology?" He closed the refrigerator door and now had a tall glass of orange juice in hand.

"Keep talkin' shit. This stripper pays her bills." I pointed with my middle finger for emphasis. He hated when I did that. I hated his snide 'stripper' remarks just as much, but now something else had earned him my wrath.

"It was just one little letter. I didn't think you wanted the junk, so I threw it in the garbage."

"So you weren't even going to tell me about it?"

Gerald paused then took a drink before he uttered the simple word. "No."

"I hate it when you're childish like this."

I watched him mull it over. He took another swallow then set the glass down. "You treat me like one enough. Maybe it was time I acted the part."

"That invitation was for me. Not you. What right do you have to open my mail? What right do you have to make those decisions for me?"

"None. That's what you want to hear, isn't it? I don't have any fuckin' rights around here. Or when it comes to you."

"Damn straight," I huffed. "No man has those rights."

"Burned you that bad, huh?" he chuckled. "Screwed your head all the fuck up for the rest of us." I watched him twirl his finger around by his temple.

"Shut up. You don't know what you're talking about."

"Guess I struck a nerve. You're ready to run off to that bullshit class reunion at that bullshit school 'n' throw yourself at him like a trained lap dog, ain't ya?"

"Get out!" I screamed, covering my ears. My eyes reddened, but I wasn't crying. "Get the fuck out of my house, Shaw!"

He squinted at me as if peering through a fog. He blinked once quickly, more like a twitch, before he spoke. "I'm a grown-ass man, Janet. I think you forget that sometimes when you're on your high and mighty power trip."

I listened to Gerald cramming his few earthly belongings into a backpack and a large Army duffel bag. He began to go out the door, but extended his hand first. I didn't take it.

"That's how it's gonna be?"

"Yep."

"Over a stupid invitation," he chuckled.

"No. Over respect."

"I had that for you. Had. Too bad that was something you never had for me. I hope you find what you're looking for."

Part of me wanted to stop him, but Godiva was in charge. I refused to be weak behind a man. Even the one I may have loved.

As if sensing I had something to say, Gerald looked back. He heard nothing.

"I had news for you, too," he said. "Got a job at the Bellagio."

"Congratulations." I couldn't look him in the eye.

Gerald left, but not without his last remark, his parting shot.

"Janet."

"What?"

"When you told me to get out . . . you called me 'Shaw'."

"I called him . . . 'Shaw'," I mumbled to myself as a change of songs brought me back to my present surroundings. I suddenly found it hard to focus on the faces waving dollar bills at my feet, then I realized why. Tears.

I stumbled slightly, shocked that the club was now viewing Janet. That weak, delusional young girl they didn't deserve to know. The frat boys had stopped yelling and looked confused, not knowing if this was part of the act. Marty saw my makeup running and paused from his monetary calculations long enough to show concern. The music kept going and so did I. I cracked a smile at him and tried to get back into my routine.

A smoldering, sexy brother iced out from ear to ear and wrist to wrist was enticing me with a hundred-dollar bill. His skin, the color of smooth coal, had me interested in an up-close examination in private. It would be just the thing to take my mind off my emotions and back to business. Besides, it was obvious he was a big tipper. I slid a leg around slowly, seductively as I made my move in his direction.

I took one more step before, not noticing the dollar bills that been thrown on stage, slipping and falling flat on my back with a loud thud.

"G! G! Wake up!" Marty yelled as he shook me backstage. "Girl, don't make my insurance go up."

"Always looking out for us," I groaned, as the lights suddenly seemed bright. The girls around us breathed sighs of relief, no matter how false they were. I drank the water security handed me and felt the lump on the back of my head.

"What happened up there? Are you on something?"

"No. I just slipped on some money." I had to laugh at the notion myself.

"Uh huh." Marty eyed me suspiciously. "You scared the place with that tumble. Probably lost half the night's customers."

I turned my head from side to side and tried to shake the cobwebs off. "What happened to Chocolate Thunder?"

"Guuurl, you mean that dark, *foine* mofo?" Peaches asked, butting in, as was her nature. She still had that country twang I had lost years before. Hated it.

"Yeah. He still out there?"

She chuckled. "Yeah. You could say that. He all up in one of them private rooms with Misty."

I sucked air through my teeth, then moved the hair out of my face. Marty helped me to my feet. "Did somebody pick up my cash?"

"Right here." I did a quick count of what Marty handed to me. It looked a little light from what I remember being up there before I went bottoms up. He had cheated me.

"Do you need to go to a hospital?"

"No."

"*Whew*. Good," he sighed. "Can you go back out? I mean . . . there's a whole different crowd out there now."

"Actually, I was thinking of something else."

"Oh. Okay. You want to take the rest of the night off?"

I found my clothes and began putting them on. "I've got a better idea."

Outside The Standard, I started my car. Marty had begged and pleaded until finally giving up and returning inside. Besides, this would give Peaches a chance to prove her worth . . . to see if she was up to "The Standard." I needed some time off and she was only going to be holding my g-string temporarily. Not that she could hold my g-string.

My tires shrieked as I spun out of the club parking lot. I made a mental list of what was ahead: Shopping stops along the way at the Galleria in Dallas then Lenox Square in Buckhead and that factory outlet mall just outside Atlanta. Nothing but the best to make a girl feel like a million bucks, I thought. They weren't going to know what hit 'em.

15 Karim

"Pressing charges? *For what*? Oh, this is crazy!" I yelled into the speakerphone on my conference table. He could hear me from where I had been painting for relaxation, but I had to get my point across.

"I think so too, Karim," my attorney said through the crackly speaker, "but Jason North and On-Phire Records appear to be very serious. He claims Trouble—"

"Who?"

"Trouble . . . err . . . That's the name of the boy in that group Saint Roch," he paused. "Anyway. He claims Mr. Trouble suffered extensive damage to the tendons and ligaments in his wrist, which he uses to hold the microphone, at your hands."

"Bullshit. Clement, I only applied a little pressure to it. If I wanted to take his wrist off, it would be gone. No doubt."

"And I believe you," he said in his best Cambridge-educated English. "But you did lay your hands on him."

"He deserved it. But I didn't hurt him. I was there with him for three days on that video shoot, Clement. Three days. He acted like everything was straight between us. I even asked him. Then he wants to pull this?" I darted my hand, sending drops of paint cascading off the brush I still held. "That makes him a punk."

"It doesn't really matter. However, I don't think Mr. Trouble came up with this course of action."

"North?"

"Undoubtedly."

I sighed. "What does the snake want?"

"I'm glad you asked that. You're always so intuitive and astute."

"You could've left that sense of humor across the pond."

Clement laughed. The youngest son of a Nigerian-born English cabbie relished high stress situations. He spoke. "On-Phire Records has come up with a proposal. They claim they don't want this whole thing blown out of proportion in the media where it could ruin careers . . . or be taken the wrong way."

"I should've broken it." I fumed a few seconds longer. "Go ahead."

"They would like you to do another video . . . for another one of their artists. A way of bestowing your 'seal of approval' upon their label."

"That's all? If they're paying, I'll do another one. Those assholes are going to cough up more loot though. A whole lot more."

"Well, there may be a problem."

"Spit it out."

"They want you to 'donate' your time for the next video."

"You've got to be kidding."

"No. They appeared to be serious. They did indicate they were willing to negotiate however."

"There's nothing to negotiate. I stop their little asshole from pulling a statutory and they have the nerve to try to take advantage of me? Tell them go ahead and sue me. And if I catch Jason North in the NYC again, I'll really give them something to sue me over."

"Um . . . How do you want me to phrase that, Karim?"

"Exactly how I said it. See? I made it easy for you."

Clement put up a brief struggle before I went back to painting. I aimed my remote and turned the stereo back on. The CD I selected was Shai, a group of brothers from my alma mater, Howard University, the real HU. "If I Ever Fall In Love" and "Comforter" were the two songs that summed up my hidden feelings when I was in high school. I wondered if their music hadn't influenced my choice of college, but didn't really care. I had taken my love of music and infused it with the craft developed at Howard's Film School.

As I sang along with the acappella verses, the image of a woman became clearer with each brush stroke applied to the canvass. I still sucked at painting, but it was my therapy, my release.

"I didn't know you could sing."

"I can't."

"Oh."

I flipped my music off and took notice of the latest woman to share my bed. I was so caught up in everything else that I forgot she lay asleep. Just weeks earlier, she would've been gone by now. I don't know what was coming over me.

"I didn't know you could paint either." She rested her head against my shoulder to look at the mess I was creating.

"I can't. I just do . . . this," I said, gesturing wildly.

"Hmm. Is that me?"

I hadn't noticed it before, but there was some resemblance. Hell, a lot of resemblance. Similar eyes, the same high cheekbones, the same flawless ebony skin. Maybe that was my reason for letting her stay the night, for holding her. "No, it's someone else. Just somebody from long ago. Nothing special," I said, lying effortlessly. "Oh."

We returned to my bed one last time before she had to go. A Knick City Dancer, Jaquel also ran an after-school program in Bed Stuy. She left her business card by my Apple. Uncharacteristically, I kept it.

I slept for a few hours before being awakened by the familiar symphony. Clement was trying to reach me again. It could wait. I let Mozart play away as I threw the Blackberry onto the bed.

My painting rested there on its easel, awaiting what I normally did when I got to a certain point—throw it away with the rest. Each time, I did get a little better. The subject was daring me to maybe keep *this* painting . . . *this time*. I ran my fingers through my mop. It was time for a cut.

I walked to my desk, picked up and read the invitation I had been thinking about again.

The class of Marion High School, Home of the Mighty Eagles
Invites to you to
A spectacular 10-Year Reunion
Featuring a Fun-filled Weekend
At the
Gaffney Sheraton & Convention Center
Please R.S.V.P.
Donna LaVelle, Reunion Chair
(864)555-9876

Our reunion was being held in Gaffney, the next town over. Being a little bit larger, it always had more options.

Even when I was there, I remembered people driving down the road to Gaffney for weddings and stuff.

I read the rest of the invitation, then dialed the hotel on my phone.

A voice on the other end rambled off a memorized greeting.

"Yes, I'm calling to make a reservation. I'll be attending the Marion reunion. The invitation says to mention the special discount."

16 Trayce

"You scared of flying?"

"Not as bad as my mother. She refuses to fly."

"They always say the takeoffs and landings are the worst part."

"That's why I'm glad it's nonstop to Atlanta. I'll be having my share of Bloody Marys."

Rosalina held back a laugh as she switched lanes in her Volvo wagon. She was nice enough to give me a ride to O'Hare, as I didn't have a car yet. I looked at the signs overhead guiding us to departures for my airline. I had a case of nerves this morning, but not from my pending flight. I turned up Rosalina's music to take the edge off. One of DLG's old albums played. Figures. She loved Huey Dunbar, who'd left their group Dark Latin Grooves, so much that I teased her about going straight for him. She began shaking to their song "Gotcha" and I joined in.

"Get it, Trayce!"

In a rare moment, I allowed myself to just be silly as we danced in our seats. We didn't stop until the skycap opened my car door and took my luggage.

I leaned over and gave Rosalina a hug.

"Thanks for the ride, mami."

"You just be sure to have a good time, okay."

"Okay."

I rolled my carry-on bag behind me and went through the automatic doors. The first thing I felt was the icy breath of air lashing at me. I closed my eyes and recited John from the Bible.

"Greater is He that is in me, than he that is in the world."

I hadn't spoken those words in over eleven years. They were what got me through my lowest point in life. Now I was confronting that low point.

I was going home.

17 *Solomon*

"**I**s it too late to register for the reunion?"

"No, not at all," Donna, the event chair replied. "We might have a problem with rooms though. We had a few extras, but some last minute registrations took them yesterday. There's also a wedding going on at the same time. *Can you believe it*?" She still had that singsong tone to her voice. In school, she was involved in everything and loved to talk.

"I won't need a room." *Couldn't afford one.* "I live here."

"Oh," she said, her curiosity piqued. "*Is this Renaldo*?"

"No. It's Solomon. Solomon Muncie."

"Who?" I heard papers rustling.

"You might have me listed as 'Solemn'."

"Oooh. I am *so* sorry. I'll be sure to get this corrected, Solomon." She hadn't a clue as to who I was. "I'm trying to do all this by myself and things go wrong sometimes."

I forced a laugh. "I forgive you."

"Didn't you used to hang with Renaldo?"

"No."

"Dwight?"

"No."

"Rico?"

"No," I sighed.

"I know! Michael."

She wasn't going to stop. I took pity on her and put her out of her suffering. "I kinda kept to myself, Donna."

"Oh. I see. Are you married, Solomon?"

"No. Not anymore."

"Well, you're going to have to save me a dance then," she chuckled.

I had plenty time for dancing on my schedule now. Missing too many days at work had ensured that. I had just been fired from my job.

18 Janet

"So, I'll see you when I'm in Vegas then?"

"Yes you will," I gushed as I bared my teeth, playfully biting my tongue. "Just bring that VIP card and tell them Godiva sent you. If I weren't in such a hurry for my daddy's surgery, I'd give you a sneak preview."

He adjusted his sunglasses, trying to hide his blush. "That's a fine car, but try 'n keep the speed down, ma'am."

"Will do, officer." I played up my southern accent for his benefit and gave him a cheerful wave. "Thank you for being so understanding."

I waited for the police car to drive away, then sat there for a moment. Once he was over the hill, I shot a middle finger up and threw his business card, *which included his home telephone number*, out the window. I had a car full of shopping bags and had made it as far as Alabama without getting a ticket yet. I was damn proud.

I retrieved my cell phone from my purse and dialed home. I waited anxiously with each ring, hoping on the off chance that Gerald might be there and pick up. My voice answered.

"Gerald, I know you probably won't get this message. But if you happen to stop by, I didn't want you to be worried about me. I've got some things I need to work out, so I'll be gone awhile. If there's an emergency . . . or if you just want to talk, call me."

I flipped the phone shut. I counted the seconds to see if it would ring. It didn't. I started my car again and looked in my rearview mirror. I spent a few moments playing with my hair and applying some lipstick.

"That's my girl," I said with a confident smile. I then sped over the hill, roaring down I-20.

19 Karim

I looked at the arrival and departure schedule broadcast on the overhead monitors. My connecting flight to Charlotte was delayed due to bad weather, so I was going nowhere fast. After asking a few questions, I found out my wait would be pushing on five hours. I rolled my travel bag to the nearest bar where I planned to take the load off.

I ordered a beer and watched the TV that was turned to ESPN. They were talking about Kobe Bryant and something that had occurred on the court. I restrained myself when I overheard an old white man mutter something about "stringin' him up" over those prior allegations back in Colorado. As much as he obviously would've liked for those days to return, they weren't coming back. I took some solace in that and wondered how he would've felt knowing my mom was a white woman who had the nerve to sleep with a black man AND have a kid by him.

"Dumbass," I cursed.

"You're talking about Kobe?" my nosy bartender asked.

"Yeah. Him too," I said, taking a swig of my Shiner Bock. "Get me another one. It's going to be a long day."

I didn't know if she would be there—or she would be married or pregnant with her fifth bigheaded child, Jarvis.

I didn't have room for self-doubt in my life. She was going to be there.

Lost, like the tears that used to tide me over . . .

"Go ahead, Shaw. Your turn." I was drunk but recognized his gleeful cackle. It was Michael, one of the biggest assholes at school. He was Shaw's best friend and rode his coattails everywhere. My head was ringing. I had given up trying to focus on the shadows swirling around and concentrated on what was being said about me.

I strained to speak. "Please. You don't have to do this." It was so soft, I don't know if anyone heard it. I just hoped he had. "Please," I pleaded. "Don't."

I still tried to make sense of what was happening to me. I thought my life had turned around after the horror with Coach Taylor. Shaw seemed so sweet. Clear out of the blue; he spoke to me one day after school. I didn't trust him at first, but then he introduced me to some of his teammates. They all seemed friendly, except for Michael. Maybe I was star-struck that people in The Crew would give a nerd like me the time of day. Maybe I was just naïve and desperately seeking some acceptance.

I had never been to a real party, so didn't know what

to expect when Shaw invited me as his guest. I had begged my mother to put a dress on her Sears card for me. As I preened and pranced in the mirror, I wasn't the dumpy big girl anymore. I was popular. I had friends.

My mother wondered why the school quarterback hadn't been gentleman enough to pick me up. I explained to her that he wasn't my boyfriend and that since the party was in our neighborhood, I would just walk over. So I walked . . . and walked. I had worked up quite a thirst by the time I got to Michael's house, where the party was. Even Michael seemed happy to have me over. Shaw shooed him and the other guys away and led me over to the punch bowl. Shaw explained that I had arrived first and that the other girls were on their way over.

He was so nice. He sat with me and kept bringing me drinks. I was thirsty anyway, but felt warmer and warmer as time passed. It started getting harder to think, but Shaw assured me everything was going to be okay. My breathing became shallow and I remember Shaw whispering in my ear. Telling me everything was going to be okay and to relax. I felt his hands on me and kisses on my neck. He reached up my dress. At least I think it was Shaw.

"What's wrong, bruh? You got the ho here. Do yo' thang." Michael's voice boomed, stirring me toward consciousness again.

"I don't know 'bout this," Shaw said. "She looks kinda sick, y'know."

"Sick from all this dick!" one of the shadows belted out. The rest of them laughed.

I blinked, then Shaw's face came into focus. His eyes looked desperately into mine. My clothes were off and I was spread across a bed. I tried to move, but my arms were held tightly. It looked like most of the boys in the room were either in their underwear or wearing nothing at all. Michael, a bottle of Mad Dog 20/20 dangling in his hand, was in Shaw's ear, egging him on.

"I think Shaw's afraid of sloppy seconds. Too good to get a piece after his boys."

"Shut the fuck up," Shaw replied, still lingering over me. "I got a girlfriend, man."

"What's Janet got to do with this, nigga? If you afraid of it, you need to move aside. Some of us want another turn." They laughed again. It was a laugh absent joy, but filled with eagerness.

"No," I cried as Shaw looked at me once more. "Please. Stop."

From my view, I was the only one to see into his eyes. Those eyes. Shaw had a deranged gaze, as if he were at war with himself. It scared me more than my predicament.

He pulled his underwear down and entered me. Vigorously, he pumped as the boys hooted and hollered. He was their leader. He had set me up and he was one of them.

In that moment, all I could think of was my dress my mother had bought for me. I didn't know where it was and didn't want anything to happen to it.

21 Trayce

"Will you be needing one key or two, ma'am?" the weary-eyed manager asked. I had overheard her saying she was supposed to be off six hours ago, but couldn't because somebody called in sick.

"Just one, please."

The lobby of the Sheraton was filled with people arriving for a wedding. I had waited patiently in line to check in behind most of them, eavesdropping on the bride and groom's honeymoon plans. Sprinkled among them were faces that dared me to recognize them. I avoided eye contact with those.

Upon instructions to my room and the usual "enjoy your stay" from the manager, I headed for the elevator. After the flight into Atlanta and the two-hour trip up I-85 in my rental, I had visited with my mother and put that smile on her face. She wasn't around now and I was in need of a smile of my own. I counted down the numbers as the elevator headed my way.

"Trayce! Over here!"

It was too loud for me to ignore. Damn. Donna's voice

hadn't changed and the elevator was just descending to the third floor. I feigned looking around before turning toward the waving lady. She stood behind a long, covered table outside one of the conference rooms. I squinted, causing her to wave even more frantically.

Oh well, I thought. The elevator door opened for me, but I walked away.

Donna was jumbling packets around on the table and rearranging lists. There was a covered box for some sort of drawing and a large basket of candy arranged at the end. Three children who looked to be hers provided her slave labor as they hauled boxes of shirts in and out of the room behind her. Donna had filled out a little since high school, but was still the tiny girl with large, round eyes I remembered.

"Give me a hug," she said, extending her arms to say she wasn't taking no for an answer. I leaned over the table. "Oh, I'm so glad you came."

"Hey, Donna."

"Well, you sure look good, girl. Haven't changed a bit."

"Just a little."

"Good thing I saw you. You know you're going to need this for our reunion." She grabbed stuff off the table, shoving it into my hands, and hollered at her son to bring a shirt out. "Here's your packet and your T-shirt. The largest they come in is extra large. Is that okay?"

"That'll be fine." I blew off her remark as I have most of my life. I really wanted to wrap the shirt around her neck though.

"Now, everything in there should be self-explanatory. But if you have any questions, I'll be down here most of the day. We are going to have so much fun!"

"I can't wait."

"Get yourself situated and we're gonna have to catch

up, okay? I hear such good things about you, girl. *Black Enterprise* and all. You're really putting our town on the map."

"Hey. Just out there trying to make a dollar."

She giggled. "Looks like you're making several of them, Trayce. We always knew you'd make it."

Whatever. "Thanks. Still have a long way to go."

"Listen. We're having blue lagoon martinis out by the gazebo for five. I'm calling them 'Mighty Eagle' martinis for this weekend, okay? There will be a live jazz band playing too."

"Sounds good."

"Yes it is. We'll be mixin'and minglin' in style. Everyone will be there." Her voice sped up the more excited she became. I saw her eyes trail off before she waved at somebody else checking in. I was about to make my escape. She continued, "Dinner's at eight in the ballroom. Be sure to wear your best."

"I don't know about this."

"Trayce, you've taken such a large step. Has somebody said something?"

"No. I haven't seen anyone. They're all downstairs getting reacquainted." I stretched the phone cord and walked to my window. I had a direct view of the mixer below. Little people milled about, some wearing the same T-shirts as the one I'd been given. I tried to imagine who was who. I didn't know if I was prepared to be among them just yet. "I feel like such a whiner calling you over this."

"Trayce, I said call me any time and that's just what I meant. You're going to get through this."

"Yes," I said, sucking in air. "Even if it kills me."

"Are you going downstairs?"

I waited to answer. "Yes. Just not yet."

22 Solomon

When I arrived at the hotel, I parked my car as far off as possible. I hated how it would continue to sputter and choke when I turned it off and frankly was embarrassed that somebody might witness it. My old sport coat was still holding up. Very presentable, I thought as I looked at my reflection in the window tint. I had worn it to my first job interview. Here I was wearing it again and in need of another job. It was never me, but I wore it on the off chance of providing me with some luck.

Inside, I strutted past the front desk as if I had a room there, whistling for no good reason. Donna, who I had spoken with, was in the hallway to greet us. She was taking a sip of bottled water as a few other classmates talked nearby.

"May I help you?" she asked.

"I guess you can." I put on my best cheerful smile. "I believe one of those packets there is for me."

"Solomon?"

"Yes, you remember me then?"

"No," she said, dashing my feeble hopes. "You're one

of the last people on my list. But I do remember your voice. I felt so bad after I got off the phone with you."

"It's okay. I'm used to it."

"Will I still get that dance with you later?" she asked. I thought she was just fronting at first, but now I wasn't sure. Donna always smiled, but she was holding it longer this time. Her pearly whites glistened.

"Sure," I said. "Why not?" I remembered Donna as the too-talkative gossip of Marion, but time had a way of changing us all. True, we were two of the shortest people around and she seemed nice enough. Unfortunately, she wasn't my type. Maybe it was the "Mighty Mouse" in me, but I liked a larger woman. Besides, I wasn't here for that.

"Good, good," she asserted. "Oh. Let me introduce you to my children." The three of them stood behind her in a single file line, like she had given them *the lecture* at home before coming here. She must've had her first one early, I thought. "This is Jordan. This is Monica. And this little thing is Dex."

"Dex?"

"Short for 'Dexter'. That's his daddy's name. I'm not with him anymore," she made a point to mention, adding a heaping spoonful of smiles on top of it. "Matter of fact, they're waiting on their daddy to pick them up. Lord knows they've been here all day helping me. He's taking them to Chuck E. Cheese." I watched the three of them, especially Monica, smile at the mere mention.

"One of my kids is named Jordan too."

"Must be a fan of Number 23 too, huh?"

"Yep. Weren't we all? How could I not be with him up the road?"

"Mmm. Something in common," she said.

I shuffled through my packet intentionally to bring her back to the matter at hand. On cue, Donna regained her composure and found a T-shirt for me. She then gave me the rundown on all the activities as I listened intently.

The jazz band played that song from Spike Lee's *Mo Betta Blues*, taking me back. The piano player tickled the ivories as the bass player strummed. The trumpeter wiped his forehead with his handkerchief, waiting for his spot. It was early evening, but still warm. A few couples, getting reacquainted as the drinks worked their spell and peeled away the years, swayed to the music.

I stood by the gazebo, helping myself to a few pieces of cheese as the tray passed, and sipped a bit of my martini. My stomach growled as it longed for something heavier, but I ignored it. I was doing my thing. Watching. And waiting for someone.

There were the locals, the ones like me who never left. Michael, always the dumb jock and probably still a rude asshole, owned his own string of check-cashing and payday loan places these days. They covered at least three counties and his commercials blanketed every channel. Shauna, one of our cheerleaders and runner-up in several beauty pageants, became a beautician. She lived in Gaffney and filled her prescriptions at my store. My store. I smirked at the sad irony, recognizing that I wouldn't be filling them anymore.

"Excuse me. Where'd you get that drink?"

"The bar's under that tree," I said, turning around to look at the guy as I pointed. "Cameron, right?"

He laughed politely. "Hey, man. How've you been?" Our former drum major and editor of the school newspaper was crisply dressed in a pair of slacks and a linen shirt. A very thin, defined mustache adorned his upper lip. He gave that look that said, *I'm pretending I know who you are, but I don't.* I knew that wasn't the case this time. He was faking it.

"Fine. Are you just getting here?"

"Yeah. Nice setup."

"Donna did a great job."

"She still can't shut up," he muttered, avoiding all eye contact.

"Haven't seen you around here. You moved, right?"

"Yeah. Down in Atlanta—the ATL." He shifted around. "Well, I need a drink. Nice seeing you again . . ."

"Solomon," I answered for him. "Yeah. You too."

I was watching Cameron's beeline for the bar with curiosity. Something had him agitated, but my attention became diverted. A new arrival to the party. Hello.

Just as Shauna was always runner-up, there had to be a winner. Shauna's best friend, Janet was that winner. A tall, drop-dead gorgeous dream of chocolate, she was. The queen of The Crew wore a black designer pantsuit, its jacket barely covering her breasts. Hmm, not a bra in sight. I guess she held them in with some of that tape. I saw a lot of that in those videos Jordan liked. Black shades covered the windows to her soul, leaving just her smile to rely on.

Shauna spotted her and came running. The two of them hugged and began chatting it up. Not bad to look at, but not what I had come for though. I finished my drink and continued to wait . . . and watch.

23 Janet

"No valet parking?" I sighed. "I guess I really am home."

The bellman was nice enough to remove all my shopping bags for me. He seemed a little awestruck at not seeing any luggage. As spontaneous as my trip across America was, my shopping reflected it even more. After raising the retractable hardtop, it only took a smile to get him to park my car for me too.

After checking in and making sure the hotel had my suite reserved for me, I sashayed over to our reunion table to face the music.

"Janet!" Donna screamed, not helping my road lag in the least. People milling about in the lobby turned to see what the commotion was about. I hoped I wasn't going to be barraged with questions over Shaw and how that went down. I had enough of those saved up myself.

"Hey, girl. You haven't changed in all these years."

"And neither have you, Janet," she gushed. Like most students, she wanted to be a part of The Crew. And like most, it stayed that way. On the outside looking in. "You're still as beautiful as ever."

"Ain't it the truth," I said with a false laugh. Actually, I thought I looked way better now. "What you got here?"

"A gift bag with some goodies and this here is your T-shirt."

I fished around inside the bag, coming up with a sheet of paper with most of our class listed on it. "What's this for?"

"That sheet has everybody who signed up for the reunion," she said proudly. Donna was always big on lists and stuff. "I have a big surprise in store."

I stepped into the warm evening feeling refreshed. I had ironed my clothes and treated myself to a long soak in my bath salts before slipping in a brief nap. On my way out to mingle, I had made a quick detour to the ballroom. Dinner was being served in there later and I had one tiny detail to change. Weave looking tight; I let folk at the mixer take in my black designer outfit and me. With the jacket outlining my bare breasts, a platinum drop lariat adorned my neck ending in a snake-like frill at the center of my chest.

It was a trip reading the faces of men I once knew. Wedding bands were being nervously twisted while the single ones were mentally putting their resumes together. I was so naïve of the power I possessed back then. I could if I wanted to, but I wasn't here to bleed their wallets dry. Besides, no one here knew where I went when I left or what I was doing. None of their fuckin' business anyway, I thought to myself.

Out of the assortment of faces, a familiar smile greeted me.

"Janet!"

"Shauna!"

Of all the people I wished I had stayed in touch with, Shauna was the one. The rest of The Crew be damned. I was happy to see she didn't bear me any ill will.

"Da-yum, girl. You are looking like a million bucks up in here."

I did a little turn for all to see then hugged my friend again. "You look great too, Shauna." I lied, but it seemed like the right thing to say. She looked "all right", but the years hadn't been as kind to her. Shauna had added some pounds, probably from child-bearing and good old Southern cooking. Her hairstyle was straight from last year, but I guess things like that didn't matter when it came to friends. I had spent too many years in Vegas assessing other women as competition, threats, or as just plain weak. Shauna was none of those. She was my friend and we were back together.

I lowered my sunglasses and surveyed the people in attendance. No Shaw. "Donna actually got our class to show up. I can't believe it."

"Yeah. She lives for this stuff these days. Donna's an elementary school teacher in town. Went through a divorce a year ago from what I heard. Her husband was principal here in Gaffney and got caught doin' the mom of one of his students."

"You keep track of all that? You must still live around here."

Shauna looked embarrassed to answer. Of the two of us, she was the one with the dreams of moving away. I was too focused on becoming Shaw's wife and settling down. Life can be a joke sometimes. "Yes. Found me a good man and settled down." She motioned toward a tall, attractive man the color of coffee with two spoons of creamer. He cracked a smile and raised his martini glass. "Two wonderful kids too," she continued.

"Good for you," I said, placing my hands on her shoulders. I meant it genuinely. "So what other gossip do you have on our classmates?"

"Girl, you better get one of these martinis first. It's going to take some time to fill you in," she chuckled.

24 Karim

"Here's your hotel, sir."

"About damn time." I had given up hiding my disgust from the limo driver. He was supposed to be from around these parts, but had missed our exit twice. I had delays every step of this trip, as if I wasn't supposed to be here. Just a minor setback, I told myself. Now that I had committed, I wasn't going to miss this for anything.

Once the limo stopped, I ran inside to the front desk. I was glad I had my reservation held with my American Express black card. By the time the limo driver brought my luggage in, I had received my key. I had an extra and gave it to him to bring my bags up to my suite while I went in search of Donna.

I couldn't find Donna, but saw an empty table in the hallway with a banner hanging from it. The Mighty Eagle crest was dead center. I looked at my watch then hurried over.

A large brown envelope lay atop with my name handwritten on it. Underneath it was a T-shirt. I took a quick read of the itinerary enclosed in my packet, then looked at my watch again.

I had missed the "mingle session" and judging by the time, I was going to miss the big dinner reception if I didn't get my ass into high gear.

From where I stood, I could see people beginning to congregate in the ballroom. I took a deep breath then ran for the elevator so I could change.

25 Trayce

"Excuse me," I said as I maneuvered around the waiter. I arrived a little early so I could find my table and take a seat. I wasn't about to walk the gauntlet of filled seats that would've awaited me later. I had been in executive boardrooms a hell of a lot more impressive than this ballroom, but never did they scare me this much.

I'd spent hours toiling over what I was going to wear. That was after I decided I was really going to do this. My braids were pulled up and swept to the back where I had them pinned. I wore a strapped full-length black gown handpicked back in Chicago by Rosalina. I was never much of a dresser, so it took over half an hour of pleading on her part to talk me into paying the insane amount on the price tag. I must admit, it did make me feel good wearing it. Little things like this were comforts I needed to get through this.

The ballroom was larger than I would've imagined in this town. There was a high ceiling adorned with paintings with a brilliant chandelier in the center. Small intimate tables were spaced all around with a stage setup to the front of the room. On each table, there were lit candles with nameplates positioned evenly around them. Each one consisted of a name, *of course*, and a yearbook photo with a brief description underneath. I dreaded what mine might say.

It took some time to find my table, but in looking around I noticed a pattern. People were set up as close to their old cliques as possible. The Crew occupied most of the larger tables in the center with lesser groupings on the fringes with tables that seated only four. I belonged to no group, not even the Honor Society, so I may have been left out of the room altogether. At a small table near the wall, somebody waved at me.

The smallish man, who was seated, pointed to my nameplate then stood up like a gentleman to greet me. He wore a basic penguin suit. His close haircut barely concealed his receding hairline. He smiled as he took my hand. That's when I recognized him. His eyes still made me nervous.

26 Solomon

I toyed with my nameplate at the table. At least it was spelled correctly this time. I wasn't in the yearbook, so a simple black square adorned the spot where my photo would've been. From looking at the names of my table-mates, things were going to be interesting to say the least.

I had arrived early and took a seat. The only person who may have had some interest in talking to me at the mixer was Donna, but her duties were keeping her busy.

A beautiful full-bodied woman in a black dress came in first, almost colliding with one of the waiters as he sped to deliver iced teas to all the tables. I watched the game progress as she went from table to table looking for her seat. It wasn't til she came closer that I recognized her. Bingo. Her hair was much different than it was in her magazine picture, but the sweet face was still the same.

I smiled and waved my hand to get her attention. But-terflies filled my stomach. I couldn't tell if they were from what I had to do or from what I was suddenly feel-ing. I told myself to be patient as I stood to greet her.

"Trayce, right? Looks like we're going to be table mates."

"Yep. Looks like it," she replied. She seemed very nervous. I pulled her chair out for her, trying to put her at ease. "I'm sorry, I don't remember your name."

"That's quite alright. It's Solomon. Solomon Muncie. I think we took PE together." Bad mention. I knew it once it came out my mouth.

Trayce fell silent for a moment, eyeing me by candlelight. "I remember you."

"You do?"

"Yes," she chuckled. "You're not as quiet anymore."

"True." I joined her in a laugh. "You ain't seen nothin' yet. I'm a social butterfly these days."

"That's good to hear. I'll need some laughs."

"Marion sucked for you too, huh?"

She laughed again as she warmed up. "Buddy, you don't know the half."

But I did know.

27 Janet

I entered the ballroom with everybody else. While most of the dresses were full-length for this occasion, I unveiled my new strapless, short Italian number complete with matching handbag. I accessorized things with matching diamond earrings and a choker.

Unlike the others who fumbled to find their places, I walked in a straight line to my table. I let a slight smile break as I admired my craftiness. I had found my name-tag earlier in the evening and switched places with someone. I didn't want to be anywhere near The Crew. Shauna was still my girl, but that other stuff was in the past. Okay, okay. I was fooling myself. I mainly didn't want to be seated next to Shaw. I figured somebody was trying to get a laugh out of that and I simply wasn't the one.

Two people were already seated at my table and carrying on from the looks of it. I watched the two laughing and talking like old friends. I didn't recognize them at first and wrote them off as members of the "nerd patrol". The little man noticed me first, then went right back to his conversation, not missing a beat. *I'll be damned*, I thought, caught off guard by the unnatural reaction to me. *Either the conversation was REALLY good or this little bugger had the hots for big mamma across the table from him.*

I recognized the woman on the second look. Damn. It was the class ho, Trayce. I knew I should've read the names on the table. Maybe I would've swapped hers instead. For all her obvious flaws and shortcomings, I wanted to attack her, tear her down. But I couldn't. From what Shauna told me, she was one of those millionaire dot.com-ers or on her way to becoming one. If she were still a ho, then she certainly was a *driven* ho—and that I had to admire. Nice dress too, I begrudgingly admitted.

"Hello, all," I said as I walked up.

Both of them smiled politely and mumbled their greetings. Little man didn't even have the nerve to get up from his seat. Trayce probably had his little pecker on hard and he was too embarrassed to stand, I thought.

Trayce seemed uncomfortable with my joining them. I could hear whispers from other tables as they realized where I was sitting too. That suited me just fine. The waiter filled my glass with tea and I sent him back for some lemon. Trayce overheard me and asked for some also. I took the break in their conversation to play nice.

"So how have you been, Trayce? I hear you're pretty successful."

"I suppose. Word sure travels fast."

"You know how it is. Same as it was in school." It was my not-so-veiled way of reminding her of the time she screwed my boyfriend and possibly half the football team. I honestly didn't know who she was until then. We all knew of Trayce the ho after that. I guess that incident could be considered her coming-out party. The little guy cut an evil look in my direction, as if he took the remark personally. I could see the "S" on his chest beneath that horrible rented tuxedo. I tasted my salad and winked at him.

"And what is your name?" I asked now that I had his attention.

"Solomon."

"Oh." I'd never heard of him. I finished chewing. "Pleased to meet you."

"You too. It's good to see everyone's grown up around here," he sighed.

"Amen to that," I said with a laugh and a raised glass of tea.

"What do you do, Solomon? I can tell by your accent that you still live 'round here."

He was preparing to speak when applause cut him off. We all looked to see what was up.

My playfully catty personality suddenly soured.

Shaw was here.

Shauna had provided me some scoop to help prepare me. After graduating and kicking me to the curb, Shaw went on to quarterback and run track for FAMU. He was now playing in the Arena League and living in Stone Mountain, Georgia, a suburb of Atlanta.

My former boyfriend sucked all the air out of the place, leaving us mere mortals gasping for breath. He still had that way about him. A black-on-black Antonini Loretta Elite tux engulfed his fine body as if he had been dipped in it. The buttons were a dead giveaway. It was as stylish and high dollar as the high-yellow heffa on his arm. Long curly brown locks and blue eyes were what this one got by on in addition to her tight body. At least it wasn't the typical Blonde Bambi from Bumfuck, Iowa that our brothers seemed fixated on if they were athletes. That didn't really comfort me though. Was she the reason Shaw did what he did? Why he never wanted to make love to me?

Was he just holding out for "something better" in his mind? Had he been waiting to "upgrade" me?

Part of me wanted to tackle him and scratch his eyes out until I had my answer. I had way too much respect and confidence in myself for that. For my own peace of mind, I was going to leave here with my answers though.

As Shaw and his trophy made their way through the handshakes, cheers and high fives, I picked up on how uncomfortable Trayce had become. She had a sour grimace worse than mine as she watched Shaw take his seat at the nearby table. Being the woman I am now, it made me reconsider what I had so easily taken for granted about her. I began to think that this reunion might be enlightening in more ways than one.

Everything quieted down as people went back to their private conversations and the dinner salads at hand. I saw Donna darting about, as she appeared ready to take the stage. The three of us at my table were all taking a sip of tea when a hush fell over the room. I looked back at the stage, expecting to see Donna ready to speak. She wasn't there. She was still at someone's table, but was hushed like everyone else. We had a late arrival. And the women all paused.

A man stood in the doorway to the ballroom. Not just a man, but also a *sexy* man. He had an exotic quality to him, as if some Boris Kodjoe/European model-type, but with a hard edge in his eyes like Rick Fox. His reddish brown hair looked hastily combed back, like he normally wore it wild and free. He went black on black like Shaw, but the tux he wore was tailor-made. He had muscles too, but of a wiry sort. He looked like the kind of brother that would have you sweating and speakin' in tongues as you hung butt-naked upside down from the bed. Most of the women in the ballroom, by their open mouths, would probably agree with me. Can the church say, "Amen?"

He looked around for an open table, to which everyone started checking nameplates to help him out, especially the ladies. The rest of The Crew hastily checked their tables for an open spot, naturally assuming he had been one of us. I could hear names of people being tossed about that maybe had been left off accidentally by Donna. Donna looked confused too. He began walking toward our end of the room.

And didn't stop until he got to our table.

Trayce just stared while Solomon seemed unfazed.

He looked me in the eyes and smiled.

"I believe that's my spot," he said, raising one finger to the nameplate and vacant spot at the table.

Oh shit. *"Karim?"*

28 Karim

"Yep. It's me. Glad you remember," I held out my hand and she took it. Man, Janet looked off the chain—simply incredible. All that was missing was a rose to hand to her. If I hadn't been so late I would've done just that. I wanted a hug, but she didn't stand up. "What's wrong?" I asked.

"Nothing," she said. Her voice didn't say that. I knew I would shock a lot of people, but not like this.

"Hey, Trayce," I said calmly, acknowledging the smart girl with the grade point average second only to mine. She seemed less tense than I remember her, but even she seemed startled by the new me.

"What up, man," I addressed the other guy at our table. "Karim."

"Solomon," he replied, touching fists with me.

"Right, right."

Nobody said anything else. "Man, yo. Why is everybody so quiet? It's like a funeral in here."

I looked around and all eyes were on me. Somebody who I think was Donna, the reunion chair, had walked onstage and approached the podium. "Oops. Guess I better sit down."

The waiter came up and asked if I wanted a salad. I passed, seeing that everybody else was finishing. Janet was seated to my right and on instinct I clenched her hand again across the table. It was so soft. I imagined it caressing my face. It was good feeling she was just as excited to see me as I her. It was even better than I imagined.

"Good evening, class," Donna giggled, her voice booming over the microphone.

"Good evening," we replied in unison with a hearty laugh.

Donna went on to welcome all of us to our class reunion. I wished I'd arrived earlier to get acclimated. People at the other tables were whispering and trying not to be too obvious as they attempted to place me. I tried to ignore it as I was here for one thing. Surprise, surprise, the one thing wound up sharing the same table with me.

Smelling her perfume, feeling her aura so close to me after all these years was intoxicating. I thought about how many canvases I'd ruined trying to capture the essence of something that was never mine. *Never was and never will be* was an internal verse I refused to hear for fear of it being true.

"Carrot Top," someone hissed. Those words shot at me as if fired by a sniper, hitting me in the pit of my stomach. I was usually on the receiving end of a fist when I heard those words. I was recognized.

I glanced over the nearby tables, trying to find the mouth that uttered those hateful words. Curiously enough, I was just noticing how most of us were arranged. Most of The Crew, from the faces I remembered, was front and center.

Solomon, seeing that I was just figuring things out,

held back a laugh. "Welcome to the outcast table," he said with a smile.

Just then, I'd recognized Michael as the reminder of my pain. The tubby man in the white dinner jacket was staring at me while elbowing Shaw to get his attention. I wondered why Shaw wasn't with Janet until I saw the woman seated next to him. He had great taste, I'll give him that. Michael, still lacking any tact, kept staring and even dared to smile at me. I smiled back, nodded my head, signaling I'd remembered him too, and shot him the bird. "Fuck 'em. Fuck 'em all," I replied to Solomon.

"I couldn't have said it better."

Janet, perhaps hearing too much, whispered over her shoulder, "You sure have changed, Karim."

"Mmm hmm," Trayce agreed. I seemed to amuse her.

29 Trayce

"If you have looked in your bags I gave out earlier," Donna instructed, "you've noticed a list of everyone in attendance. From putting this whole thing together, I know for a fact that a lot of you haven't kept in touch."

A lot of heads nodded.

She continued, "I've had an opportunity to learn about some of you, but I want everyone to know. I'd like a couple of people to stand up."

Everyone fidgeted in their chairs, not wanting to be called out or put on the spot. First up was Michael. He seemed pretty happy receiving some recognition and tried to go on stage to talk some more. Next up was Shaw, who seemed even more of a celebrity now. Janet was most uncomfortable then. She always seemed vain with no clear direction, but I couldn't help the tinge of pity I felt for her.

We learned about three other classmates, mostly from the large, *privileged* tables before Donna wrapped it up.

"I have one other person that I want to mention. Probably because she would refuse to do this herself." I laughed along with everybody else, but started feeling uncomfortable. "Trayce . . . would you stand up?"

I shook my head "no," trying to talk her out of it. Anyone who knew Donna knew that wasn't happening.

I stood up, palms sweaty, as a roomful of eyes looked me up and down. To calm myself, I looked down at the table. My eyes met those of Solomon, my new friend. His nod told me everything was going to be fine.

"Our very own Ms.— *It is Miss, right?*" I shook my head. Donna continued to read what she knew of my life story after graduation. I was forced to endure the oooos and awwws as people who formerly ridiculed me were now privy to way too much of my life. My therapist didn't prepare me for this.

Donna went on a few minutes longer before finishing with the *Black Enterprise* article. My mother would've been so proud if she were here. I was given a big round of applause with a few people, including all my tablemates, standing up. At the large table nearby, Shaw was standing too. I'm not sure how that made me feel.

Things died down and Donna finished. "Well, now y'all know a little something about some of our classmates. I need y'all to complete your information on those lists and to tell your neighbors all about yourselves over dinner. Does anybody remember the box out in the hall? Well, when we're all finished we are going to vote on Mr. and Ms. Marion High and we will announce the winners tomorrow night during the dance. *Isn't that great?* Oh . . . By the way, we will have another surprise tomorrow night, so be sure to be there. Our school may be gone, but we ain't. Soooooo LET'S GO!"

"MIGHTY EAGLES!" the room erupted in unison.

30 Solomon

Our options of chicken or fish were being served for dinner. "You were a great sport," I said to Trayce as my waiter put my plate in front of me.

"Yeah, you handled that well, girl," Janet added. All traces of sarcasm and cattiness had dropped from her voice.

"Thank you. I feel kind of odd saying this, but y'all made me feel at ease. At this table, I mean."

"That's because things are so *intimate* with us," Karim joked as he exaggerated our lack of space. "If I breathe in too hard, Solomon might faint."

"You are just too outgoing, Karim," Janet gushed. "C'mon. Spill the beans. What woman got you open like that?"

Karim seemed to debate over his response, before deciding. "None," he replied. "You're just seeing the guy I always was."

"Boy, please. You were always wrapped up in your music. Used to walk around with those headphones on all the time."

"Yep, I remember that." Even Trayce was unwinding. "So what are you doing now, Karim? You're dressing like a million bucks."

"Amen," Janet agreed with a naughty glint in her eye.

"Well," he began. "I'm living in New York now."

"The city or upstate?" I asked.

"Good question. Most people don't think to ask that. It's the NYC though. I'm a director."

Janet, already intrigued, lost it. "Like a movie director?"

"No movies yet, but perhaps a short film next year. I direct music videos."

I did a double take and pondered it for a second. "Do you use your own name?"

"Sometimes. I usually work under my nickname. Special K."

It was my turn to lose it. "I knew it! You're Special K!"

The ladies at our table were startled. Even Karim was taken aback.

I regained my composure. Didn't want it to seem I was jocking him. "I . . . I mean, *my son*, Jordan. He watches your videos. I have to get your autograph before this weekend is over."

"You mean those videos that exploit women?" This was Trayce.

Karim simply grinned. "No. I direct those videos that *employ* women. And pay them very well, thank you. Ain't nobody being exploited. Besides, if a woman is confident in herself then it shouldn't matter what she does. Melyssa Ford, for example."

"That's just it," Trayce retorted. "A lot of women aren't confident. And it's those booty shakin', *twerk sumthin'*, *drop this and drop that* videos that are sending the wrong message to them."

"Trayce, videos go in phases just like everything else.

Let's just say we're in one of those phases. I direct *all* kinds of videos. It's just those you're referring to that bring me the most notoriety."

"Do you have a problem with that?" she probed.

Karim took his napkin off his lap and placed it on the table. "No. I'm proud of my accomplishments. But . . . if you must know, I've recently stopped doing that particular style. It's a personal decision, but I know there's somebody waiting to take up the slack as soon as I step aside. It's the way of the world."

Trayce backed off from the "non-confrontation" and started into her fish.

Karim swiveled in his chair, agreeing to the stalemate. "Your turn, Solomon. What's your story?" he asked.

Trayce stopped eating and Janet put her iced tea down to listen. I felt so outclassed. I didn't know what Janet did, but it was obviously paying very well too.

I gulped then took a drink of my tea to stall. Me, the guy nobody paid attention to now had three people, two of them mega successful, wanting to actually know about me. Me. I'll be damned. It scared the hell out of me. I didn't have a job. Nobody knew me. I could've said whatever I wanted.

They waited.

"Uh . . . I work for Walgreens. I manage stores in the area. I'm district manager." I hoped they'd talk now and bail me out before I added more lies to my story. "That's all," I hurried to stop the bleeding.

Trayce sensed my discomfort and sought to alleviate it. "What are you up to these days, Janet?" she asked.

31 Janet

"**M**e?" I knew this was coming. It wasn't that I was ashamed of what I did; it's just that whatever life I kept to myself stayed that way. These people were my past and to let someone in was a sign of weakness. And I refused to be weak again.

"Entertainment," I said. Same thing I'd told Shauna. I had time to think of that during my cross-country drive. Besides, if Trayce disapproved so much of my boy Karim's thing, then she'd have a coronary if I was up front. *Come to think of it, that might be fun*, I devilishly thought. "I live in Las Vegas."

"Are you a performer?"

"*Excuse me*?"

"Y'know . . . like a singer," Solomon clarified.

"No, no. I'm a show coordinator for the casinos."

"That doesn't surprise me," Karim said. "You were always a fantastic cheerleader. Good dancer too. That sounds right up your alley. I'll have to check you out next time I'm in Vegas." Thinking that he might've overstepped his bounds, he added, "Or at least one of your shows."

He made me smile even though I had just lied to him. I couldn't believe how fine Karim was. At the moment, baby boy was getting me wet just with his eyes and making me stow Gerald in my memories. Who was this man that had replaced my Karim, the nerd that used to help me with my homework? Maybe he was right. Maybe I was finally seeing the guy he always was. Had I been that blind and self-absorbed?

I had to be self-absorbed right now for being here. To leave my boyfriend and drive thousands of miles because of a bad taste in my mouth was surely the sign of a disturbed individual. I knew it, but didn't rightly care. I wanted Shaw to say to my face his reasons for leaving me.

As the evening wore on, I spied on Shaw. Shaw would speak when spoken to, but wasn't trying to be the center of attention. I watched our classmates stopping him in the middle of his meal. I watched Mike laughing at his own jokes that Shaw wasn't reacting to. Shaw's woman, on the other hand, continued to politely smile and immerse herself in her dinner. I expected her to be clinging to him, but she wasn't. Maybe that's why I lost out. Maybe I had pressured him too much. I wondered how he would be reacting if I hadn't switched places. Would he have been able to look me in the eye? Would he have choked on his water? Too many questions going through my head and I was weary thinking about them.

I closed my eyes to ease the strain. When I opened them again, I was focused on my former spot. I hadn't paid attention when I did it, but I had switched places with Cameron, our drum major. Cameron looked like he had a bad headache. He wasn't saying much and seemed to be playing with his food. Shaw and his lady friend were conversing again and began laughing about something. It got my attention and Cameron's too because he was staring across his table directly at them. I watched Shaw whisper in her ear then slip a tiny bite on her lobe. It was all I saw before Cameron abruptly stood up, blocking my view, and stormed off.

32 Karim

"I guess the fish didn't agree with him," I joked, as Cameron bumped my chair on his way out. Janet had been playing it off, but she was burning a hole in Shaw over there. I didn't get it.

First off, I didn't understand what happened between the two of them. She was Barbie to his Ken. When I left for college, I assumed Janet would be married to Shaw and having his babies. You know what they say about assumptions.

"Want to tell me about it?"

"Huh?" Janet had gone back to the pretense of eating her food.

"I'm a good listener. Really."

"Things didn't work out." She was too smart to insult me by playing dumb.

"His decision or yours? Never mind."

"Yeah. Never mind."

I was pushing. It was a bad habit, I acknowledged. I guess after being pushed so long, it was my turn. Besides, my years in New York had taught me to speak my mind, even if nobody wanted to hear it.

"Here comes the dessert." That was Solomon, trying to be a diplomat and saving me from the scorching of Janet's gaze.

"I need a drink. Anybody else want one?" Trayce and Solomon passed. "Janet?"

"If I want one, I'll get it myself," she said dryly as she eyed the banana cream pie being placed before her. "But thanks for asking."

"Suit yourself," I shrugged.

Everybody and their momma was lined up for the good stuff at the bar. It had been set up in the hallway outside the ballroom for convenience, but the bartenders were overloaded. It looked like the hotel had another group scheduled at the same time. Some really bad hair-cuts in really bad tuxedos made it apparent. Mullets and the infamous *pornstache*, that thick bushy cropping of hair that might be mistaken for a moustache by a few, had lost their luster, even here in the heart of the south. Some folk were rebels to the end I guess. Yee-haw and all that.

The hotel was considerate enough to have seats and couches lined along the walls and by the restrooms. I decided to have a seat and wait it out rather than stand in line or return inside to face the dragon's flame.

Somebody plopped down beside me, jolting me. My eyes were closed, but you know how it is when you sense someone watching you.

"Hey." I was casual enough in my greeting.

"You're Karim, right?"

"Yep. It's me."

"You don't remember me?"

I opened my eyes again, checking the drink line first. It

still wrapped around the corner. Two of the guys with the other party had begun singing Dierks Bentley's "Settle for a Slow Down." Nice story in that video, I thought. Still typical country with its reference to lost love though. Kenny Chesney had tighter songwriting. Maybe they needed me. Actually, Garth Brooks needed to return for good and quit teasin' mo-fos.

Turning my attention to her, I replied. "Sure do. Naomi?"

"You do remember me," she beamed.

"And you're Shauna," I said, acknowledging her friend. She was standing silently near my outstretched legs. "Would you like to sit?"

"No. I'm fine right here. Just checking you out," she giggled. I raised an eyebrow on that one. This was the same Shauna, Janet's best friend, who used to tease her about being seen with me at lunch. It gave me some sick comfort that Shauna had fallen off over the years. She was still hot, I'm sure, for our hometown and here in Gaffney. She never held a candle to Janet in my eyes, but now she couldn't even see the candle.

"Like what you see?"

"We both do," Naomi said. I think she was feeling left out. "Damn, you smell good. What's that cologne?"

"Prada."

"I knew it," Shauna chimed. "Told you, Naomi."

Naomi ignored her. "So, are you married?"

"Nope."

"Oh. Seeing someone?"

"As often as I can," I laughed. These two weren't smooth at all. "And how about y'all two?"

"Nope," they said in unison. "Naomi has a room here," Shauna volunteered. "306. We'll be hanging out there and reminiscing all night. Are you staying at the hotel?"

I looked at Naomi again. She looked good—one of

those thin-bodied girls with long legs that could go in so many different directions, a screamer for sure. It would be so easy. "Yep. Have a suite," I replied.

"It must be pretty big."

"It suits my purposes."

Naomi made the move. "Are you going to sit here all night or would you like to hang out with us?"

I blinked twice to shake off the eyestrain I was experiencing. "Neither."

Naomi and Shauna were still talking when I stood up and left without another word.

Back at my table, it looked as if Janet was waiting on me. Trayce and Solomon had left the Homecoming Princess by herself. Her arms were interlocked defiantly across her chest.

"Where's your drink?" Janet asked.

"Sober's better right now."

33 Trayce

"How do you like Chicago?" he asked. If it weren't for the magazine article, I would've sworn Solomon had researched me. His eyes were still way too intense, but our conversation and his warm smile made him disarming.

"I love it. I really enjoy the culture and history of the town. I'm trying to buy a place in Bronzeville now."

"I've heard of that neighborhood, historic section of Chicago. The Black Metropolis, right?"

"Very good," I replied. "You must travel a lot."

"No, unfortunately. I just do a lot of reading to keep my mind active."

"More of us should do that," I remarked, cutting my eyes toward Michael. He was standing now and being overly boisterous. "Where'd you attend college?" I asked of Solomon.

"I went," he began. "Well, actually I . . . I never went. I never went as far as I would've liked." His voice had tapered off to where only I could hear him. His hand made a clink-clink sound against his glass as he tapped it. It was then that I first noticed the wedding band on his finger.

I had some curiosity, but didn't get a chance to ask him about it. Shaw approached our table just then. He had walked off from whatever story Michael was trying to tell. He looked dead at me up until he reached us. Then he faced his ex.

"Hello, Janet," he said in an articulate voice matured by experience. Janet looked like she wanted to slap the taste from his mouth. I felt three times worse. When Janet didn't reply, he simply smiled and walked toward my side of the table. Solomon sensed my unease and adjusted his seat. Shaw could've walked around him, but he kept his distance.

"Hello, Trayce. I just wanted to congratulate you—"

His lips moved, but I didn't hear him. I was too busy hearing slurred voices from years ago. Tears welled up and I lost it. Years of therapy down the drain.

I stood up suddenly, causing my tea to splash onto the tablecloth.

"Excuse me."

Before anyone saw me cry, I ran for the restroom.

Donna saw me and tried to speak, but I rushed past her. In the hallway, I quickly found the ladies room and ran inside. Rather than being able to let loose with my emotions, I was greeted by Shauna and Naomi. The two of them were apparently closet smokers had been sneaking a few drags. I wasn't even given the courtesy of a fake smile. They hastily put out their cigarettes and left after checking themselves in the mirror.

A handicapped stall on the end was where I chose to hide from the world. I latched the stall door shut then took a seat on the toilet. My smudged makeup stained my cheeks and my throat was tight. I unrolled a wad of toilet paper and did my best to wipe my eyes.

I wanted to call my therapist to tell her this wasn't going to work. That's when I realized my cell phone was in my purse, which had been left in the ballroom.

I reached out to unlatch the door, but couldn't. I looked at my outstretched hand as it trembled. It was as if my body refused to get off the toilet. I drew the same hand back and covered my eyes with it.

34 Solomon

"The least you could do is apologize to her, Shaw. She really deserves it, don't you think?"

"I don't know what you're talking about."

I looked up at him. "I think you do. Matter of fact, I know you do."

"*Who are you?*" he asked, his face scrunched up.

"A friend. Something she didn't have back in the day."

"So, she's pissed at you too." Janet joined in. "I ain't running away though."

Trayce's purse was left on the floor next to her chair. Neither Janet nor Shaw were that important to me, so I grabbed the purse and left them to their quarrel.

Running into the hallway, there was no trace of her. I asked around for those who bothered speaking to me, but they didn't help.

Shauna and Naomi, of the sorry-ass Crew, had left the ladies room. It was the logical place for Trayce to have gone so quickly. I decided to risk asking them if they saw her.

Before I could get a word out, I overheard them.

"*. . . bitch still fat as hell.*"

"*. . . no amount of money in the world gonna help her sorry ass.*"

"*. . . ho think she all that now. She still ain't shit.*"

"*. . . don't know why she bothered to come. Nobody wanna see her.*"

I was standing right in front of them now. They continued talking and ignoring, until they walked into me.

"Can I help you?" Shauna asked, irritated by my invasion of their space.

I didn't speak. I tightly clinched Trayce's purse that was in my hand.

"Are you deaf?" Naomi asked, making one of those fake sign language gestures with her hands. Shauna cackled.

I thought before speaking my peace.

"Shauna, how long did it take to clear up that STD? Did your husband know? I noticed he was never with you when you picked up your prescription." Hell, I didn't work there anymore, so it didn't matter.

I paused and smiled, watching it set in with Naomi. She put her hand to her mouth as if holding back a laugh. It was her turn now.

"Naomi, did Shauna know you used to give her boyfriend head out by the tennis court? I guess that was the best use for it, since none of us played tennis."

It was my turn to ignore them.

I decided to look for Trayce out back where we had the mixer. It was dark and quiet now and as a good a place to get away as any.

No sight of her. I was by the gazebo when I felt my cell phone vibrating. I entered and took a seat to see who was calling.

A view of the screen showed Linda's number. I should've expected her to call and nag me about something. She'd leave a message if it were important. I guess I owed her for my being at the reunion anyway. If she provided a safe, healthy environment for our kids, then I wouldn't have been fired and I wouldn't have thought up this desperate scheme. Except, I wasn't scheming. For once, I was really having a good time and enjoying Trayce's company. And someone besides my kids didn't mind my company. I liked it. A lot.

I had rehearsed my story about how I had graduated from college and was very successful. I was going to use my knowledge to get in good with Trayce, then try to worm a job out of her. As with all desperate attempts, there was a problem. The more I talked to her, the more I backed out of it. All for my kids, I told myself. Yeah. I was being a real man. Piece of shit was more like it.

I heard some voices and peeked up from my seat, thinking it might be Trayce. It was just the person who had caused her to run off in the first place. He had company.

The woman that was Shaw's date was outside in the night air with him. She wasn't too happy.

He was apologizing to her about something, but she wasn't very accepting at the moment.

They didn't see me, so I clung to the shadows of the gazebo and listened.

35 Janet

"So, she's pissed at you too. I ain't running away though."

"Look, I'm sorry you have hard feelings over what we may or may not have had, Janet, but you need to let it go."

When I looked, Solomon wasn't there. Probably chasing behind Trayce. Hard-up little fella, that one. I was glad he was gone. It gave me a chance to get a decade of shit off my chest.

"You come over here to talk to Trayce? *And just ignore me*? Oh, you will hear my mouth, boy."

"You're acting childish."

"And I should slap your bitch ass." I clinched my fists and thought about what I'd considered doing when I first saw him. I didn't care that I couldn't beat him. Right about now, I just wanted to tee off. "You must be crazy thinking I'm gonna put up with your disrespecting me here."

"Can't you just leave well enough alone?"

"No. You wouldn't sleep with me as much as I begged

and pleaded; yet you somehow wound up with your
dick in Trayce? What the fuck, Shaw! How do you think
that made me feel back then? I only came to this shit to
tell your ass off to your face. Now I wonder why I even
bothered."

"I did love you."

"Hmph. Damn funny way of showing it. Do you tell
your little toy the same thing? Watch her. It's obvious she
has expensive tastes. Would hate for her to bleed you
dry." I stood up and got in his face. I noticed him brace as
if he expected me to swing or something. I continued, "I
should know because my tastes are expensive too and
your Arena League-playing ass couldn't afford me now
anyway. You see, maybe I owe you for how you treated
me because it only made me stronger."

"That's good to know," he smirked, trying to claim his
backbone again. "So why don't you just move on?"

"I have," I smiled coldly. "I don't know why I'm even
talking to you when someone as sexy as Karim is here.
You think you're hot? *Please.* Every woman's panties got
drenched when he showed up. And he can be all mine,
like you refused to be, *Mr. Big Man.* How does it feel not
being the big man this time? Huh? I'll bet your woman is
wishing she weren't here with you so she could have a
crack at him too."

Shaw seemed not so indestructible now—almost
small. I relished giving my pain back to him.

"I don't have time for this," he muttered as he looked
to work his way around me. Every time he would move,
I would move. He was still trying to be discrete. His
woman walked over, scowling in her red dress.

"What the fuck are you lookin' at?" I asked, not appre-
ciating her position or timing.

Sistergirl's nostrils flared and her blue eyes widened

into orbs. For whatever reasons, she was already in a foul mood and I had just pushed her over.

"What?" she snapped. I saw I had mistakenly questioned her legitimacy as she began stepping out of her shoes. "Look, I don't know who the fuck you are, but I didn't come here for this mess. I only came—"

Placing his hand over her mouth, Shaw immediately snatched her up and spirited her away before she could utter another syllable. He did stop, however, to grab her shoe.

Instead of an explanation, I was left with more questions about why he simply left me. Fucker broke my heart the day he told me he was leaving for college. And that I didn't fit in with his plans.

Just like that.

Always felt I deserved more after being so faithful.

I had gotten most of it off my chest, so I resigned myself to that victory. I resumed my seat and waited for Karim to come back. He was looking more and more appealing and a damn good distraction for the rest of the weekend.

After what seemed an eternity of sitting alone, the man of the hour returned. I wondered if he'd witnessed any of my trip down memory lane with Shaw.

"Where's your drink?"

"Sober's better right now," he remarked. "You look like you could use one though. Wanna rethink my offer?" He smiled. It hinted of cockiness and I liked it.

36 Karim

"Yeah," she replied. Something about the way she held her mouth at the end of the word, her bottom lip hanging like so, was so . . . so damn *hot*. "Let's get outta here. I've had enough of this little table and this little town."

We roared through the hills in her car. The bottle of cheap wine we had purchased from the liquor store was still in its brown paper bag. "Are you sure you want to drink this?" I asked, trying to hide my case of nerves. This woman drove like a devil.

"Crack it open," she yelled over the noise of the road. The wind whipped her hair wildly in the moonlight. "It's what we used to drink."

"I could've called for a limo, y'know."

"Showoff."

"Me? You're the one showing off with this big blue torpedo."

"It's extravagant and fast," she hollered, "like me."

"Whatever," I sighed.

Her dress was already short, so it slid up her thighs more and more as she drove. A woman wasn't meant to drive in that much less do anything else. A great choice on her part as my eyes locked in on her ebony smooth skin and the thong between her legs that became more visible with each sharp curve she zoomed through. I contemplated how she would feel, how she would taste.

"Well?"

"Huh?"

"Are you going to open the bottle or what?"

"What was I saying?"

I repeated for the third time, "You were saying how much you missed this school."

"Yeah, that's it," she giggled.

We'd finished the bottle of wine and were now sitting in the parking lot. Janet played Kem's new CD as I tried to impress her by stating I'd met him at a music expo. That was childish, as I thought she was feeling me anyway. Marion, our old high school, was right across the street so I guess it was bringing back the dorky kid in me.

"So they're really going to put a factory outlet there?" I asked.

"That's what I heard."

The high chain link fence wrapped around the entire block, giving our old school the look of some kind of prison. "Good riddance."

"You really mean that?"

"Yep. My only good memory won't be in there when they level it." *It's right beside me.*

"How'd you wind up a video director? You were so smart, I thought you'd wind up being a rocket scientist or something."

"I could have," I asserted. "I just loved music and images way more."

"What do you think of this image? Think I could be in a video?"

She turned sideways to give me a better look. One of her arms rested on the steering wheel, the other on her seatback. She leaned her head back and tilted her neck from side to side in a provocative manner. One of her legs slid onto her seat as her foot went atop the armrest. She was tipsy, but it was like another person was talking to me, tempting me.

"Yeah. You're workin' with something."

"You think?" Janet leaned over in my direction. She placed her hand on my knee and positioned herself even closer. As she came forward, her breasts heaved out from the fabric holding them. I reached up to cradle them with my hands. Perky and smooth to the touch they were. My thumbs teased her chocolate covered nipples, drawing her in further.

Our lips came so close to touching, but not yet. I could feel her panting breath on my face.

"Know what I wanna do right now?" she whispered . . . softly . . . seductively.

"Hmm?"

"Karim!" she shouted.

"Huh?"

"Did you hear me?"

"What?" I asked, trying to play off the buzz from the wine as well as the fantasy from which she'd just jarred me. Jetlag had whipped my ass more than I knew.

"Know what I wanna do right do now?"

I shrugged, sure that it wasn't what I was wishing for. "No."

"I wanna take one last walk through Marion."

"It's locked up."

"So. Is that supposed to stop us?" Janet asked.

37 Trayce

The door to the restroom creaked.

"Trayce? You in there?"

I paused from my sniffling, trying to recognize the voice.

"Trayce?" He called out again. It was Solomon.

I cleared my throat. "I'm here."

He took one step in. I could see his shadow on the tile under the stall door. "You left your purse back there."

"Oh. Thank you."

He walked further into the restroom, probably afraid of some woman going off on him. "Trayce?"

"Right here," I responded. He followed the sound of my voice until his shoes stood directly in the space under the stall door.

"Are you okay?"

"I'm fine. Just hand me my purse," I demanded brusquely in a voice not mine.

He hesitated, probably thinking of what to say, but gave up and slid the purse under the door.

"Thank you."

Solomon left me alone. I wanted to scream out for him to stay, to lend me his strength, but I didn't. He hadn't a clue as to what I bore on my shoulders. I'd sat in a smaller bathroom stall like this, afraid to death of coming out. Years ago.

I waited until my eyes were incapable of tears and emerged from the stall once the noises died down. I wasn't wearing a watch, but knew hours had elapsed. A stranger in the mirror mocked me with every step I took, until I decided to face her. Dried salt trails scarred my makeup. The black on my dress was covered in specks of tissue lint and my braids had come loose, dangling across my swollen cheeks. I would've splashed water, but I was too tired. Too tired to care anymore. My outside now matched the inside they'd created. This place had broken me again . . . and so easy, I thought.

The hotel staff was stacking chairs in the ballroom when I left the ladies room. No one else was in sight. Slipping out of my heels, I grasped my gown at the sides and ambled over to take one last look at the smallish table I'd recently shared. I knew Solomon wouldn't be there, but thought it'd be nice to see him one last time. I was going to see my mother then return to Chicago as soon as I could get my plane ticket switched.

"Trayce."

"Oh," I gasped. "You scared me. Where'd you come from?" Solomon stood there silently. The bowtie on his tux dangled loosely around his thin neck. His eyes were red.

"I've been waiting. You've been in there a long time. Must've really stunk it up." He smiled, but I wasn't in the mood to smile back.

"You didn't have to wait."

"I know," he sighed. "I wanted to."

"I am glad to see you though."

"Really?"

"Yes. I wanted to say 'Bye' "

"Bye?"

"Yes, I'm going upstairs to pack. I'm going home. Back to Chicago."

"But you just got here," he spurted. Solomon had a hint of desperation in his body language. "You can't."

"*I can't?*"

"I mean . . . whatever upset you couldn't be that bad."

"You just don't know."

"Try me."

I shook my head in the negative. "Take care, Solomon."

He kept talking, more than I've ever heard him say. And I still kept walking.

I was at the elevator when he yelled out, "Are you going to let him do this to you, Trayce? You don't have to, y'know. I know things!"

It dinged, its doors opening up to take me away. Not the absence of pain, but simply the lessening of it. I took one final look at the peculiar little man. In his tux and through my weary eyes, he looked kinda handsome to me. Kind of how Humphrey Bogart wasn't at all cute, but still had Lauren Becall swooning over him in *Casablanca*. A final smile, a polite wave and I was walking rather than running away this time.

I pushed the button to take me to my floor. Solomon's voice was silent, replaced by rapid footsteps that came closer and closer. I pushed the button again in the hopes I could get away before he made another attempt to talk me out of it.

The doors began shutting just as I heard a yell. From out of nowhere, Solomon's head flashed into view, crashing against the edge of one of them with a nasty "thunk".

38 Solomon

"My God! No!" she shouted. Her hand braced against the elevator door and she ran out to attend to me. "What happened?"

With my hands pressed firmly against my forehead to stem the bleeding, I parted them enough to direct her attention to the cause of my hurt.

Michael still stood where he had just tripped me. Trip is being nice. I felt the forearm shiver he had snuck in as I fell forward into the elevator door. I cursed at him for almost losing an eye instead of the piece of skin above it. In my haste to run behind Trayce, I had chalked up the glare in his eyes to just being drunk. I was way off. He'd been looking for me. In what had been a deserted lobby, it was now filled with glee. Two familiar voices melded together in their taunts.

Standing behind Michael were Shauna and Naomi, drinks in hand. They had obviously put him up to this and were savoring my payback. Having gone through most of life unnoticed, I was suddenly finding myself mixed up in a lot of shit.

"Aww, man. I'm sorry. You need to watch where you're going," he bent over, straining his white suit to contain his gut. "Here, let me help you up."

I took my bloody hand off my forehead and seeing he was already having difficulty balancing himself, yanked him onto the carpet.

Naomi first, then Shauna screamed as I lurched toward the fallen Michael in an attempt to pay him back. I punched at his head, but he covered up with his arms. Bloody streaks lined the forearms of his white jacket. Michael, slowed by alcohol and the easy life, took a few seconds to recover from my reckless assault, but it didn't last. He managed to get his foot between us, sending me rolling backward into the feet of a stunned Trayce. She almost went down like a bowling pin, but righted herself against the wall.

"What are you doing?" she demanded as she helped me to my feet.

Blood in my eye, I gasped. "Cheapshot. He tripped me up on purpose."

"The little fucker's crazy," Michael said as he shrugged off Shauna and Naomi's attempts to help him up. He stopped to rest on one knee. "That was an accident."

"Bullshit." I growled at the two ladies. They didn't blink, having gotten a measure of revenge through their dumb tool.

"Whatever," Trayce muttered bitterly. She looked at Michael as a mother would a child whose ass she was about to whip.

Michael, sensing her question, answered again. "I said it was an accident. Look at this. Bled all over my tux 'n shit. You need to control your little boyfriend. Shit, he's lucky I'm a man of the community. Back in the day, I woulda stomped a hole in him just for somethin' to do."

I went to lunge at Michael again, but Trayce blocked me. As small as I was, that's all it took. She turned and shoved me on the elevator, then waited for the doors to close.

"What's your floor?"

"I'm not staying here."

"Oh." She didn't hesitate to push her floor. "We have to get you cleaned up."

"I'm . . . I'm okay."

She looked at me hunched over, out of breath and dizzy from the blood that still flowed out. "Uh huh," she sighed.

As we rode the elevator up, I looked at my tux in the mirror-lined wall. "Shit."

"What's the matter?"

"The tux. It's ruined."

"So. At least you're alive."

She didn't get it. She couldn't. She could buy a hundred of these. I couldn't even afford to rent this one and was going to be in a bad way when I tried to return it. Bye-bye, deposit.

The elevator dinged, announcing our arrival. Trayce helped steady me as she fished her room key from her purse. "We'll see if we can soak it in some cold water, okay?"

"Thanks."

Trayce took her arms from around me, but I held onto her hand as she led me into her room.

It was a standard brownish room with a single king size bed. I knew she could have afforded a Presidential suite, but as I was learning, Trayce lacked all pretentiousness.

On the desk, her computer was open, its screen flashing alive with color and activity. She was linked up to her company's website, but the session had timed out.

"The bathroom's over there," she said.

In the bathroom, I removed my tuxedo jacket. I let the cool water dance off my fingertips as I scrutinized the cut over my eye. A lot of dried blood masked it, but I could see the wound wasn't all that large. Perhaps just a deep scratch.

"It's always like that," Trayce said. I turned to see her in the doorway. "You have so many capillaries in your face that you bleed like a stuck pig. It usually looks worse than what it is."

She approached me. "Watch a lot of Discovery Channel?" I asked.

"No," she chuckled. "My roommate in college was pre-med. She broke a bottle upside her boyfriend's head once and explained it to me." She fetched a washcloth from off its ring. "Come here."

She adjusted the water in the sink to make it warmer. Dampening the end of the cloth, she used one hand to steady my head. With the other, she dabbed gingerly around the area at first. When she saw I didn't flinch, she applied a little more pressure. "Just want to get it clean. Don't need it getting infected. Sorry I don't have a Band-Aid."

"Uh huh." I hadn't been with a woman since a relapse with Linda last Thanksgiving. That didn't count. We were so close I could feel Trayce's breath on me. I imagined it becoming as shallow as mine. Imagined her large bosom rising and falling at my urging. "Can I talk you into staying? It's just two more days." My agenda had changed. Definitely.

"Is that what all that was about downstairs? Did you stage that with Michael?"

"Yeah. Me and Mike go waaay back," I said, sarcasm oozing from my mouth. "You guessed it."

She put the cloth under the water once more, letting

the blood rinse away down the drain. "No, really. What was that about? I don't remember him having any bad blood with you in high school. Come to think of it, I don't remember you interacting with anybody."

"Do you really want to know?"

"I asked."

"If I tell you, you have to promise to stay. You can be Michael's bodyguard. Keep me off of him." I winked at her as I forced my arm to make a bicep.

She let out a bellowing laugh, filling the tiny confines of our bathroom. "Okay . . . but you have to promise to stick nearby."

"I wouldn't have it any other way . . . friend." I stuck out my hand and we shook on it. "You."

"Me what?"

I looked down at the bathroom floor then met her eyes again. "Michael was giving me some payback for Shauna and Naomi."

"I'm not getting it. What would they have against you?"

"I heard them talking shit and had a few words for them earlier tonight."

An eyebrow raised on Trayce's forehead. She turned away and looked at her worn makeup in the mirror. "They were talking about me." It wasn't even a question, rather an assertion.

"Yes."

"Mmm. Now I know why I hate skinny bitches."

In the mirror, my reflection now stood behind Trayce. "They're just jealous. I've watched them smack their lips and roll their eyes ever since Donna spilled the beans about you. You have everything and they have nothing."

"You really feel that way?"

"Yes," I said into her ear. My hard-on was bulging through my pants and grazed upside her hip. I took my hand and moved her braids aside. Instinctually, she tilted her head, exposing her neck to me.

In the mirror, something glistened. It caught Trayce's attention. She abruptly sidestepped me before my lips could touch her skin. She closed her eyes and pinched the bridge of her nose, as if to alleviate stress. "When were you going to tell me?"

"This?" I asked, waving my wedding band with my fingers outstretched.

She chuckled, but not from amusement. "You say it all nonchalant. Yes, *that!*"

"Trayce, I'm divorced. I wear it out of habit."

"Prove it. I want to see papers."

"Not very trusting, are you?"

"No. Nobody ever gave me reason to be."

"I could call my daughter, but I'd wake her up. She'd tell you. She teases me about it all the time."

"You have a daughter?"

"And a son," I added, sensing her mood lightening again. "Twins. Jordan and Justine." They were supposed to have been my reason for being here with Trayce, but I couldn't tell her that.

"I love kids. Do you have a picture of them?"

I reached to oblige, then remembered what I was wearing. "I left it at home."

"Just like a man," she huffed.

We shared a polite laugh as the tension eased again. My mind and body began returning to the groove they were in previously. Trayce leaned against the wall next to the hair dryer.

"Take it off."

"Huh?"

"Your shirt." She stuck out her hand. "You have some blood on it too."

"Yeah."

"Unless you want to try to get it out yourself."

I knew I sucked at that sort of thing. After unbuttoning my shirt, I held it out for her. She had already begun holding my tuxedo lapel under the cold water. "Just set it over there. Some of this is about to come off." Her thumbs worked at the almost-blended stain on my rental. Water had splashed up on her, which she seemed to ignore. Her mind was focused on a problem and nothing distracted her. I knew characteristics like that were what had made her such a success.

"You're getting your dress wet. Here. Let me take over while you change."

"That's pretty presumptuous of you, Solomon," she teased. "Maybe I like to lounge in evening gowns."

"Whatever," I laughed.

I had scrubbed all that I could off my shirt, when Trayce finally came back. She nervously slid in the door.

"Y'know, I think I got all of it out—"

She now wore a purple silk robe. It descended just past her ample hips, exposing bare legs and manicured toes. Her braids had been pulled back and wrapped. I watched her hand as it rested on the bathroom light switch. All the other lights in her room were off. "Be honest with me," she said.

"Okay."

"Are you feeling what I'm feeling?"

"I've been feeling it." She flipped the light switch off, bathing us in the orange-red glow of the power bulb on the hairdryer.

"Are you attracted to me? Honestly."

"Yes."

"Are you seeing anyone?"

"No. Are you?"

"Not in a long time. Things just don't seem to work out."

"Oh." I let go of my wet shirt and walked closer. "Maybe it's just timing."

"Is that what it is?"

"Yes."

"Should I take this chance?" Her hands massaged my shoulders. I could feel them trembling as her nails dug in ever so slightly. Hurt had been so much of her life here; she couldn't help but consider the worst.

"Not a chance," I answered. "A sure thing."

"You promise?"

"Yes, yes, yes." Each affirmative was delivered with a kiss across her neck. I undid the sash and pressed myself against her.

"Make me believe, Solomon. Make me believe."

39 Janet

"What happened here?"

The hotel night worker was on his hands and knees. "Excuse us, ma'am. Some of the hotel guests got a little carried away tonight."

Karim and I shrugged and stepped around the bloodstains they were trying to clean up at the foot of the elevator.

"Probably that redneck wedding party. Somebody found out somebody slept with someone's sister. If we look around we might find a tooth. A good tooth," Karim joked.

The two bottles of wine and our stroll through the old school had made for an interesting night. I think both of us were thinking of taking this to the room, to see just how interesting things could get, but we were still feeling each other out. We decided to look for some empty chairs outside what was the hotel's club. Karim pulled mine out for me, then took a seat across the art deco table from me.

"I can't believe we just did that," he said, his head

shaking while he smoothed his coif of hair back. The red strands he had been teased about those years had given way to deeper brown.

"Why?"

"Breaking and entering for one."

"So, you're still all goody-goody."

"Janet, I wasn't back then. And I'm certainly not now." He flashed me that cocky smirk. This tall, fine nigga got much pussy, I could tell. He'd never had some like mine, though. I smirked right back to let him know.

"You didn't think running through the old hallways was fun?"

"It was okay, but you know we're back in the South. All that shit said 'Off limits' and 'No Trespassing'. I don't take no shit, but I also don't start none. *Knowhu'amean*?" he grunted, going into that overly New Yorker thing of his.

"Well, how 'bout when you busted the window to Mr. Anderson's door?"

"Now that was fun, yo!" His hands gestured wildly in the air, probably aided by the buzz he was still feeling. "That mother fucker gave me a 'B' in computer science. Can you believe that mug hated blacks? Hell, he taught at a school full of 'em."

I listened as Karim filled me in on things at Marion from a nerd . . . *err* . . . smart kid's perspective. He was so much of a man now, but it was nice seeing the other side of him wasn't completely lost. From my own unique perspective, I knew a thing or two about the little boy that hid inside most men.

". . . but enough about me."

"You were doing just fine."

"Nah, I want to hear you talk. I want to know everything about Janet, *Janet*."

I chuckled. "Cute. A woman's allowed to have some secrets."

"Alright then. I'll go slowly. Simple stuff. How do you like Vegas?"

"I love it. You can be so free there."

"So I've heard. Is that why you picked it?"

"Maybe."

"I mean . . . Well what I'm trying to say is," he paused to put things together. "I think we all expected you to wind up with 2.5 kids for Shaw. In my honest opinion, I think you've come out a lot better."

"Really?"

"No doubt. Look at you then look at these sisters that stayed around here. You're gorgeous. Straight quarter."

"Quarter?"

He smirked. "When a dime just won't do."

"How many other women have you used that on?"

"None. I invented it when I saw you."

"That's sweet."

"Uh huh. Sweet. Don't use that kinda language around me." He pretended poking his fingers into me. I really did want him to touch me though.

"Sorry."

"You're forgiven. Now, like I was saying," he continued as he leaned back. "You're much more decisive than you used to be. Confidence. Now that's the real turn-on."

"Are you saying I turn you on?"

"Always have. Always will."

I flushed at Karim's revelation. He was so straightforward. Like Gerald. But Gerald, who knew the complete me, was gone. "I have something I want to tell you."

"Yeah?"

Karim grimaced just as I was about to speak. He raised one finger, begging me to hold on. From out of his pocket, he pulled out his cell phone that had been set to vibrate. He surveyed the number of the incoming call.

"Excuse me for a second. It looks like I have to take this."

I stood up, preparing to give him some privacy, but he motioned from me to stay.

"Clement, this better be good," he said to the party on the other side.

"What?"

"*What?*"

"I'm still telling you that wrist injury is bullshit."

"So what if he gets surgery. The asshole probably hurt it jerking off to Black Tail or sumthin'."

I tried not to listen, but let out a giggle. Witnessing him bark into the phone with such authority was moistening me to no end. He was right. Confidence was the real turn-on. Maybe once I let him in on Godiva, we could get down to some real business.

He put his finger up again, letting me know he was about to end the conversation.

"Look, if he and On-Phire gonna keep fuckin' with me, then I'll give them their fuckin' free video alright. I was thinking about getting out of this business anyway. Cheap bastards."

"No, no! Tell them I'll do it. I'll give them one of those cheap, unimaginative numbers. Y'know, up in the strip club. Probably get some real strippers in there too. Yeah, the low-end ones. Some of them that'll do anything for a buck."

"That's it. Low class. Real nasty and skanky. Yeah. Yeah. Maybe North will catch sumthin'."

40 Karim

"I'll relay your answer to them, Karim. Sorry about disturbing you."

"It's okay," I answered Clement.

"Occupied with a female are we?"

"Oh yes. The one."

"It's about bloody time," he laughed. "Goodnight, sir."

"One."

I clicked my cell off, then stowed it in my pocket.

"Now where were we?" I asked of Janet. Her smile was missing. She sat at a distance. A defensive posture was obvious; closed arms, legs crossed tighter than my grandma's Christmas wrap. "You were about to tell me something."

"It was nothing. I just want to go to my room. All that wine has given me a headache."

"That's it?"

"Yes," she replied dryly. "That's it."

"I didn't turn you off with my cursing, did I?"

"Baby, I was never turned on."

"Oh. Okay." I nervously fumbled like the Carrot Top of old; trying to regain ground I had lost somehow.

No words were spoken on the elevator ride up. I saw Janet had pushed the same floor as mine, but left any conversation over that alone. When we exited, I saw our suites were on the same side of the building. Being a gentleman, I walked her to hers first.

"Hey, we're neighbors," I remarked. She was still stoic. She inserted her key into the lock. The green light flicked and she grasped the handle.

"So, I'll see you tomorrow?"

"Yeah. Sorry about my headache. I just need to sleep."

"No prob. I understand. Thanks."

"For what?"

"For letting me hike you over the school fence in that dress tonight. Da-yum."

Janet's dimples returned. "Goodnight, Karim," she said wearily.

As nice as the suite I'd barely used was, even down to the chilled bottle of champagne I'd requested, it all seemed hollow. I looked at the connecting door, which separated me from Janet. She was supposed to be here, sharing this champagne with me now. I discarded my ruined tux, shredded from my climb over the fence at Marion. The things I did for this woman.

As much as she tried pretending, I knew Janet wanted to be with me tonight. There was something she wanted to tell me, but didn't. Maybe she was a married woman trying to play the field like her girl Shauna. Maybe I'd done something wrong. Or maybe she simply hadn't found me up to her standards. The latter hurt me the most, but a woman like her had to have a legion of admirers at her beck and call. I gave up stressing over the possibilities and resigned myself to a nice, long shower.

After clearing my head and letting the warm spray relieve some tension, I lay in the bed. I flicked the TV on to see what kind of local happenings they had. Unimpressed, I turned it back off. I was tired, but still not ready to sleep. I looked at our adjoining door again, imagining what Janet might be doing.

"Get it together, man," I said aloud then exhaled. From the gym bag at my bedside, I found my iPod and put my headphones on to listen to some music. Track four was an underground mix tape joint I'd downloaded back home. I closed my eyes, imagining a video for this rapper none of the MTV watchers or large record labels had ever heard of. Maybe I'd try to find this kid when I got back.

"Huh? Whazzut?"

A knock at the door startled me. I'd fallen asleep without realizing it. I looked at the time. Less than an hour had passed. I must've been more tired than I thought. A knock came again. Maybe Janet had come to apologize. It would've been easier for her to use the connecting door, I thought, but I guess she didn't want to be presumptuous. I took my headphones off then went to the door.

"Are you busy?" she asked.

"No. Just sleeping."

"Mmm hmm," she grunted as she eyed me from head to toe. She stopped at the bulge in my boxers. A smile let me know it met with her approval. "Well, can I come in?"

She tried to barge past me, but I wouldn't budge from the doorway. Taking advantage of our proximity, she allowed a hand to caress my back. That little voice was calling out, telling me how easy this would be. I was deaf tonight.

"What are you doing here?" I asked. Shauna was still up celebrating, but hadn't brought Naomi with her. She wore some sort of powder blue sleep set with matching furry slippers. Something that could be sexy, but seemed kinda inappropriate for her.

"Just figured I'd stop by. You know you didn't give your room number when we talked earlier. I had to check with the front desk."

"That was intentional."

"You like making things a challenge, huh? You never came by our room either. We were so disappointed."

"I was busy."

"With Janet? You know she got a boyfriend."

It stung like it was meant to do, but she may have been lying. "And you have a husband," I countered.

Shauna was flabbergasted that I knew. I had merely guessed, but the large orbs that used to be her eyes gave it all away. She tried to recover. "Yes. Yes, I do. I wasn't trying to get with you anyway. See, I was trying to help my girl Naomi out."

"Oh, so that's what this is?"

"Yeah. She wanted me to stop by . . . to see if you were interested in her."

"That sure was nice of you. I must've been confused, seeing you at my door like this."

We heard a lock click. Janet must've heard the noise from the hall. She looked at us through a crack in her door, me in just my boxers and Shauna in *whatever*.

"Yeah. You were confused," Shauna said gruffly before she huffed off in the direction of her girlfriend. I wondered what Shauna was going to tell her, but decided just to go back to sleep. The school was going to be torn down, but Marion still had its drama.

41 Trayce

Solomon was still beside me when morning came. He lay asleep with his mouth open, spent from our night of lovemaking. So tender, so passionate was this man. He'd taken me to levels I didn't know existed. From his instinct with his touch and his mouth that lavished praise upon every finger, every toe, every curve, every crevice . . . *whew* I found myself getting hot again . . . he had turned me into an addict—*fiendin' for a feel*. I guess that's why I was already awake, watching for any sign of him stirring to continue the campaign of sweet war our bodies had engaged in. Except in this war, there were no losers. I had tasted victory, free of my pain and memories if only for one night.

In the midst of my cravings, I thought about something. I didn't know a lot about him, other than his intense love for his kids and his exceptional way around my body. I doubted that anyone really knew who Solomon Muncie was or had taken the time to learn. I was guilty of being in this category too and that left me feeling not so good about myself.

I kissed him, a gentle peck at first. When I pressed my lips to his the second time he began stirring.

"Good morning," he said. "How long have I been asleep?"

"Not long."

"Oh."

He moved the sheet aside for me to join him. I straddled him and we kissed once more.

"I'm not hurting you, am I?" I asked, self conscious about my weight atop his little body.

Solomon chuckled, still delirious. "I'm not hurting you, am I?" he mimicked. That was when I felt it poking up between my legs. I smiled wickedly at him and kissed him once again. On the dresser beside the bed, I reached for the last condom. If there was going to be a "next time," I was going to buy Trojan Magnums for him.

"You want me to go with you? To church?"

"Yes. Remember. You have to stay by my side," I teased.

"On a Saturday?"

"Yes, I'm . . . well, I was raised Seventh Day Adventist."

"I never knew that," he said curiously.

"You act like you're supposed to have a file on me. Now stop that. I haven't been devout in a long time, but I really feel the need to go this morning."

"Because of what happened between us?"

"That's some of it. Look, I normally don't sleep with . . ."

"It's okay. I understand. I don't do it either," he confided. "But I don't have any clothes here."

"Then we'll pass by your house. Now hurry up and shower."

If Solomon had any more excuses, he kept them to himself. I finished dressing.

I'd found some strength from Solomon, but had to attend services this morning to truly give thanks to the
Man upstairs for granting me the one true strength. If
Day Two was going to be like the first day of the reunion,
then I would need it.

While Solomon showered, I checked my voicemail. I
had two messages. I returned the call from the first.

"I.T., Ms. Hedgecomb's office."

"Hey, mami."

"Trayce? Is this THE Trayce Hedgecomb?"

"You know it's me, Rosalina."

"Are you the Belle of the Ball yet?"

"That's not likely," I laughed. "Look, I just called to let
you know I'm okay."

"Okay? I want to know if you're gettin' some."

"Rosalina!"

"Aww, mami *is* gettin' some!" Rosalina's raucous laughter caused me to pull the phone away from my ear.

"I didn't say that. I—"

"Whatever. Who is it? The QB?" I winced at that. She
continued, "The water boy? That hot girl all the boys
used to lust after?"

"No, that would be Janet and that's more your style."

"True," she remarked. "But I'm a one-woman woman
these days."

"Good for you."

"So, you're not going to tell me."

I smiled. "No. Stay outta grown folks' business."

"So he's hung."

"Bye, fool!"

I hadn't finished my smile when I heard a cell phone
ring. Mine was still in my hand. I tracked the little chime
to Solomon's tuxedo trousers thrown across one of the
chairs. I didn't want to pry and had planned on retriev-
ing his phone and bringing it to him. I was nosy though.

Solomon had told me he was divorced, but that ring on his finger still lingered on my mind.

The caller ID on his old Nokia read "LINDA." He'd received enough calls to program Linda's number in, whoever she was. I went to carry it to the bathroom, but decided to answer it . . . for him. It was about to hang up anyway, so I called myself helping out.

"Hello?"

"I'm sorry. I must have the wrong number."

I could've let it go. "Are you calling for Solomon?"

She mumbled something. "Who's this?"

"Trayce, a friend of his. You must be Linda."

"How'd you know that?"

"Solomon's told me all about you." I made that up. I wasn't normally a messy person, but something in her tone pissed me off.

"Put Solomon on the phone," she growled. "I gotta talk to him about somethin'."

"He's in the shower right now. Can I take a message?"

"Nah. I ain't leavin' shit with you."

I heard the shower being turned off.

Solomon was reaching for a towel as I held his phone for him. The little well-endowed man wiped the water from his eyes.

"Did I get a call?"

"Yep. Linda."

"What?" he asked, suddenly coming alive. I didn't like his reaction. "Did you answer it?"

"Would it have mattered if I did?"

Solomon finished toweling off his legs and stepped onto the floor. He smiled. "Actually, I would've liked it."

42 *Solomon*

"I'll be out in a minute." I struggled to find some suitable church clothes in my junky bedroom. After being fired, things had gone downhill quickly. I never expected to have company, especially her. I wondered what she thought as she waited for me in the tiny living room.

After finding a nice pair of slacks, I threw on one of my dress shirts I used to wear at my job. A dash of cologne and I ran out to join Trayce. She had helped herself to a photo album from under the coffee table.

"You have gorgeous children."

"Thank you," I answered. "They get that from their mother."

She flipped back a few pages, turning back the years, and found myself and Linda in happier times. It made me fidget, but I tried not to let on. She eyed the woman who bore a passing resemblance to her then brought her gaze back on me. "No, they definitely have your dimples and your eyes."

I smiled.

"I take it the two of you don't get along."

"You could say that."

"Was it always like that?"

"No. At least, I didn't notice it. Young. We got together right out of high school." I remembered the lie I'd told her about some college I'd attended. That had been so stupid of me.

"Oh." I couldn't tell whether she'd remembered what I'd said or just wrote it off as "reunion boasting" on my part, but her demeanor stayed the same.

"Yeah. Things just didn't work out no matter how hard I tried."

"A shame. For your children, I mean."

I nodded and tried to put my original motives for seeking Trayce out of my head. "So, ready to go?" I prodded.

I hurried Trayce as we were going to be late, but the real reason lay on the coffee table beneath the opened photo album. She had missed the magazine article I'd circled and the pages I'd printed off the internet on her.

Trayce read over the paper while I drove her rental. Back at the hotel, she'd been kind and took my explanation about my car without question. I'd never been to her church, or any in recent years, but I knew my way around town.

Looking up to enjoy the beautiful morning and the wild radish blooming alongside the road, she spoke. "It says here that we have a dance tonight, the results of the voting, and a special surprise."

"Special surprise. I wonder what that could be."

"Who knows what Donna thought up. She's certainly put her all into putting this on. Think she meant for us to get together?"

"I doubt it."

"Why'd you say it like that?"

"Just because. I don't think anyone saw that coming." I saw no reason to bother Trayce with Donna's flirtations when I first checked in. I'd experienced such an intense union with Trayce, on both an emotional and physical level, that it didn't matter. I needed a high-paying job away from here now more than ever, but I would go about it in a different way.

"True. I didn't come here for *this*," she joked as she pointed between my legs. I fought off a blush and concentrated on the road.

"So what did you come here for?" I asked, curious as to her answer. I knew my reasons. "If you don't mind my asking," I added.

"Let's just say it's something I had to do for *me*."

"Demons?"

"What?" she asked, surprised by my question.

"Things troubling you that you want to put to rest."

"Oh. I thought you were being religious."

"I've never been that religious. I've always been about hard facts."

"With a name like Solomon, that's too bad. Maybe you need a little spirituality in your life."

"Maybe." I wondered if that would have led me to someone other than Linda after high school. I was blessed with two great kids, so I assumed it was all part of God's plan.

"I'm one to talk," she laughed.

"Has spirituality helped you?"

She hesitated as we drove into the church parking lot then broke into a smile. "Yes," she replied.

I watched Trayce as she took a deep breath before exiting the car. Service was about to start and she leaned into the car before closing the door. "Are you coming?"

I nodded then undid my seatbelt. The sun glinted off my finger drawing my eye to the golden wedding band I still wore. I looked up to see Trayce motioning to me once more to hurry along.

She wore a red dress, ablaze with brilliant splashes of yellow. She smiled as she playfully moved one of her braids aside. As I stepped out the car, I slid the band off my finger and deposited it in my slacks pocket.

"Let's go do this," I said as I took her arm in mine.

43 Janet

"You've got to be kidding," I muttered, lowering my designer shades. After receiving his way-too-early wakeup call, I'd applied my makeup, slipped into one of my jogging suits, and made my way downstairs. He was waiting on me out front as promised.

"Get in," he replied. Karim extended his hand from the open door of the limo. He wore a New York Jets jersey and a pair of baggy jeans that looked slightly odd on his lanky frame. A pair of throwback Nikes adorned his feet. The driver stood silently at attention. "C'mon, we're wastin' gas here."

The driver snapped to attention when I got closer and grasped the car door in his hand. I took a seat beside Karim. Rather than moving over like a gentleman, he stayed his ground, making me share his space. I could've found another seat in the spacious cabin, but my head still hurt and it was too early for all that moving around. I gave in, this once, and made myself comfortable.

We circled out of the parking lot.

"Why the limo?"

"It's how I usually travel these days," he replied as if an afterthought. With some people it would have reeked of pretentiousness, but I could tell he was just telling it like it was.

"Where are we going?"

"So many questions. Good morning to you too, sunshine." He placed his hand playfully on my knee and gave me a kiss on the cheek. He was trying very hard to put how our night had ended behind him. I wasn't that easy.

"If you're not going to tell me where we're going, could you at least give me some room?"

"My breath's that bad?" He faked blowing into his hand then blinked his eyes from the smell.

"Yes," I replied. "Your cologne too."

"Other people like it."

I closed my eyes. "I'm not other people. I'm Janet." Still sleepy, I almost called myself "Godiva."

"No, I think your name's 'Grumpy,' but I'll cut you some slack anyway." Karim moved to another seat and reached into the bar. "Can I get you something to work that mood off? Iced coffee? OJ?"

"OJ . . . with vodka."

He laughed it off and gave me straight OJ on the rocks.

The limo turned onto the highway and merged with traffic.

"You're not kidnapping me, huh? I need to be back for the dance tonight." I made a mental note not to show off too much when I danced. I wasn't at work.

"We'll have you back in time. Trust me."

"Trust you?" I didn't mean to say it like that, but I couldn't help but think of him talking to Shauna in the hallway the night before. She said they struck up a conversation by accident when she was looking for my room, but something about it unsettled me. Shauna was happily married and not about to give Karim the time of day, but you never knew with men. I knew the type, those who took a wedding ring as merely a challenge on their way to another notch on their dick, but I didn't want to recklessly cast Karim in with them.

"You don't trust me?"

"I'm just saying that I don't know you that well."

"And I'm trying to change that, but you gotta work with me."

"What makes you think I want to?"

"Simmer down, sister. It's me, Karim. You don't have to be the hard ass around me."

"I'll consider it if you tell me where we're going."

"To get a bite to eat."

"Then why does it look like we're going back by the school?"

"Good eye," he said.

I watched as the limo retraced the route I had driven, but Karim was still being mysterious. That cockiness that I liked before wasn't as enjoyable this time.

When the limo got to the fenced Marion High, it kept going. A block away was a new strip mall, part of the revitalization at the expense of history in these here parts. I vainly wondered if there was a D&G or Coach store to do some shopping, but it was too early for them to be open . . . *unless*. Maybe Karim was surprising me with a shopping spree? *Definitely a way to get back on my good side*, I thought. My toes curled with delight.

"Here we are," he said as the driver came to a stop. I tried to feign surprise as I turned to see the open doors of . . .

"*Krispy Kreme*?"

Karim beamed with excitement. "Yeah. I'm hooked on those things. When we were out here last night, I saw the sign."

"You've got to be kidding me."

"Nah, see that sign right there?" I humored him. He continued, "When it's turned on, that means the donuts are hot."

"You are crazy. And I want to go back to sleep."

"And miss part of this weekend? *With me*? Ain't havin' it. You can sleep when you get back to Vegas. C'mon, share a donut with me," he said as he took my arm and gently tugged at me to get out. "I know you ain't one of those shorties who likes to purge. All your stuff is in the right places."

"And I want to keep it there."

"Whatever calories you put on, I'm sure you'll work them off tonight at the dance."

He just stood there, arms folded, with that silly smirk on his face. The driver stood calmly by, waiting for this to play out.

"Besides . . . you owe me for helping you with that math you never got all those years."

"Low blow."

"Call me 'Carrot Top' later and pay me back."

Carrot Top was fine and sexy now. That won out.

44 Karim

It was warm inside and she'd lowered the zipper on her jacket, revealing some more of that cleavage. Damn. It was robbing me of the pleasure from the hot donut I'd tossed in my mouth. Talk about a dilemma.

"Are you going to eat the whole dozen?"

"Not if you help me." I slid the box toward her then blocked it with my hand, preventing her from sliding it back.

Janet gave in and daintily picked one free. She placed it on the napkin, then broke a piece off. I watched her suck the remaining glaze off her two fingers, one chocolaty digit at a time. As she brought her lips together, I promised myself I would kiss them at least once before this weekend was over.

"Do I get a dance tonight?"

"That's all you want?" The donuts were more magical than I thought.

"Don't want to push," I replied. "But you know I came to see you."

My bluntness surprised her. I knew she wasn't expecting an announcement like that. Surely her reasons for being here had been different. As different as four little letters: S-H-A-W.

"How'd you know I would be here?"

"I didn't. Took a chance."

"That's so sweet."

"Uh huh. The old brush off. Like you did last night when I got too close."

"It wasn't that."

"Oh? Then what was it? Why'd you suddenly turn off? What's up, ma?"

She took another donut despite her earlier protests. I drank my orange juice and waited for an answer, but none ever came.

Then it came down on me like a ton of shit. It could've been bricks, but a ton is a ton, no matter what it is. I laughed because it was the only thing I could do. "You think you still have a chance with him."

"Excuse you?"

"You're still holding on. For Shaw."

"You've lost your damn mind."

"All right. Prove me wrong."

"How? By sleeping with you?"

"Not what I meant, but that would be cool," I chuckled.

"Real bad psychology. I get that from most of these little boys."

"You're funny."

"What?"

"I mean 'funny' in a sad way. For a woman who's had men at her beck and call her whole life, you sure are bitter. What kind of men are you running into out there? Are they that bad in Vegas?"

"I come across all types. Doesn't matter what town. Most want something."

"What did Shaw want?"

Silence. She went to speak, but there was silence again.

"Fuck him." A mother nearby overheard and gave me *that look*. I lowered my voice out of respect. "I want to talk about you. That's the only reason this reunion is worth my time—because of you. What do *you* want, Janet?"

"Look, I don't want to talk about this here." She rolled her eyes at the same woman, sending the woman leaving with her child. "This isn't the place."

"Janet. I ain't seen ya in ten years. It might be another ten years . . . or never. I just want to put our cards on the table."

"I'll say it again. I'm not talking about this here." With a simple shrug, she got up from the table and went back to the limo. A manager was about to ask me to leave when I shooed him away and left on my own. My *cards* remained behind, there on the table, mine and mine alone . . . alongside three warm donuts.

45 Trayce

"This is some dance," Solomon said over the sounds of Zhane's "Groove Thang."

His foot would bump against mine as he tapped it under the table. I'd politely smile and ignore that he was a little off when it came to rhythm.

"Yes it is," I answered, my mind on the twirling figures and wondering if I should dare join them out on the floor. I didn't dance in high school, but now you could catch me at the Dragon Room or Spot 6 whenever I got that itch back in Chi-town. I wasn't a bad stepper either.

The ballroom we'd been in the night before had been transformed into probably the best dance club for miles around. Balloons lined the walls like wallpaper and the lights were dimmed except for the area cleared for photographs. I assumed this is how the prom would've been if I'd attended. This night, we were free to sit wherever we chose as the tables were arranged on the perimeter, leaving the middle section open to groove. We'd angled our chairs at the table so we could watch the dance floor as the deejay took us on a trip down memory lane.

It was funny watching the familiar old patterns people were slipping into. Most of The Crew had assembled at a table on the opposite side of the room. In their midst I saw Shaw. I hoped that he would stay away, but didn't feel as uptight about him this time. After going home to change into a nice white button-down and pair of gray slacks, Solomon had returned tonight to stick right by my side.

As it was a larger table, we had more company this time. Donna, between checking with the deejay and admiring her handiwork, sat on the other side of Solomon. Still being the inquisitive reporter, she was using every free moment to question me to death. Every time she would call out at me, which was right in his ear, he would scrunch his face. As the night wore on, I think her voice was working on his nerves. Once her barrage would end, he would go back to smiling at me . . . and tapping his feet.

Our table was also shared with Cameron, who appeared to be drinking the night away. The scowl stuck on like glue kept Solomon and me from talking to him, but Donna, being Donna, would still dare from time to time. They had worked together on the school newspaper, so she assumed she had immunity of some sort. Most of the time, he would simply flash a smile then go back to whatever spirits were whispering to him in his latest glass.

"What's wrong with Cameron?" I asked my companion. "He looked all sour yesterday too."

"Let's just say this reunion hasn't been enjoyable for some people," Solomon replied cryptically. His nonchalance when he spoke told me he knew more than he was letting on. Every time I felt more comfortable with this man I'd been intimate with, he'd do something like this again.

It was like Solomon was privy to a world most of us didn't see and frankly it unnerved me.

Tevin Campbell's "Can We Talk" had just begun playing. I watched a few more couples take to the floor and bumped Solomon's leg.

"C'mon."

"I . . . I don't dance very well."

"So. Neither do I," I asserted. I didn't plan on wasting this nice lavender dress sitting down all night. "It doesn't matter. C'mon."

Solomon was still hemming and hawing when another man's hand planted firmly on my bare shoulder. Shivers went down my spine as I dreaded who it might be.

"Feel like dancing, lady?"

Dressed all in black, which appeared to be his favorite color, Karim flashed his teeth. I breathed a sigh of relief because of who it was, before confusion set in on my face.

"Huh?"

"Dance. Wanna dance?"

I looked at Solomon, who shrugged his shoulders. Donna, over his shoulder, sat with her mouth agape. Cameron looked up briefly to smirk.

"Sure."

"You didn't have to do this."

"I wanted to," he replied as he went into a turn. I watched his footwork—smooth, real smooth. "How else are you going to get Solomon up?"

I held back a laugh. Karim nodded, seeing that I got what he was saying.

"Trust me," he said with a wink. "He'll dance with you from this point on."

"You've turned into quite the character."

"Hey, we honor roll students gotta stick together."

"I thought you'd forgotten about us and made new friends tonight. Seeing as you're Mr. Man now."

"Nope. I'm hardly that. I was working my way over to y'all."

"Where's Janet?"

"Around here somewhere I suppose."

"I thought ya'll two would be inseparable."

"You mean like you and Solomon over there?" he chuckled. "Nah. She's still nursing some wounds."

I knew a thing or two about that. Ironic that it was owed to the same guy. "That's too bad. Ya'll two make a beautiful couple."

"Maybe you can make her believe that."

"I doubt Janet would want to listen to anything I'd have to say."

"She should. After everything you've been through . . ."

"What do you mean?"

Karim mumbled to himself, indiscernible to my ears. He moved closer, leading people around us to believe he was trying to put the moves on me. He whispered. "You and I both know things weren't too easy for you in high school. Everyone here knows about . . ."

"My rep?"

"Yeah," he said as if trying to chase an awful taste from his mouth.

"You're a bastard, Karim." The song was ending anyway, so I began walking off.

"Wait. Hold on," he said, grabbing my arm. "Hear me out." I balled my fist, but restrained myself. He continued. "I didn't say I believed it. What I'm tryin' to say is that you didn't let that keep you down. You didn't let all this bullshit twist you up and turn you out. You're a success, girl. You handled your business and moved on."

"Then why am I back here?" It was a question I asked myself.

Thinking I was talking to him, he replied, "I think we're all asking ourselves the same thing."

When the next song ended, the deejay decided to slow things down. As we parted, Karim had a few words.

"We're cool?"

"Yes," I smiled.

"Good, 'cause I admire you. Really."

"Thanks for the dance."

"Nothin' but a thang, ma," he replied. "Solomon's waiting."

"And I think someone's waiting for you," I said as I pointed to the woman waiting for her chance to dance with Karim. I watched the boyish smile return.

46 *Solomon*

"Is she your girlfriend?"

"No." I felt kinda uneasy seeing Trayce dancing with Karim. I was self-conscious about my two left feet, but was about to do the damn thing when his dopey ass showed up. The fact that other women were taking notice of it pissed me off even more. Who did he think he was barging in like that? Trying to be *Mr. Peanut Butter Smooth*, I guessed. Hell, I remembered when he used to run for his life after school. "We're just friends," I answered sourly.

"Good," Donna blurted out loud enough to get my attention off the floor and on her. "Thought I was going to have to separate y'all two. Not that I blame you. You'd have to be crazy to pass up being her 'Stedman.'"

"What are you talking about?" She already talked way too fast

"Stedman. As in *Oprah and Stedman*. Hello! If you were to get with Trayce, you'd be set for life."

"Are you insinuating that I . . ."

"No, no," she protested. "Not you. I'm just saying . . ."

"Well whatever you're saying, stop."

"Okay. Damn. What's got you so riled up?"

Did it piss me off more that Donna would imply that or because she was telling the truth? When I came up with this crazy scheme, I had no plans on trying to be Trayce's "Stedman" and still didn't. I simply wanted a decent job so I could raise my kids free of the insanity and would've busted my ass proving my worth to her. With the way things were now, I'd dumped that idea too. Somehow, watching Karim dancing with Trayce made me wonder if maybe some people had other intentions.

"Sorry, Donna. I didn't mean to snap like that. I don't do well on little sleep."

"Okay, I'll forgive you this time. But only if you give me a dance."

"Right now?"

"Yes, silly. Are you busy?"

"Well, no." I looked at Trayce's empty chair. She was still *tripping the light fantastic* with Karim, her Stedman. "I did promise you, huh?"

Donna rested her head against my chest and hummed along to the music of Shai, very popular during our school days. As we rocked back and forth, I wished she'd picked a more up-tempo song for us to dance to. I would've looked awful then, but I certainly would've felt better with less intimacy between us. I took solace that it wasn't "Let's Get it On."

"Solomon?"

"Hmm?"

"Are you enjoying yourself?"

"Yeah."

"I'm so happy," she sighed. "You don't know how much I wanted this to succeed. When this is over, I'm going to sleep for an entire week."

I laughed, using that to end our embrace.

"Since you still live in the area maybe we could go out sometime . . . once this is over."

I wasn't ready for this from Donna. Glancing at our table, I saw Trayce had returned. She'd noticed me and waved to get my attention. Karim was nowhere to be found.

I was spared from answering Donna when someone walked up and whispered in her ear just then.

"I gotta check on a few things," she said. "Just, think about it, okay?"

I nodded and smiled.

"I hope you voted for Mr. and Mrs. Marion. There'll be a big surprise later," she gleefully promised as she gathered her dress and scurried away.

Ironic as it were, the two classmates I'd voted for were Trayce and Karim.

47 Janet

"Donna did all this?" Naomi asked rhetorically. "Fantastic, isn't it?"

"Yeah, for someone like her."

She and Shauna laughed in unison. That used to be me and Shauna's thing. I felt a little out of sync when the two of them were together, like the outsider, even though they did everything to reassure me it was just like old days. Old days.

"You could've done better, Naomi?"

Naomi's eyes narrowed as if she didn't understand me. "Well, yeah."

"What would you have done to make this better?"

"Um . . . well, you know."

I took a sip of my champagne, not as sweet as I liked, then giggled. "No, I don't know."

"Well, if I would've been in charge, this whole reunion would've been better."

I turned to Naomi, feeling some kind of need to fuck with her further. "Okay. Better. But how?"

"Just because," she proclaimed, proud in her ignorance.

"Because anything The Crew does is better?" I questioned, my sarcasm evident.

Naomi's eyes widened. "Yeah," she said as if coming out of a fog. "You're right, Janet! That's it exactly!"

So much for that. I shook my head in frustration. Some people just didn't get it.

"Why you stirrin' stuff with Naomi, Janet?" Shauna asked, the only one nearby to pick up on my intent.

"Just having a little fun."

"Speaking of fun, somebody better get out here and dance with me," Mike said as he made pelvic thrusts in a futile attempt to arouse someone. "Nice dress, Janet." I knew he was more interested in what was beneath it and rolled my eyes in defiance. After a few more seconds of coaxing, both Shauna and Naomi joined him to Chubb Rock's "Treat 'Em Right."

"Yep, just like old times," said the deep voice echoing what I was just thinking.

"Almost. Where's your woman? Did I offend her last night?"

"Andrea's not feeling well," Shaw replied. "She's up in the room."

I'd heard someone saw her with her bags packed catching a taxi, but remembering what Karim had said decided to be cordial. "Is that why you're talking to me now?" Okay. Maybe *semi*-cordial.

"C'mon, Janet. Can't we put all that behind us?"

"I just want to know one thing."

"What?"

"Did you find the Lord with Andrea?"

Shaw looked confused.

"Forgot it already, huh? I assume you're sleeping with her."

He shrugged. "So?"

"Remember when you used to keep me at bay? *Just wait, Janet. I can't do this now, Janet. When we're together forever, Janet. I love you so much, Janet.* Blah, blah, blah. Talk. Talk. Talk. That's all you were then when you were stringing me along. So now Andrea sees the action while all I got was the shaft."

"Please. Wasn't last night enough?"

He was uncomfortable, but trying to make peace. Whatever he'd wanted, it obviously wasn't me, so I had to deal with it and move the fuck on. I understood it in my business. Sometimes the customer wanted vanilla, sometimes strawberry, and sometimes chocolate. I would never be 31 flavors, but what I could *and did* do was provide the best damn chocolate to those with the sweet tooth.

I winked at Shaw, signaling an uneasy truce or time-out. "Tell you what," I paused. "I'll think about it and let you know if last night was enough."

Naomi and Shauna interrupted us just then as they'd managed escape from Mike's clutches. Shaw looked relieved to have them back if only to act as a buffer. I was trying to get another glass of champagne, but Mike slapped his meat hooks on me next and wouldn't let go. I decided to humor the oaf and maybe embarrass him a little on the dance floor.

Janet Jackson's "If" played and Mike did the best he could to keep up with me. I liked this song and went through my moves as the old video replayed in my head. Ms. Jackson, the other Janet, had such control over her audiences, especially the men, which this ambitious country girl had drawn on when she brought Godiva to life in Vegas.

Some of the couples cleared a path for me, cheering me

on. I took a few side steps, moving my shoulders with the groove, then turned to circle a perspiring Mike.

"Mmm, mmm, Janet. You still got them moves," he panted as beads of sweat collected on his forehead. When he tried to put his hands on me, probably to stop me from showing him up, I'd teasingly dance out of his reach with a smile.

"How would you know? I never danced with you."

"Yeah, but that didn't stop me from lookin' at those dances and proms. You were wastin' all your time with Shaw."

"But Shaw's your boy," I teased, dancing closer. Toying with him, working him like that mark that he was.

"Yeah, yeah," he agreed. "Shaw's my dawg, but he did you wrong after school." He licked his lips. "That mother fucker was crazy to let you go."

"He looks like he's getting along okay."

"I'm doing much better." Uh oh. Here came the bragging. Probably as a way to overcompensate for a small dick, I thought. "Trust me. I've seen his condo in Atlanta."

"He and Andrea's?" I asked, attempting to pry and correct him at the same time.

Mike laughed. "Nah. Shaw's a straight-up bachelor. She tight and all that, but this my first time seein' her. Anyway, like I was sayin', you need to be thinkin' about me."

"Uh huh."

"I've taken over out here since you left. I got businesses in four counties. Four. Ask anybody. I'm the man."

"I can see," I said facetiously. His shirt was about to pop open because of his gut. A few more minutes of dancing and it might bust out.

"I can take care of you, Janet. Whatever you want. *However* you want."

"You don't have a family by now?"

"Of course, I'm all about family," he beamed. "I got a nice wife and kid at home, but this ain't about them."

"It's about you," I said, completing his tired, predictable pick-up line. A Tevin Campbell song had begun playing. In the days, I'd danced all my songs with Shaw. Now Karim was on my mind wherever he was right now. I really wanted to see him, to be with him.

"Yeah. You get it," he smiled with whatever delusions running through his big head. "You need to move back. Or maybe I can see you in Vegas. I'm out there a lot. I'm a really big gambler."

And a really big loser too. "Nah, I couldn't fit that into my schedule."

Mike froze as if struck by something. "What casino do you work at?" he asked as he focused on my face more closely. "I could've sworn I've seen you out there before."

He may have been fishing, but before this went any further, I called it a wrap. "Doesn't matter because Mike baby, you couldn't afford me anyway . . . and that's *if* I were interested."

"Who you got? Not Shaw," he boasted with a guffaw.

I brushed against Mike, letting his sweaty hand touch my waist. I looked into his eyes as they widened, then stood on my tiptoes to whisper seductively in his ear. "Mike?"

"Yeah, baby?"

"I hope you enjoyed your dance, you fat, no-dressing, cheating piece of shit. This is the closest you'll ever get to this," I said as I smacked my ass. I was walking off when

I gave him a parting shot. "Oh. And I don't know what's receding worse—your hairline or that pimple in your pants you call a dick."

Mike waited until I was almost off the floor. "That's why you ain't got a man," he shouted.

I think he looked more the fool for it.

"Girl, what's gotten into you?" Shauna was the first one in my face. If she weren't my girl, I would've had words for her too. "First you messed with Naomi—*poor thing didn't know it*—now you and Mike are getting into it. We're your friends. Did those weirdos rub off on you last night? Remember?"

"Y'know, Shauna. They weren't that bad. You should try hangin' with them."

"No thanks. I'll pass."

I smugly pushed. "Not even Karim?"

"Uhh, that one there." She smacked her lips with distaste.

"What?"

"Look who's dancing together!" Naomi blurted before Shauna could comment.

I thought Naomi was just being obnoxious at first, but saw that everyone else in the place was riveted also. Karim and Trayce were dancing. I didn't take too kindly that she was dancing with Karim, who could be my man if I weren't so *me*, while I got sweaty-ass Mike.

48 Karim

If this was one of my videos, I couldn't have dreamed it up any better if I tried.

She stood there like all those years of awful paintings suddenly made beautiful and come to life. My vision wore her hair curly this evening with long ebony locks that framed her face. Janet was wearing some kind of navy blue wrap dress that ended in ruffles at her shapely thighs. Her sleeves were sheer and stopped at her forearms where they formed bracelets. The high collar that dipped deep between her breasts reminded me of the wicked witch from *Sleeping Beauty*, except despite her attitude Janet was no witch. She was my queen and had been since that day I first laid eyes on her.

"*The very first time that I saw your brown eyes,*" I mouthed silently along with the words to Shai's song.

"*Your lips said 'hello' and I said, 'hi,'*" I saw her mouth back with a smile.

We met in the middle of the floor, both of us rushing headlong to one another.

"I missed you," she said. Her skin was so smooth and

flawless. "You could've come to look for me instead of dancing with Trayce."

"Shhh. I don't want to ruin this, so stop complaining." I put my arms around her slender waist, leaning over as I pulled her to me. She opened her mouth to ask questions, but quieted as our lips touched for the first time. Hers were as soft as I'd imagined and tasted liked fresh strawberries and champagne.

"Karim, what are you doing?" she asked, catching her breath.

"Do you want me to stop?"

Janet nervously paused, blinking her eyes and looking around as emotions overcame her.

"No," she said as she looked back into my eyes.

The second kiss was even better.

If somebody commented, I didn't hear it. If someone was offended, I didn't care. If someone enjoyed the display, I gave a damn. I finally had her.

"Karim, are you alright? You look like you're day-dreaming."

"Yeah. I'm a dreamer. I do that a lot." There she was, just as beautiful. Those lips touched by my imagination only. The night was early though.

"Dreaming about what? Trayce?"

"No. You."

"Then you should've been looking for me instead of dancing with her."

"I saw you," I said, wishing things between us were progressing in a more positive direction. "Didn't know you wanted to be found. Remember at Krispy Kreme?"

"I've been thinking about that." Janet's lip curled as if she were a naughty school kid. That would've been a different fantasy altogether.

"While you were being Ms. Soul Train with that balding asshole?"

"You saw me and Mike? Why didn't you come get me?"

"Didn't want to interrupt your fun."

"Fun?" She made a mock gagging sound. "That was NOT fun. He made me dance. I just decided to make the most of it."

"C'mon. You were with your *friends*."

"Why do you say it like that?"

"No reason," I shrugged. "I was never a big fan of The Crew."

"Did you ever give them a chance?"

"Just you. Besides, the rest of those morons were too busy laughing at me or trying to beat my head in . . . or both."

Janet laughed. "I don't remember it being that bad."

"Sure you do. It's just that when it's not happening to you, you don't care."

"Was I that bad?"

"No. You were just preoccupied in those days." I gestured in the direction of Shaw.

She looked at him too then moved closer. I felt electricity shoot through me as we touched. Her eyes, her breath on my neck was incredible. "I'm not preoccupied anymore."

"Straight?"

"Did you mean all this shit you've been telling me?" she countered. "Or were you being a man and just trying to . . ." she laced a few subtle kisses on my neck—no dream—before continuing, ". . . get in my pants?"

"I'm a man all right," I proclaimed as I fought to maintain my cool, unfazed demeanor. "I've meant everything I've ever said to you and I'd like *that* very much too."

She pressed her chest firmly against me. "I can tell if you're lying, y'know. By your heartbeat."

Our bodies moved to the music—Jodeci, I think—but I

wasn't hearing the song. "Are you sure? Maybe you need to get closer." Janet complied without hesitation. "Can you feel it?" I asked.

"Yeah."

"How does it feel?"

"Good. *Mmm*, real good." She closed her eyes, savoring my hardness through our clothes as she rocked up against it.

"Well, what does it tell you?"

"That you're about to get in my pants."

"Where are we going?"

"Oh, just come on."

I stumbled down the stairs as Janet led me out back past some of our other classmates. A few winks and smiles were cast as we hurried beyond the gazebo and toward a dark area by the pond.

Janet's grip on my hand tightened as she searched for seclusion—seclusion for us. The excitement was overwhelming. I wondered if she felt my palm getting sweaty.

When we came upon a large knotted tree almost off the property, she grinned and I knew she'd found what she was looking for. She had difficulty walking through the thick grass and removed her pumps. I slowed to watch her stumble barefoot haphazardly at first, but then she began running.

"C'mon!" she urged. I would've followed her through a wall of fire.

In the moonlight, we reached the tree at the same time, laughing like kids. Then the kids had to go. Grown folks' business was afoot.

"Why don't we go up to the room?"

"Un uh," she answered. "We can do that later. I don't want to miss the votes."

Curiously enough, I didn't want to miss that either as I'd voted for the two of us.

"Nervous?"

"A little."

"Why?"

"Because it's you."

" 'Bout time you got over that, Karim."

"Yeah. No doubt."

I slid my hands along her arms and grasped her shoulders. Squeezing gently, I began massaging them. Janet rotated her head as she moaned softly with pleasure.

"You have strong shoulders."

"Mmm, you have strong hands."

She turned to face the old tree, bracing herself against it as I came close behind her. I moved my hands to her neck then slowly worked the knots out as I traversed between her shoulder blades and down her back. At the base of her spine, I worked my thumbs to relieve the pressure of carrying such an exquisite frame around. That was the key with most women, getting them to relax and feel comfortable around you. My actions were now accomplishing things with Janet where once words were the only possibility.

My dick flexed and throbbed with each circular gouge into her muscles, entrancing and enticing me more and more. I roamed further south, sliding my hands underneath to grip her tight ass. She showed her approval and responded by rubbing it against me, harder and harder. It was like she had an itch to scratch and I was her fence post. I began to grind back in turn, our bodies locked at the pelvis in a bizarre dance of sorts.

"You're making me so hot, Karim," she gasped between rearward thrusts. "Don't tease me like this."

I reached around the front of her dress, finding buttons, which I unfastened. She gasped at first, feeling the cool night air reaching in, then her breathing became shallow and desperate. I inserted my hands, feeling her warm, soft skin. No bra. Just those gorgeous, lovely mounds she was so proud of. I took ownership of them, squeezing and caressing until coming to a stop at her erect nipples, which I pinched.

"Ouch, that's it. That's it. You want 'em. Take 'em, baby."

Savoring the moment, I kissed the back of her neck, dragging my tongue to taste her essence. "Give it to me," she said, bucking her ass into my dick again. I looked in the direction of the hotel, wondering if anyone could see us behind the tree from one of the upstairs windows. It was dangerous and fantastic all together.

"Do you have a condom?"

"Yeah." I reached down and slid her g-string off, letting it fall. From out of my wallet, I frantically reached for it, tearing the foil seal with my teeth. I undid my pants and let them fall to my ankles.

"C'mon. Put it in. I want to see if you feel as good as you look, boy."

Letting go of the tree, she reached back to kiss me. Those lips were finally mine as I felt their mutual longing, her tongue darting about to find mine. As she put one of her long legs up to steady herself, I slid Janet's dress up onto her bare chocolate ass—devil's food for the devil, for the devil was me at the moment. With the leg still against the tree, she bent over slightly and invited— no, *ordered* me to come inside. Being the obedient gentleman I am, I pressed myself firmly against her backside and took her like she wanted, adding another story for the old tree to tell.

49 Trayce

"Where's Karim?" Solomon asked as he scrambled back to the table.

"Did you miss me?" I asked in turn as I remembered Karim's remarks.

"I didn't want you to go in the first place." The sincerity in his answer was evident.

"Is that why you were out there grinding with Donna?" I enjoyed watching Solomon riled up. Karim's dance with me had set him off. He held so much in check with that calculating manner of his that I couldn't resist.

Solomon stuttered as he went to explain then choked on his own spit. I stood up to slap him on the back then helped him to his chair.

"Relax. I was only playing."

"It wasn't funny because I wasn't grinding," he snapped. "I wanted to dance with you."

"Really?"

"Well . . . yes."

"Then why are we sitting here?"

* * *

The group Troop told me to spread my wings and fly away to a place that I long for, just as it had during my time at Marion. Solomon had loosened up and stopped being self-conscious with his dancing to the point where he even surprised me.

"I remember this video," he said as he mimicked some of their moves. He looked so silly. "I used to do this in my mirror."

"Never went to the dances either?"

"Just one," he admitted. "Senior year. The last dance."

"Who did you dance with then?"

"No one." He smiled. "I guess I'd been waiting on you."

"That's a long wait, my friend."

"But it was worth it," he commented as he planted a kiss on my cheek. I was beaming so much that I'd failed to realize Solomon had just done this in plain view of everyone.

Over the next hour we danced nonstop, more and more couples joining us. Even Karim and Janet returned from wherever they'd been hiding and were right beside us as if lifelong friends. Amid what appeared to be genuine smiles and congratulatory nods given by those around us, what amazed me most was that Solomon and I fit in. There would always be people, like most of The Crew, who would never accept us, but this wasn't about them. It was our time . . . time for the rest of us, the rest of us where life wasn't summed up by just those four years, but rather by our whole journey through life and what we had learned. My therapist would be so proud of my moment of instant revelation, I thought with a pleased grin. I then gave Solomon an unexpected kiss of my own square on his lips.

"Did you vote yet?" he asked.

"Sure did."

"For us? No, don't answer that."

"It's okay," I answered. "I voted for you." I never could vote for myself as Ms. Marion, but I'd felt Donna had done such a wonderful job organizing this, that she got mine instead. With my vote for Mr. Marion, I was allowed to play favorites.

"Well, I voted for you, so maybe I'll see you up there."

"Aren't your legs getting tired?" I asked more for my benefit.

"Nah. I've saved up all these moves," he said, laughing at himself. "If only my kids could see me now."

He got his wish. Solomon stopped dead in his tracks as if struck by lightning. Confusion set in on his face before anger gained the upper hand.

"What the . . ."

I began to ask him what was wrong, but followed his gaze instead.

A woman, roughly our age, in a tight red velour jogging suit with large blonde tresses layered atop her head prowled the room perimeter.

She was questioning whoever would listen to her, at which point they'd mostly shrug. She looked vaguely familiar and I tried placing her from our class . . . until I saw the two children that followed her five steps back.

Solomon's ex-wife and kids were here and he was now making a beeline for them.

50 Solomon

"What the . . ." *She couldn't be here*, I thought. *She wouldn't do this*, I thought. Yeah. She would . . . and did.

I'd been having the time of my life, something oh so rare, when my life intruded. Not that I was unhappy to see my lovely children, but Linda being here meant something was wrong.

Before she could terrorize anyone else, I was up in her face.

"What are you doing here?"

"You don't know how to answer yo damn phone?"

"Is something wrong with the kids?"

"They all right. Thanks for askin' about me though," she sneered.

"Then why are you here?" I asked again, getting her to focus on me instead of the partygoers. She'd had her shot to be here with me at my side, but had cast her lot elsewhere.

"Look, you need to be a father to your kids."

"What are you talking about, woman?" I waved my

hands around in the air rather than give into dark temptation and lay them on Linda.

She huffed. "Just what I damn said."

She'd attracted people's attention now by being so loud. I think she was doing it intentionally, to embarrass me. Trayce stood within earshot, but politely kept her distance.

"Linda, stop this shit. Just tell me what you want."

"You need to watch your kids."

"What?" I asked as if slapped.

"Bo and I have plans tonight and you need to watch Jordan and Justine."

"Let go of my arm," she shouted as I pulled her out of the ballroom. Jordan and Justine followed behind us as I'd instructed.

"Y'all two, sit right there," I barked at them. "I need to talk with your mother."

Linda was loving this. Once we were clear of the kids, I lit into her.

"You knew I had this planned, Linda! Why here? Why now?"

"Well, your little pity party was no big deal until Bo came up with some tickets to the Katt Williams concert. He's outside waiting for me." She flashed her teeth, daring me to escalate things.

"I'm not supposed to have Jordan and Justine this weekend. And you know that."

"All I know is that suddenly you got some ho answering your phone calls for you and now you ain't got time for the kids that *you* helped make. *Hmph*. You ought to be lucky I'm giving you time."

"This is some bullshit and you know it. I bust my ass for those kids and put up with your shit only because I love them. Now you want to just dump them because you have tickets? Tickets! What kind of mother are you? What if I weren't here? Would you have just left them on the curbside?"

"Always so damn dramatic. That's why I'm glad I got a real man now," she remarked with a roll of her eyes. She took a look at her watch. "You don't want to watch your own children, fine. I'll guess I'll leave 'em with my sister."

"Stella? *The crack head*?"

"She ain't no crack head no more."

She knew just what she was doing—as manipulative as ever. Linda knew I wasn't letting them stay with Stella. Child Protective Services had taken her kids just last month. "Go."

"What?"

"I'll keep them. Now get out of my face."

"That's what I thought," she said with a mock kiss. She sauntered off toward the lobby without even saying goodbye to Jordan and Justine. "I put some stuff in Justine's overnight bag. Drop them by the house tomorrow, but call first. Bo likes to stay overnight when we go to the city."

"You'll see them when you see them," I shouted. If she heard me, she didn't react.

I took a minute to compose myself before returning to my kids. I didn't have a room at the Sheraton and couldn't afford one, so I began preparing my explanation to Trayce. I was pleasantly surprised to see her in the hallway entertaining Jordan and Justine.

"Hey," I said as I returned.

"There you are," she said with a smile. "I was just getting acquainted with Jordan and Justine here."

"Hey, she knows our names!" Jordan blurted out, which was uncharacteristic of him.

"Of course, I told her all about you two."

"See," Justine said as she hunched her brother with her elbow. "Toldja!"

"Trayce, I'm so sorry about all this."

"Relax. It's okay."

"No, it's not. I hate to do this, but I have to go."

51 Janet

"Act natural."

"Natural? After that?" he scoffed. I continued walking past the partygoers as if nothing happened. Yeah. Nothing but the wildest sex I'd had since . . .

"Gerald," I gasped out unintentionally, startled by the sudden unexpected pangs of guilt I felt.

"What'd you say?" We'd kept our distance intentionally since coming back from our excursion, but he moved closer to hear me.

I'd already recovered from the lapse. Gerald and I were through; he probably already packed up and left for LA to sell his paintings on some beach. "If you must know," I mumbled in one of my low sultry tones. "I thought it was incredible too."

Harder, harder, oooo that's it. Yeah, yeah, yeah. That's it, baby. Give momma that dick, my mind replayed, my pussy still throbbing from every thick inch he'd labored on me. I really wanted to see how Karim handled his business down south, but we had time to do that later back in the suite. I was making myself wet again with anticipation. I quickly pulled Karim into the ballroom before we wound up undressed on the elevator.

Once I cleared with Donna we hadn't missed the Mr. and Ms. Marion announcement, it was time to dance again. Besides, Salt-N-Pepa's "Whatta Man" seemed appropriate for the two of us.

Little Solomon had tamed his woman Trayce and was making like a man finally. Being in a playful mood and perhaps missing their corny charm, I found a spot on the floor for us right next to them. The four of us laughed and danced and laughed some more. I couldn't say we were reliving the past because I had none with them. Rather, this was a new animal that shouldn't have felt right, but did—maybe because it didn't really matter who I'd been or who I was now. Here were these three people, two who I knew nothing about until yesterday, along with one I thought I'd known, but just discovered in a whole new way. Kinship of some kind was not what I'd come here for, but maybe it was what I needed.

Just when I thought Solomon and Trayce would outlast us, they left. Probably to go do what I should be doing with Karim, I thought. Peering through the crowd, I saw Mike again. He was sparing us his pelvic thrusts, but seemed to be holding an intense conversation with Devon and Dwight, the terror twins as they were known. Normally, they wouldn't have held my interest, especially with Karim being mine, but their gesturing and high-fiving meant trouble for somebody back in the day. I focused my attention back on Karim, but eventually found myself drawn back to them, especially when one of the twins—Dwight, I think—looked dead at me and laughed. I tried ignoring it, but the other two got in on the act and began pointing.

"Something up, ma?"

"Nothing I can't handle," I answered. "I'll be right back." I should've left it alone, and in hindsight, I would've.

I stormed into the area staked out by my old friends,. Devon was the first one to clam up, hastily hushing his brother. Mike kept talking, unperturbed.

"So what lies are you telling now, Mike?"

"Shit, this ain't 'bout me, Janet," he said with a hearty laugh, meant to be heard. "This is all about you this time."

"Let it go, Mike. I ain't even sure."

"Sure about what, Dwight?"

"I'm Devon. *He's* Dwight." The other twin flashed a gold tooth differentiating himself from his brother.

"Whatever."

Mike urged Devon. "Fill her in, man. Tell her what you told me."

I waited, arms folded, to see what kind of shit was being stirred up.

Dwight grew tired of the silence too. "Call it like you see it, Devon. I wasn't there."

Devon hesitated. Mike looked like he was about to burst at the seams with whatever it was. "Where did you say you work in Las Vegas?"

Devon's question sent my stomach into convulsions, but I kept my eyes calmly on the three of them, looking for some confirmation. "It's none of your business, but since you're dying to know, I work at . . ."

The Standard where I'm the best paid woman there. Now. Say sumthin'.

". . . The Bellagio. I work at the Bellagio," I continued, sounding so damn weak. Ironically, I'd grasped and said the place I last knew Gerald worked before he left me. Gerald didn't love me any less because of my occupation and maybe that's why he was suddenly on my mind.

"You entertain there?" Mike asked.

"I coordinate for shows," I answered, slipping back into my rehearsed routine.

"I'll bet coordination's a prerequisite," he insinuated with a sneer.

"Fuck you, Mike."

"Nope. Not me, but maybe Devon's cousin." He looked at Devon, who gave him the okay to let out whatever he'd been holding. "Devon says he remembers you from Vegas. His cousin got married out there last year and had a bachelor party. He says he saw you in some titty bar."

I took major offense at Mike's taunting. I didn't work at any fuckin' *titty bar*.

"She looked a lot like you, Janet." Devon overemphasized for the amusement of the rest. Shauna and others moved closer, wondering what was going on.

"Cat got your tongue, Janet? Or maybe you got a dick in yo' mouth."

Just as I leapt at Mike, Karim appeared, snatching me from the air with his powerful arms. He stumbled back into Mike, still close enough for me to pop him in the eye with my fist. Mike struck back, but hit Karim instead.

I screamed, struggling to free myself from a dazed Karim. Mike and the twins laughed all the while, until Karim's hand found its way around Mike's throat in a death grip. In a fit of rage, he forced the larger man back until he slammed against the wall. People were screaming by then as the twins pounced on Karim. I jumped onto the back of one of them and attempted to get him off. Karim took his free hand and jabbed the throat of the other, causing him to keel over wheezing and coughing.

Above the fray, a voice could be heard pleading.

"Please! Stop this! Please!" Donna rushed about frantically; desperate to erase this nightmare into which her event was degrading.

Someone stepped up and answered Donna's prayers. It was Shaw. He forced himself past the crowd and began prying everyone apart.

"What is wrong with you, people? Can't you act like adults? We came here to enjoy this weekend and reflect on the good times and all you want to do is trash it. I couldn't wait to get away from here after high school, and now I see why." Shaw's glance cast at me didn't escape my notice. "Look at you! You're all too old for this!" he shouted, awakening vivid memories of him barking out orders on the football field. Even with their age, Mike and the twins yielded. Karim still held his fingers around Mike's neck, albeit not as tightly.

"He started it," Karim affirmed.

"You're the one who came sticking your nose in this. This don't involve you, faggot. Besides, you ain't even gettin' any of that unless you pay."

Karim's grip tightened again. "You ain't in a position to be calling names, *knowhu'amean*?"

"Stop it, Karim" Shaw said as he grabbed Karim's wrist. "As much as he deserves it, stop it."

"Huh?" Mike gasped in a garbled breath.

"Shut up, Mike."

"Not 'til he apologizes."

Mike's eyes met Shaw's. Enough could be understood even though he croaked like a frog.

"Not to me," Karim said. "Apologize to the lady."

Devon and Dwight began to snicker, but Shaw froze them with his gaze. Whatever else they had to say would keep for the night. Mike cut his eyes at me, hate radiating out, but he gave in.

When Karim let go, everybody was hastily separated. Shaw recommended the twins take the coughing Mike to get some fresh air and cool off before walking over to us.

"You okay, Janet?"

"I'm fine. Didn't know you cared."

Shaw looked as if he wanted to answer, but smiled politely and moved on. Donna had hurried over to the deejay, coaxing him to mellow things out with the sounds of Babyface.

"That was something," Karim said. It was obvious he still didn't particularly care for Shaw.

Karim had bombarded me with questions and I'd done a good job avoiding them, even sending him to get me another glass of champagne.

Shauna was keeping me company, curious in her own right about why there was so much angst between Mike and me. Mike was outside cooling off, but I knew my time at the reunion without my life being questioned was limited. Karim was the person with whom I needed to come clean. He would be the first and then maybe Shauna . . . *after* I'd picked up the title of Ms. Marion.

"Janet, you're hangin' with me and Naomi the rest of the night, right? It'll be just like old times. Once they crown you Ms. Marion, this party ain't gonna stop until the sun comes up."

"I wish I could, Shauna," I said, lying through my teeth. "But I've got other plans for ending this night."

"With Karim? I *know* you're not talking about him." Shauna sucked her teeth. "Troublemaker. If he's not starting a fight with Mike, then he's trying to sleep with every woman he sees. Making up for lost time, I guess."

"What'd you say?"

"Oh. You didn't know. He tried to pick up Naomi and me last night—*both* of us, girl. Pure player, that one. I guess that's how they do it in New York, but not down here and certainly not with *this* married woman."

"Shauna, you're so full of it."

"Girl, I'm serious. Ask Naomi."

We called Naomi over, who was fixing herself a plate of hors d'oeuvres, and I listened as Naomi nodded in agreement with everything Shauna had told me.

"He was still tryin' to get me in his room when I was coming to visit you last night."

"How come you didn't tell me about that?" I asked, hating that I hadn't inquired when I first saw that exchange.

"What did it matter? I didn't take him serious. He's a joke, Janet." I raised an eyebrow.

"Don't tell me you're serious about that boy."

Serious. I had been serious about Shaw for four years. These two days weren't enough time to gauge where I was with Karim, but the humiliation I was feeling was the same.

52 Karim

"She still doesn't want you, Carrot Top! She's after your money! That's what she does! Don't think I forgot about that middle finger yesterday either!" Michael taunted as his friends shuttled him out the back door. "Oh yeah, come on out back. Once I get my wind, I'll kick yo kung-fu ass." I was the bigger man, trying to ignore him, as I went searching in the opposite direction for a drink for Janet.

I took several deep, meditative breaths, trying to find my center as I'd been taught, but my head was too screwed up. A lot of pent up rage from those years of abuse from idiots like Michael had me wanting to snap someone, but that was the smaller issue at hand. Janet had more going on than what was apparent and I needed a resolution to some of it before I stuck my neck out for her again. It was time for "the talk."

Champagne in hand, I brought it back to Janet. I was about to get her attention when some classmates delayed me with questions about the fight. She was occupied with her girlfriends, so I took the time to be vague with them, blowing it off as a misunderstanding.

Gerald.

The name caught my attention, but I didn't know why. I tuned out the people around me. There. I heard it again. This time I concentrated on hearing what was being said.

"He's wonderful, I tell you."

"Then why didn't you bring him with you?" I heard Naomi ask.

"That would've been like taking sand to the beach," Janet chuckled. "Besides, Gerald knows I'm coming home to him when this is over. I'm just having a little fun."

Shauna saw me eavesdropping, but for reasons known only to her, let Janet continue.

Naomi laughed. "Karim? You slept with Karim?"

"Is that what you've been doing? Having a little fun, Janet?" Shauna continued to prod. "You have to give your girls all the juicy details."

"Well Shauna, 'little fun' is right. Don't let the boy's shoe size fool you. He's got a lot of growing to do in other areas."

"For real?" Naomi asked, to my credit, seemingly in disbelief.

Shauna cut her eyes at me again. "I find that hard to believe. Looks like he's packing to me."

"Believe it. He'd be on my last nerve if he weren't so eager to please. When this reunion is over, so is he."

The bitch had played me like an old Atari and it hurt like hell. I downed the drink meant for her and left.

53 Trayce

"Trayce, I can't let you do this."

"Sure you can. We're not using the room." I gave Solomon a wink, hinting at what had taken place here last night.

"I should get them home."

"So what you're saying is you're going to let Linda ruin this night. Our night."

"I don't want to, but . . ."

"But nothing. Jordan and Justine can stay here as long as they want."

Justine smiled ear to ear as I had opened my laptop for her, allowing her to look up a website on Beyoncé. Jordan, who was yawning, had staked out a spot on the couch. I found the controller to Nintendo games on the TV and handed it to him.

"Kids, feel free to order whatever anything you want from room service."

"Anything?" they said in unison.

"Anything. The menu's on the table, kids."

Solomon went to grab the menu before his children reached it. "C'mon. I can't impose like this."

"You're not. You're having a good time and so are your children. It's a win-win."

"Is that the businesswoman I'm hearing?"

"No. It's the woman that really loves children," I said as I grabbed Justine and put my arms around her. "And who thinks you're not so bad either."

Justine reached up and grasped my hair. "Ooo, who did your braids?"

"A nice lady in Chicago. Why? Do you like them?"

"I love them!"

"Well maybe your mother can braid yours like this."

"My momma doesn't like you."

"Justine!"

Jordan guffawed; probably thinking his sister was about to get in trouble.

"It's okay," I said to Solomon. "Justine, why do you say that?"

"I heard her say your name when Bo was bringing us here. She kept saying you were disrespecting her."

"Do you know what that means?"

"No. Not really. I just think she doesn't like you because Dad likes you."

"Oh? Do you really think your dad likes me?" I sat on the bed with her. Jordan left his Nintendo game and came over to join us.

"Yeah. Dad was dancing with you. He never dances with anyone."

"Except the mirror!" Jordan added. The three of us had a hearty laugh at Solomon's expense.

He had raised some fine children no matter what influence their mother had exhibited.

"Daddy, can we stay the night here? Please." It was Jordan this time. He was starting to warm up.

Solomon didn't answer. "Trayce, I need to talk to you."
He smiled, but I sensed something had him disturbed. It
was probably his thoughts of Linda screwing around
with him.

"Sure. I'm listening."

"Alone."

54 Solomon

Trayce let Jordan and Justine order some late night dessert from the menu, then joined me in the hallway for a talk.

"If you're going to try to change my mind. Give it up. You have a pair of great kids."

"I know. They're my life, but you shouldn't be involved in this."

"I really don't mind." She took my hand, but I pulled it away.

"Okay. What's up, Solomon?"

I glanced down the hallway to make sure we were undisturbed. The elevator chimed as it went past our floor. "I have something to tell you. And you're not going to like it. I've been trying to come up with a good time to say it, then this happened with the kids."

"Is it about them?"

"Yes and no."

"Will you quit being mysterious and just spit it out?"

"I came to this reunion looking for a job."

"So? I mean . . . I'd feel better if you said you came here looking for me, but . . ."

I cut her off. "I did come here looking for you."

"Oh." Trayce digested what I'd just said. Her look soured.

"I've been lying to you and everybody here. I don't work at Walgreens. Well, not anymore. I was fired."

"What for?"

"Same shit like this—Linda dropping my children off unexpectedly. They're the real reason I came here. It was because of them, but then things changed."

"You mean with us?"

"Yes."

She sighed before taking a deep breath. I watched her pace for a few seconds, half expecting her to hit me. I deserved it.

"What do you want from me, Solomon?" The way she said my name now had changed. It was marked and pointed, symbolizing the distrust that had crept in.

"I *had* wanted a job. Had."

"Why me? Did you think I would be that big of a sucker?"

"It wasn't like that, Trayce. I saw your magazine article and got to thinking. I just thought if maybe I impressed you that maybe you would . . ."

"Sleep with you?"

"Wait. Wait. Let me finish please. It wasn't that sort of party."

"Well. Finish then."

"I had this crazy, desperate idea to ask you for a job . . . a chance to prove myself. I want to fight for custody of Jordan and Justine. You see how Linda uses them like pawns. I need a job to do that . . . a good job. I'll never win that fight with a job around here and that's *if* I could even get another one. I told you it was a crazy idea. The point is that I never . . . *never* planned on the rest of this happening and that I'm truly sorry."

"You can't plan everything, Solomon." She said it as if it were more for her benefit.

"My motives in the beginning weren't pure, but all of this," I said taking her hands in mine. "*This*, this is real. I just hope you can forgive me for not being honest with you in the beginning."

"Y'know, I have a lot of trust issues with men to begin with," she chuckled. "But I kinda understand."

"You do?"

"Yes. My therapist would be proud," she sighed. "Kids hold a special place in my heart. I've seen you with yours and as twisted as it sounds I sort of understand where you're coming from."

"What I'm feeling for you is real. You have to believe that. I'd decided to dump this stupid plan before we . . . umm . . ."

"I got it. I have something I need to admit too."

"Go ahead."

"At your apartment today, I saw the 'research' you had on me. I was just waiting for you to come clean about it."

I opened my mouth to apologize profusely again, but she put two fingers to my lips.

"I would've helped you with the job stuff . . . without all of 'this'."

"Without really knowing me? I knew how bad you were treated in high school and never said a word. Never offered to help. Would you really have helped me out of the blue?"

"Putting it like that . . . maybe not. You used to creep me out back in the day." We both laughed nervously, trying to reclaim that comfortable place between us.

"How about now?"

"No. I think you know what you do to me now."

55 Janet

"Don't tell me you're serious about that boy." I heard Shauna's remark over and over in my head before I answered. "Hell nah, I'm not serious about that boy." I'd just found out that Karim had been trying to fuck not just me, but my friends as well. I couldn't have been a bigger fool at the moment.

"You're good, Janet," Naomi giggled. "I thought you were serious about him."

"Girl, puh-leaze. I've got a real man by the name of Gerald waiting on me at home. He's wonderful I tell you."

"Then why didn't you bring him with you?" Naomi asked, eager for details.

"That would've been like taking sand to the beach," I chuckled as I tried to hide my pain somewhere deep inside where I couldn't find it ever again. "Besides, Gerald knows I'm coming home to him when this is over. I'm just having a little fun."

Shauna smiled, but didn't say much. I wondered if she

believed my act. *Of course she did*, I reassured myself smugly. I was the best at this. A facade was my weapon and best friend all rolled up in one.

"Karim? You slept with Karim?" Naomi laughed with delight. "Damn!"

"Is that what you've been doing? Having a little fun, Janet?" It was Shauna's turn to join in. "You have to give your girls all the juicy details."

"Well, Shauna, 'little fun' is right. Don't let the boy's shoe size fool you. He's got a lot of growing to do in other areas." Of the lie I'd just told, only my pussy knew and it wasn't one to talk to strangers.

"For real?" Naomi seemed almost disappointed by my proclamation.

"I find that hard to believe," Shauna commented. "Looks like he's packing to me."

"Believe it. He'd be on my last nerve if he weren't so eager to please. When this reunion is over, so is he." After uttering those words, I wanted to cry. The more negative things I said about him, the more I realized that Karim had scarred me in such a short time. I was stupid to even consider letting him into my world.

"Maybe one of these single ladies around here might want to give him a try when you're through with him."

I didn't respond to Shauna at first. Karim hadn't returned with my drink. The ho was probably trying to slip his tongue down someone's throat. Good for him because I probably would've splashed the drink in his face after what I'd just learned. "They can have him for all I care." I laughed while crying on the inside. The group BBD's song "When Will I See You Smile Again?" played as if the deejay were taking cues from my soul.

Donna came by to let us know the announcements we'd been waiting for were to take place shortly. She was wondering if we'd seen Trayce or Solomon. I hadn't and it didn't matter anyway. She was probably just trying to dot her *i*'s and cross her *t*'s before I got my crown. *At least that will cheer me up*, I thought. In the back of my mind, I did wonder who was going to win Mr. Marion though.

56 Karim

"Karim, where are you going?"

"Up." I hated being rude to Trayce and Solomon when I pushed by them onto the emptying elevator, but wasn't up for "Twenty Questions."

"Did we miss anything?"

I laughed at Trayce's question and shook my head.

"Karim?" Solomon called out as the doors slid shut. To me, they couldn't have closed fast enough.

As soon as I got to my suite, I stripped bare. I balled up my clothes, still imbued with Janet's essence, and dropped them into the garbage can. Each stomp of my foot drove them down further and further until they were compacted. I'd come to this stupid reunion just for her and now I'd just been used like some toy. I couldn't believe this whole thing had been a big joke to Janet, but I heard the words. Her words. They left nothing open to interpretation.

I looked at myself in the mirror. I didn't see the man I had become. Rather a skinny, nervous redheaded child looked back with eyes wide.

"You're gone, kid," I said with a laugh "Shit. Been gone."

A quick check of my voicemail and I'd be off to the shower. Just a few messages were present, stuff from Clement and my assistant, Brady, which would keep until I returned to New York. Just for a distraction, I checked my other number. This was the non-VIP number I gave most people. There was an old message from On-Phire Records threatening me along with the usual cast of ladies from coast to coast. After listening, I deleted them all save one, not sure of my reasons.

I ran the shower hot and steamy, just how I liked it. Suds and hard scrubbing were my cure to a rough night. I worked to rid myself of any of her love juices that had missed the condom. When the complimentary soap bar was almost non-existent, I climbed out and toweled off.

I went over my itinerary, checking into any possibility of leaving early, but bad weather had rolled at both Charlotte and Atlanta. All flights were stalled until morning. Torn between hitting the bar downstairs or trying to do some work, I broke out my laptop.

Someone knocked at my door before I could even turn the computer on.

"Go away!" I yelled out.

The knock came again.

"What part of 'Do Not Disturb,' don't you understand?"

There was silence briefly. Then the knocking started back up. I muttered a few choice words before sliding from under the covers. I grabbed my robe and headed to the door.

"You really weren't going to let me in?"

"Who says I'm letting you in now?"

Shauna slid in under my arm and into the suite. She

still wore her black evening gown. For the first time, I noticed she looked rather hot.

"You alone?" she asked as she took her heels off one at a time. She circled the room, surveying my quarters.

"Yeah, but you already knew that."

"Did mean Janet hurt your feelings?"

"Nah. Just figured I'd come up and get some work done."

"Told you she had a boyfriend," she huffed in one of those I-told-you-so tones. "Oh. They're about to announce Mr. and Ms. Marion. You don't want to see who wins?"

"Nope. Doesn't matter to me. You better get back there. Don't want you to miss it." I was still in the doorway, hinting to her she wasn't welcome.

Shauna instead sat on my bed and began massaging the arches of her feet. *"Ooo, those heels were killing my feet. Don't matter to me either. Janet will probably win. Just like old times."*

"What's up, Shauna? Here for your girl Naomi again?"

"No. I'm being selfish this time." She shut my laptop and pushed it to the other side of the bed.

"Or maybe just honest for a change."

She giggled. "Probably both. Admit it. You need the company tonight."

"I don't need shit from you, ma."

"Can't tell." Shauna grinned as she stared at me. My dick was throbbing and bobbing beneath my robe. Sensing someone's call, the pheromones thick in the air. "Looks like someone has a lollipop that needs a lick."

"You don't know when to quit, huh?"

"Why don't you close that door and find out."

57 Trayce

"What was that about?" I asked after the brush-off by Karim.

"Dunno," Solomon shrugged. "Guess we had to have been here."

"Bet you it had something to do with him." Michael was going inside the ballroom. He looked pissed off despite the claims of "I'm all right" he was throwing around to those worried about him. Seeing Solomon and me, he frowned, but continued on as if we weren't worth the trouble.

"I wonder if something happened with Karim and him."

"It wouldn't surprise me. He used to pick on Karim heavily. Or maybe something blew up over Janet. Michael has been trying to put the moves on her."

"You don't miss anything do you?"

"Not much."

"Know any other secrets going on around us?"

Solomon smiled. "I'm sure I do, but let's not worry about that now."

"I think we should at least find Janet and make sure she's okay."

"Even if she's with Shauna and them?"

"Yes. I'm not worrying about them."

"Getting kinda close with Janet?"

"We'll never be best friends, but I've warmed to her a little in this short time. It would be nice to see her and Karim make it."

"Mm hmm." Whatever Solomon's thoughts were he kept them to himself. Again.

Inside the ballroom, I got the vibe something big had happened from the whispers and mumbling taking place. Donna was just turning on her microphone and testing it as she prepared to speak.

"You see Janet?"

"No. Maybe once they raise the lights." He squinted as we walked through the crowd.

Just then, Shauna bumped into us. She appeared to be in a hurry as she simply kept going.

"Bathroom break," Solomon joked.

Retracing Shauna's path, I saw Janet. Naomi was talking to her and it was apparent Janet was upset. Her arms were folded painfully tight and she kept tapping her foot, despite the smile affixed to her face. I told Solomon I was going talk to her even though she was surrounded by a lot of The Crew.

"Do you mind if I talk to her alone? Girl talk."

"Suit yourself. I'll be nearby if you need me."

"I know," I responded with a reassuring grin. "Thank you."

He gave me a kiss on the cheek then melted away.

Everybody greeted me pretty warmly when I walked up, except Naomi. I was glad Shauna hadn't returned because she would've been one more trying to put me in my place.

"Hey, Trayce." Janet seemed genuinely pleased. Her arms unfolded and her posture changed.

"You're okay, Janet?"

"I'm fine. Couldn't be better."

"You sure?"

"That's what she just said," Naomi chimed in. She tried to do it under her breath, but stupid wench that she was, she failed.

Janet cut her eyes at Naomi then led me away by the arm. I looked for Solomon, but assumed he was around, even if not in sight.

"She's been annoyin' the fuck outta me to no end. I don't remember her like this."

I laughed. "What's up, girl? Michael started something again?"

"Why? *He told you something*?"

"Uh . . . no. I'm not on his list of people to talk to. I just saw him in the hallway and he was looking pretty crazy."

"Oh." Whatever had riled her up had gone away. "Yeah. There was a little scene you missed. It's okay now. I've been waiting for Karim to bring my drink for the longest . . . the bastard."

The way she called him out of his name surprised me. I didn't know Janet well enough, so I paid it no mind. "I just saw him, but he didn't have a drink in his hand. He was taking the elevator up."

"With who? Was he by himself?"

"By himself," I answered before she ripped my head off. "Is something going on here?"

"Nothing. Nothing anymore."

"What happened between you and Karim? You seem perfect for each other."

"I guess he felt he was perfect for everyone else in here too."

"I refuse to believe that."

"Honey," she called me as her southern drawl rolled out. "I don't mean to be rude, but I've had a hell of a lot more experience with men than you. I appreciate what you're trying to do, but he's gotten to you. He even had me fooled for a second."

"Have you talked to him?"

"No, he cut out before I got to tell him what was on my mind. Smartest thing he's done."

I wasn't going to give up, but Donna cued the deejay to stop at that point. It was time.

Janet tapped me on the shoulder. "Thanks for being such a sweetie, Trayce. You've been one of the realest women in here. Now if you'll excuse me, I've been waiting for this announcement. Does my hair look alright?"

She was hurting, really hurting. As much as she proclaimed to know about men, I'd learned just as much about hiding pain. Maybe if we were somewhere else, I could've broken through and learned about where she'd been and what she was going through now. Resigning myself to failure, I went to look for Solomon.

58 Solomon

No longer beside Trayce, I was back to being the unseen. Most of my life was spent like this, so I was used to it. Don't know if I would ever say I enjoyed it, but it was okay at times. What made it more tolerable now was Trayce. She gave me a warm feeling I hadn't felt since the early days with Linda.

I watched her and Janet briefly as they talked, just to make sure everything was fine. It was surprising that Trayce was genuinely concerned for Janet. This extraordinary woman had a ton of forgiveness in her heart, as I'd learned firsthand. The night wasn't finished and I feared even Trayce's strength would be tested before it was over.

I moved through the ballroom, picking up bits and pieces of what we'd missed. Some of it was mere gossip, but it gave me enough to figure things out. Karim and Mike had a run-in, which was on everyone's lips. At least Karim got the best of him. There was also a lot of chatter about the votes and the announcement coming up. I contained my response over what I'd overheard.

I went to rejoin Trayce, but stopped when I saw two particular classmates talking next to the Mighty Eagle ice sculpture. They were carrying on in whispers, not even looking at one other. The way you do when you don't want anyone to know you're talking. I waited, then came over after the person Cameron had been talking to walked away.

"Everything okay with the two of you?"

Cameron downed what appeared to be a Long Island Iced Tea. "Huh?" he snapped late, as if hearing my question on tape delay.

"You really should lay off the drinks. Just looks like you're about to explode. You've been on a collision course since you got here."

"You don't know me and you don't know what you're talking about."

"I think I do," I said, challenging him. "I'm just looking out for people who don't need this night ruined."

"Too late for some," he muttered as he peered at the bottom of his empty glass. "What about that?"

"Do you really want to do this tonight?"

"No," Cameron admitted. "This should've been cleared up before I came here."

"If it's any consolation, Andrea left him. That is what you wanted, right?"

"How do you know?" I watched his brow furrow.

"Wrong place. Right time."

He chuckled. "Damn. Are you missing that much of a life of your own?"

"Once I was."

Donna, the manic bundle of energy, cued the music to stop so I left Cameron to drown his sorrows. In the past, I wouldn't have tried to help . . . more of this gathering rubbing off on me. Of all the secrets and lies floating around here, his had the potential to be the most explosive. The problem is that when things blow up, the ones hurt are not always anticipated.

"Ladies and gentlemen," Donna uttered like a circus ringmaster. "I apologize for the earlier misunderstanding and hope it hasn't ruined your night. I promise you that it won't happen again. Right, Mike?" She winked at him, which drew chuckles. He gave her a thumbs-up and she continued. "I'm so enthusiastic over the turnout for this reunion. Y'all have been so beautiful and wonderful. Y'all should give yourselves a round of applause." And they did.

"I know you've been waiting patiently for the votes to be tallied and I want to thank you. I really don't want this night to end, so maybe I should keep y'all waiting." The crowd that had gathered around the deejay booth let out a collective groan.

"Spill it! We're not getting any younger!" someone yelled. Trayce found me just as everyone laughed. I took her hand.

"Well, I'm about to announce the Mr. and Ms. Marion of our ten-year high school reunion," Donna said, "but first, I want to give you some ground rules. We're going to announce the winners, then the two will have the dance of the evening. After that, I need everybody to stick around as we have the final surprise of the night."

"She keeps talking about that darn surprise," Trayce muttered.

"Probably a free trip to Cancun or something."

"If you win are you taking me with you, Solomon?"

"If I win, I'm selling it for some cash. I'm out of a job, remember?"

"I remember, Mr. Schemer," she said with an elbow to my side. "Maybe I can have someone call you for an interview next week."

"Trayce, I don't need a handout."

"I know. Just a hand up."

59 Janet

"Come on. Come on. Will you shut up and get on with it."

The little woman was stretching her fifteen minutes of fame for all it was worth.

"We're going to start first with Mr. Marion," Donna acknowledged. "I was lucky enough to have some of our great hotel staff count the ballots. Y'all remember our junior year. When that girl who wound up transferring demanded a recount? Well we're not having any 'hanging chads' around here."

Donna talked a while longer while two staff members approached with envelopes. She took them in hand and everybody started buzzing.

"I'll have you know that I haven't seen these envelopes until just now. I'm so excited."

Karim was supposed to be my Mr. Marion tonight, but the dog was nowhere to be seen. I felt a little concern, probably due to Trayce's guilt trip, but I held firm. To think I threw away my vote on him. I did find it odd that my girl Shauna wasn't around to back me up. She'd been present at every Ms. Marion I'd won, like my good luck charm. I asked Naomi, but she didn't know what was up with it either.

"Deejay, could you give me a drum roll?" He complied and Donna tore open the first envelope. She read it and smiled. "And our very own Mr. Marion High School iiiiiiis . . ."

We all held our breath. It was just a silly little vote that had no meaning, but it was as if the world were about to end.

"Shaw! Shaw Underwood!"

Mike's raucous cheering was the first thing heard. He was probably more excited that somebody had beat Karim in some form since he couldn't do it physically. He and most of the jocks from our class were shoving Shaw around and chanting as if the clock were turned back. Shaw accepted his congratulations and walked up to claim his title again. Once upon a time, I would be at his side to give him a kiss for luck. Now I was standing all by my lonesome, left simply to applaud.

Donna produced a pair of crowns, one of which was for Shaw. As he'd been the whole night, Shaw was gracious and bent over for Donna to place his on his head. I sucked on my teeth as I prepared for her final envelope.

"Now to see what we have for the ladies." She tore the open the envelope, then decided to tease us. "Any guesses at who is Ms. Marion?"

There was mostly silence, but the few chants of my name emboldened me. It was just like old times.

Donna read. "Oh. Oh my." Donna surveyed the crowd from end to end, building the tension. "And our very own Ms. Marion High School iiiiiiis . . ."

60 Karim

"Stop! Oh gawd, please stop."
She didn't listen.

"Shauna . . . stop. We gotta stop."

I spoke, but the words were lost to the hot, juicy pussy I'd tasted. From beneath the neat little runway of hair, its single eye stared down at me, begging to feel my face in it again. Shauna's face was on the other end of me.

Busy.

My body jerked involuntarily as she sucked harder and harder, her wet lips locked in precision around the head of my dick.

I pleaded with her to stop again, but how do you make a woman stop with your dick in her mouth. I was in no position to piss her off and cursed that I hadn't come to my senses before we'd wound up nude on my bed and engaging in a sixty-nine.

61 Trayce

"Did you hear?"

"Huh?"

Solomon was shaking me. "She called your name. Donna called your name."

"So."

"You're Ms. Marion, Trayce."

"Trayce Hedgecomb," Donna announced again in an effort to get me to come forward. She then held up the slip of paper for all to see. My knees became weak, my chest tight.

62 Solomon

"And our very own Ms. Marion High School iiiiiiis . . . Trayce Hedgecomb!"

The room erupted in a chorus of cheers, but they were so loud I don't think she heard. I chuckled as she looked over her shoulder to see who everyone was looking at. I had a feeling about this, but wasn't going to ruin her surprise on a hunch.

"Trayce, you won!" It still didn't register. Her eyes were glazed over as if she refused to accept the moment.

"Did you hear?"

"Huh?"

"She called your name. Donna called your name."

"So."

"You're Ms. Marion, Trayce."

As Donna announced her name again, I began pushing Trayce forward. In the midst of the joy I was feeling for her, I couldn't help but think of the loser.

63 Janet

No, no, no. This isn't right. It's mine, was all I kept thinking.

I applauded just like I had for Shaw, but that was reflex. Inside I was stunned. I'll never forget that silence as people debated over how to react to Donna's words. Then came the clapping. As they did that, the stares came . . . then the whispers.

I ignored them looking at the faces of the haters who'd betrayed me tonight. Had even Shaw, who was applauding too, voted for Trayce instead of me? I refused to give them the satisfaction of seeing me break down. Damn it, where was Shauna during all this?

64 Karim

Shauna's sweet sticky juices covered me. Every whiff threatened to put me back under her spell. She spread her legs wider, lowering the kitty close to my face to give me another taste.

"Sh, Sh, Shauna, stop. I mean it," I gasped, turning my head to the side to avoid its tempting bob at my open mouth.

"Boy, who are you kidding? You love this pussy. Get back to work." She put my dick deep in her mouth, her tongue twirling around its head before plunging on it with a gag at the back of her throat.

Waves of pleasure rose up from my toes, making me shudder. I grabbed the back of her head as she hummed. This was some of the best brain I'd ever had. It didn't escape me that I wanted to push her head down and tickle her tonsils again.

"Shauna?"

"Mmm hhhhmm." She loved her work and knew I was succumbing to what she'd served up.

I was blazing past all rational thought. Thoughts consumed me of getting back at Janet, Shauna . . . hell, all of them. I was going to carve my initials in Shauna's pussy like I should've done last night. Why? Because I just didn't give a fuck no more. *Knowhu'amean?*

She moved over, allowing me to sit up as she continued sucking. I grasped some of her hair and wrapped it around my fingers.

65 Trayce

"This isn't happening." I'd begun crying, mascara was running and all. I wiped up as much as I could with my hand. Shaw, Mr. Marion for the umpteenth time, extended his hand, but I didn't shake it. Last time I'd completely trusted him, he'd betrayed that trust in the worst way.

He held his crown as he leaned over anyway. "Congratulations, Trayce," he said as he kissed me on the dry part of my cheek.

The applause was still going strong. Donna placed the tiara on my head, then waved her arms to work the crowd up even louder. The attention was embarrassing, but I stood there and graciously accepted it. I used to fantasize about moments like this. Even as an adult, I still dreamed of those what ifs. What if I were taller, what if I were thin and pretty like Janet, what if I tried harder . . . What if those horrible things never happened.

"Trayce, are you going to be okay?" Donna asked.

I looked at Solomon. "Yes. Yes, I'll be fine."

"Good, because I just want to say how proud we are of your success. You may not have noticed it, but you've been the buzz of this entire reunion. For someone to come from this school and to represent for all of us like you have is amazing. I don't know how often you heard it back in the day, but you're hearing it now. We're proud of you, girl."

Donna paused to bask in the success of all of this, then made her proclamation. "Mighty Eagles, I give you Mr. and Ms. Marion High."

This was my first time looking directly at the crowd. I'd been afraid to do it for fear that their votes were some cruel prank, a replay of past deeds. As I gazed into the room of faces, my fears and suspicions left. I continued looking around, hoping Karim had returned. Solomon had been my rock, but Karim had been there for me too.

Everyone at our little table had affected me positively. From Solomon, I had support from a good man in spite of myself. From Karim, I had a fellow outsider who didn't let the world dictate to him. That brought me to Janet, who I was sure was waiting out there to give me a hug. From her, I learned that things aren't always as good as they seem, and that it's okay for a woman to have a pair of balls.

That's why the look Janet cast chilled me to the bone. Eyes filled only with hate fixed on me before she turned and walked away. I hadn't time to think this tiara on my head might mean so much to her, but I guess it did. I began to go after her, but Donna stopped me.

"I think she needs some time alone, Trayce," she said in as soft a manner as I'd ever heard her speak.

"She has always been Ms. Marion. I never wanted this." I reached to take the tiara off.

"I know." She grabbed my arm and stopped me. "But

enjoy it anyway," she said. "The votes weren't even close. A lot of us grew up."

Donna winked before raising the microphone to her mouth again. "Now ya'll know we can't end like this. Mr. and Ms. Marion have to have the dance of the night."

She cued the deejay again.

66 Solomon

It wasn't hard to find her. I just had to look for the steam rising over the crowd.

"Janet lost? What just happened?" Naomi asked Michael as I walked by.

Michael laughed. "She got what was comin' to her."

Janet was left to herself as Donna finished the announcement. She clapped at the appropriate times, but it was forced. It wasn't like me to just walk up and start talking, but I did it for Trayce.

"Janet."

"Hey, Solomon," she acknowledged. The greeting was strained. "Looks like it's your girl's night tonight. Too bad you're not up there with her, huh?"

"You know, you're right. Maybe I'll demand a recount." I tried joking, but she didn't laugh.

"What do you want? Came around to gloat?"

"No, I wouldn't do that. I was just concerned about you. I know this kind of stuff means a lot to you."

"*Used to*. Used to mean a lot to me," she corrected. "You share a table with me, so now I'm an open book?

No offense, but it's just a bunch of cheap crowns. I can see the plastic from here."

"What about the guy wearing that cheap crown. You came back because of him, huh?"

Her eyebrow twitched at my remark. She decided to look at me. "You're about a nosy mother fucker. How does she put up with you?"

"I don't know. She's very forgiving."

Janet looked me up and down. "I can tell."

"Let somebody in, Janet. That's all I'm saying. It's something I've learned recently. It can really help when times are hard."

"What's hard is listening to your whining. You don't know me so don't step to me like that, little man. Now please run along to your queen. I'm trying to have fun and you're killing my buzz."

I left her alone to focus back on Trayce. There was no talking to her anyway. People like Janet thought they had the whole world figured out and beware anyone who told them different.

She had a lot of outer beauty, but the ugly inside was eating away at her like a cancer.

I made my way to the front of the crowd just in time to hear Donna's latest announcement. Trayce and Shaw were going to share a dance.

67 Janet

I despised Solomon. Hated the way he looked at me with those spooky eyes. Even more than that, I hated the relationship that was forming between him and Trayce. They made me sick. I'd put on as happy a face as was normal for me, but I really wanted to scream.

Trayce. This woman was wearing my crown and standing next to Shaw who used to be my man. That was all I saw as Solomon took pity on me and tried to sermonize. *I can't believe this, I can't believe this*, I kept thinking repeatedly.

"What about the guy wearing that cheap crown. You came back because of him, huh?"

He'd finally gotten to me. "You're about a nosy mother fucker. How does she put up with you?"

I'd returned to this sorry place to put things to rest with Shaw. I'd lost Gerald because of my issues, but had discovered Karim. Then he'd turned out to be worthless. Still, being here alone without even Shauna at my side had me missing him. Michael and the twins weren't going to keep their mouths shut much longer, so I decided to find him for a talk.

I took one final look at Trayce as she accepted her time in the spotlight. This woman who'd slept with Shaw when I never did, had now taken something else of mine. As sweet as she seemed, I felt nothing but hate when our eyes met. I knew their dance was coming next and couldn't stomach it. It was time to go.

On my way to the elevator, I ran into Shauna's husband. He'd remembered me from yesterday, before he left Shauna at the hotel to hang with us, and caught my attention.

"Have you seen Shauna?" he asked. From his posture, I could tell he was one of those blue-collar country boys. They sprouted like weeds around here.

"No. Not in a while," I answered. "You might want to check the room she's sharing with Naomi."

"Nah. She ain't there," he sighed. "I just came from there. She ain't in the ballroom?"

"Could be. Naomi's in there. Check with her."

"Alright. Thanks. I brought the kids to the babysitter, so I figured I'd surprise her. If you see her, tell her I'm lookin' for her."

"Aww, such a sweetheart," I gushed as I touched his shoulder. "I'll be sure to do that."

"I'll Make Love to You" by Boyz II Men began playing in the ballroom as Shauna's husband entered. Trayce and Shaw had begun their dance. I jumped on the elevator and pushed the button to take me to Karim's suite.

68 Karim

"Ow!"
"Ahhhhh! Shit!"

Shauna reached in back of her head as she rolled off me. "What the fuck are you doing yanking my hair?"

I lay on the bed, grimacing in pain. My hands grasped my privates. "Getting you off me. You, *you bit me!*"

"No I didn't. My teeth just scraped it when you pulled my head back. You're lucky I didn't bite it. What is wrong with you?"

"I told you to stop and you wouldn't!"

"Only because you didn't mean it!"

"Bullshit!" I saw the blood on my hand and ran for the bathroom. "You need to get the fuck up outta here. Now!"

"You're crazy!"

"Yeah," I agreed as I looked at my limp dick in the mirror. It was just a scrape, but it stung like hell. I thought back to my last tetanus shot. "Crazy for doing this with you. I don't mess with married women."

"Whatever boy," she said peeking in the bathroom.

She was slipping her dress back on. "You need to get some counseling."

"Get the fuck out!" I shouted.

I went back to tending to myself as I heard the room door open then slam shut. Shauna scared the hell out of me as she reappeared. She was panic-stricken.

"Janet! Janet's out there!"

"Did she see you?"

"Yeah, I think so."

I thunked my head against the bathroom counter. "Fuck."

69 Trayce

"Feeling uncomfortable?"
"Yes."
"I'm sorry."
"Huh?"
"I thought it might help if I got that out of the way."
"Maybe years ago that would've done the trick. *Before* the shame, guilt, and countless therapy sessions."
"Oh my God. I had no idea."
"Of course you didn't. You didn't care. Yep, you and your friends really messed me up. Would you like to see the bills? I keep them in a folder. A big folder."

We continued our dance, smiling politely with each twirl. Most onlookers would've thought it was small talk, but we had none of that between us. What I'd personally known about him and experienced sickened me. The positive vibes I received from Solomon were probably what kept me from breaking out in hives. Whenever I wanted to run again, I'd look and see him there. If I needed him, he'd come running. A few places over from Solomon stood Cameron, watching us intensely. A fresh drink rested in his hand. I could've sworn he bore some grudge against Shaw by the way his eyes narrowed into slits.

"Trayce, you have to believe me when I say that wasn't me. I'm a different person now."

"So am I, Shaw. So am I."

"Is there anything I can do to make it up to you? I mean it with all my heart."

"Sure. Go back in time and never invite me to that 'party.' The rest of those idiots, I could understand, but you . . . I thought you were different. I really trusted you, Shaw."

"I was different. I am different, Trayce," he pleaded. I almost wanted to believe him . . . again.

"Know why I came here, Shaw?"

"No."

"Closure. I came here for closure, but I've gained so much more. God tested me. Yesterday, I ran from you . . . hid in the bathroom like a scared rabbit. Now tonight I'm dancing with you with a tacky tiara on my head. Crazy, huh?"

He laughed, one of those nervous ones. "Look . . . there was a lot of stuff going on that you didn't know about."

"That's obvious. I was clueless."

The song ended. There was applause again as our classmates swarmed to congratulate us or simply pat us on the back. Shaw and I were separated, but there was a look of genuine sorrow in his eyes as the gulf between us widened.

The deejay kicked things back up with Tag Team's "Whoomp There It Is." The men from Marion who had gone on to pledge various fraternities started breaking out some of their step moves in response. I was moving out of the way when Solomon found me.

"Everything okay, Trayce?"

70 Solomon

"Yeah. I think so," she answered, her nerves calmed as if just exiting a rollercoaster.

I held Trayce in my arms for what seemed forever.

Donna spoke on the microphone again, reminding us of the big surprise coming up soon. I was tired of hearing about it and wished she would just get it over with.

"I don't think I can stand any more surprises," Trayce said as she lifted her head off my shoulder. She moved her braids aside and removed her tiara. "I hope Janet's going to be alright," she said as she looked at it.

"She left."

"Where'd she go?"

"To talk with Karim I hope."

"I wish I knew what happened with them."

I thought about all the different things I'd heard. "I don't think they even know," I commented.

The music stopped again. This time, tables were moved in place with large boxes atop each one. Donna and a few volunteers began rummaging through them. From her smile, I could tell this was the big surprise. Donna pulled out a list then began reading from it. One by one, she called certain classmates forward—Shaw, Michael, and others. It took but a second to realize these were members of the football team.

As they came up, Donna presented them with brand new jerseys and had them gather to the side. Behind the tables, chairs were set. A large object covered by a tarp was brought in too. Trayce was taking an unusual interest in all of this. That made me particularly nervous.

"Want to go outside? Get some fresh air?"

"No. I want to see what this is about."

"Okay."

Donna looked into the crowd. "Has anyone seen Janet and Shauna?" she asked of us.

Nobody responded. "I need the captain and co-captain to lead us in a cheer one last time."

"I'll do it! I'll do it!" Naomi screamed. The wiry girl appeared to dance on air as she ran.

Donna whispered in her ear, explaining what was going on. Naomi's eyes grew larger and she cracked a smile.

"So the big surprise is a pep rally?" I asked.

"Donna always liked them," Trayce added, seeming less than thrilled. "She was always full of 'pep'."

We were in for a treat as Naomi tried to remember the cheer and failed miserably. Michael and a few other players joined her and proceeded to make asses of themselves. We laughed at the exhibition as it was all in good fun. Trayce wasn't amused. That same fixated gaze was there. I took another look at the group assembled; those all in their jerseys, and it dawned on me.

I took her by the hand. "C'mon. Let's go outside for a second."

"No. I want to stay."

"We'll come right back," I said a little more desperately this time.

She pulled her hand free. "No. I'm staying."

Donna spoke again. "I think all those fine young men look familiar to all of y'all. And I do mean *fine*," she teased. "Does anybody remember what they did? I sure do and most of this state does too. It was ten years ago. Ladies and gentlemen, I give you the seniors of Marion High's first ever undefeated football team! C'mon! Let's give them a hand!"

Shaw and the rest of them waved at everyone and took a few bows. They filed in front of the tables for the photographer who was setting up. Two of Donna's assistants had moved to either side of whatever was covered and were waiting for their cue. I pleaded with Trayce to leave one more time, but she cut such an angry look that said it was fruitless.

"Now I know y'all remember this team here. But we can't honor them without giving props to the man that led them there."

I lowered my head, knowing what was to come.

Donna nodded, at which point her assistants yanked off the tarp.

It was unveiled for all to see. In a large golden frame, stood a portrait of Coach Taylor.

71 Janet

"I'll be damned."

The bitch tried to duck, but I saw her. As I came off the elevator, I saw Shauna's barely dressed ass coming out of Karim's suite. She gasped and ran back, leaving me wondering who'd betrayed me first. I ran for the door, but she'd slammed it shut before I could get to it.

Part of me wanted to bang on it until it opened. The other part of me wanted to take out my .25 and shoot the lock off.

A part of me I didn't know I had won out. I fell to the floor outside his suite and just sat there. My eyes were burning and my throat hurt. I didn't have allergies. Maybe it was a cold. Anything to explain the water filling my eyes would've been better than the truth.

Truth. That was something I'd hidden behind Godiva. Godiva wasn't supposed to come here with me . . . but she had. Now my "best friend" was behind that door fucking someone who may or may not have been worthy of the truth. Guess I'd never know.

My thoughts went back to Shauna. Everything she'd

said about Karim I began thinking about. With all my time in the business, I should've known. Just because you see teeth doesn't mean it's a smile. Sometimes the person is gritting their teeth, waiting to stab you in the back.

I wiped my eyes, straightened my outfit and went to the elevator. Maybe I'd congratulate Trayce after all. Her smile was real.

"You better get in there, Janet. They were just calling for you and Shauna," her husband said as I got off the elevator.

"Thank you. You're such a sweetheart. Shauna really has a good one in you," I said as I poured it on. I didn't always need a pole to work a man. "Oh . . . did you ever find your wife?"

"Nah. I don't know where she's at," he sighed.

I paused as if having a dilemma. "Shauna is my friend, so I really shouldn't tell you this."

"*Shouldn't tell me what?*"

"I think I *might* know where she is."

He stormed away promising this would be the last time she did this to him. I headed back to the ballroom to see what I'd missed.

See. Sometimes a smile is just that.

72 Karim

"Are you sure she's out there?" I asked, slipping on a pair of pants over my ailing manhood.

"Yes! I saw her!"

I peered through the peephole then unlatched the door.

"Don't do that!"

"Why not?"

"Because she's crazy!"

"Is that any way to talk about your friend?" I looked out into the hallway. Nothing. I closed it back. "She's gone," I said to Shauna.

"Are you sure?"

"I just looked. You can go now."

"What if she's out there waiting for me?"

"Now why would Janet want a piece of you?" I asked. "She obviously doesn't give a damn about me. I heard her saying all that shit to you. Remember?" Shauna looked nervous. "Something you want to talk about?"

There was a pounding at the door. Leaning against it, I felt the jarring vibration in my back and jumped away.

"Damn."

"She's back," Shauna whispered in a panic.

The pounding on the door came again.

"Look, I hate that what happened happened, but I'm going to clear this up now."

I looked through the peephole, but couldn't see anything. I unlocked the door and opened it.

Janet hit harder and faster than I imagined. Except it wasn't her. I was on the floor holding my jaw when this country bamma mofo stepped over me.

"Where she at?"

"Who?"

"Shauna! Don't fuck with me. Where she at?"

My eyes darted about the room. "Nobody's here, man. And who in the fuck are you?"

As I got to my feet, I fought the urge to rush ole boy. He was here for a valid reason, so I figured to be the peacemaker.

"I'm Shauna's fuckin' husband."

"And whoever this Shauna is, she ain't here."

He looked under the bed then noticed the sheets. "Uh huh. Looks like somebody's been sexin'," he said, glaring menacingly.

"You need to bounce before I call downstairs, man. For real."

He was stomping toward the bathroom when he knocked the garbage can over. The clothes I'd worn spilled out. He picked up the pants.

"Look, put that down. Now."

He ignored me like I expected and put them to his nose. "Hmm. That's not her perfume."

"Nah. It's sweat from my nuts, mother fucker." Actually, it was my sweat mixed with Janet's perfume. Luckily, it was different than Shauna's. "Look man, I'm'ma cut you some slack for the cheap shot, but you need to go. So, whenever you find this Shontell . . ."

"It's 'Shauna,' man. Shauna."

"Whatever, *man*. Whenever you find this woman, y'all need to work out your problems without this drama. Married folk shouldn't be playin' 'Holiday Inn hide 'n' seek.'"

He dropped his shoulders, looking defeated. I moved aside, giving him a clear exit. He began to leave then cut his eyes at the closed bathroom door.

I looked at him and shrugged. "Hey. Check it if you want. Hold your breath though. Something didn't agree with me."

He stared at it then me. "Sorry 'bout this, bro. Somebody gave me some bad info."

"It's cool. I'd be mad too if I were in your shoes. Good luck."

I was lucky he didn't decide to take a whiff of me on the way out. He would've found that perfume he was searching for.

I locked the door followed by a quick look through the peephole. Once I saw he was gone, I let out the deep breath I'd been holding. I then ran my fingers to comb my hair back in place.

The bathroom door opened slowly. The head of a frightened woman peered out.

"Thank you," she said.

Dirty deeds done dirt-cheap . . .

Coach Taylor was always letting us hang in his office after practice. Confident and in control, he sat with his feet up on his desk. His hands rested behind his head as he gave us his patented lazy smile. He demanded obedience and fire from us. In return, we got the perks that came with being one of the best football teams in the state. This night was one of our normal bullshit sessions, after Coach Sutton had gone home.

"Ya'll know that girl, Trayce?"

"You're talking about *your pet*, Coach?" Mike laughed then took a bite out of his apple. "You always got her hidden in here while we at PE."

"She ain't my pet, boy," he said dead serious. "*My pets don't eat that much.*"

The fellas all laughed at Coach's funny one.

"Why you bringin' her up?" I asked. "She didn't accuse us of teasing her again, huh? I'm gettin' tired of those laps you be havin' us run."

"No. I'm just startin' to think I shouldn't believe everything she says about y'all."

"What did that bitch say?" Mike was in his aggressive mode.

"She didn't say anything about you. I'm just wondering if she's said anything about me."

"To us? She ain't in The Crew. You know we don't talk to her."

"Hmm. She worries me. I might have to keep her out of my office."

"What happened, Coach?"

He put his feet down and rolled his chair closer to his desk. "I shouldn't be talkin' about this."

"What, Coach? We won't tell." The other guys moved in close to listen.

"This needs to stay between us only. 'Cause if it got out, she might try to lie on me to save her own neck. I value my job and what I do with y'all boys too much to let some accusations cost me it."

"Coach, did you fuck her?" Mike asked. He was going to be asking for details next.

"Coach?" I joined in.

"Nah. Y'all know I'm too old for that kind of stuff. I ain't about to go to jail over these young tenderonies. Y'all young studs can handle all of that pussy. That girl Trayce did try something though."

"Trayce?" I blurted out in surprise.

"Yeah, Shaw. It surprised me too," he answered. "I was just tryin' to be nice 'n' all. Next thing you know, she tryin' to give it to me on the desk."

Mike jumped back from the desk he'd been leaning on. "Big Trayce? Oh man!"

"Yeah, fellas. She flashed them big titties and dropped her drawers for me. I had her put her clothes back on and told her don't ever try that again. I'm only telling you boys because I trust y'all. I think she liked that I was nice to her. Hell, if you boys show her some kindness, she might even give you some. She quiet, but I'll bet she got a lot of experience."

"I got a girlfriend, Coach."

"There he goes again," Mike taunted. "Always using that 'Janet' excuse. Shit, I ain't passin' on *no* pussy. Especially if it's good!"

Coach nodded his head and smiled. "That's my boy. That's my boy."

74 Trayce

"We're sorry Coach Taylor couldn't be with us. As most of y'all know, he died in that twenty-car pileup on I-26 a couple years back. But we can still honor his memory tonight."

Ironic that there was no honor in my memories of him. He was a sick bastard and God forgive me, deserved to die. I don't know why I stayed here reliving the abuse and pain. There he was in the portrait, that smug lazy smile. There he was in the old team photo on display beneath it. Now these people had the nerve to honor him?

Donna continued talking, going over a bunch of meaningless records and stats. I swear I almost saw a tear in Michael's eye.

My hands trembled even though Solomon tried to hold them. He never said it, but from the concern he was showing, I knew he knew. He was there that day in the gym after all. I would've felt ashamed if I weren't so angry over the tribute.

My heart raced. I tried to breathe, but the more those

eyes in the portrait looked at me the more the oxygen seemed to be sucked from my lungs. I could feel his breath on me as he whispered his lies. I became nauseated as I remembered those hands overpowering me.

Worst of all, I remembered how it felt to have my virginity ripped from me . . . and how it had soiled every relationship I had with men.

"Now everybody, let's give a big round of applause for the late, great Coach Taylor."

"No!"

I hadn't realized I'd done it except for the burning in my throat. My scream had brought the whole room silent. Hands were extended in mid-clap and my classmates stared stunned. I tried so hard to shut my mouth, but couldn't contain it any longer.

"No! No! No!" I screamed again as tears awakened, flowing down ancient rivers beds.

"Trayce, what's wrong? Something the matter?" Donna asked.

Ignoring Solomon's protests, I came forward. "No."

"No what?"

"This . . . I can't," I sputtered. I was pleading with Donna to stop this as much as I was pleading with Coach Taylor all those years ago. I'd spooked the football players assembled behind her. Even they retreated with each step I took. I heard phrases like "crazy" and "possessed" being thrown about. "You have to stop," I pleaded.

"Umm . . . we're almost done with the program, Trayce."

"No. Please stop it now. He doesn't deserve this."

Solomon joined in, running behind me. "Donna, cut it. Now!"

"Bullshit!" It was Michael. "I'm sick of these retards tryin' to ruin things. This is our reunion. Ours!" Several other jersey wearers who wouldn't be denied their moment to shine joined him. Solomon cut them off, preventing them from getting near me. Someone's hand shoved him in his face.

A scuffle broke out as Donna tried to restore order; begging and pleading with us not to ruin her reunion she'd worked so hard for.

I ran for the portrait and knocked it from its easel. It tumbled to the floor; its heavy frame splintering in pieces. I sunk down on my knees and began clawing at the portrait. When that didn't work I began smashing it Again and again, I brought it over my head only to hammer it on the cold concrete. Shards of glass sliced into my hand causing drops of crimson to mix with my tears.

"Why? Why?" I demanded. Emotions gurgled up from the depths of my soul this night, laid bare for all to view. When there was nothing intact left, I curled into a ball on the floor. "Why did you do that to me?" I murmured in front of the class of Marion High.

75 Solomon

Her words were soft; almost a whimper, but they staggered all of us. I knew, but in no way did it prepare me for hearing it. The only sound that could be heard was Trayce's lone sobbing.

Shaw stood over her, his crown fallen off during all the pushing and shoving. The blood from Trayce's hands smudged the white on his jersey as he tried to help her to her feet.

"C'mon. Let me help you, Trayce."

"Leave me alone!" she snarled. He withdrew his hands just in the nick of time.

I freed myself from the mass of bodies surrounding me and ran to her.

"Get out of the way!" I shoved Shaw harder than I meant. He slid across the floor as he was already off balance.

Ignoring him, I wrapped my arms around Trayce and told her everything was going to be okay. I prayed that if I said it often enough that it would be true.

Shaw got back to his feet. "I was just trying to help, man."

"Haven't you done enough? A lot of people are fucked up because of what you and your Crew did."

Shaw fumbled for words.

"Look around you, man! Coach Taylor wasn't any good and to me you're no better."

"Aww come on now," Michael blurted out. "Do you believe this shit? I don't." His sentiments were echoed by a few of the other players. "Coach didn't rape anyone, especially her."

"Why?" It was Shaw this time. "Because he said so, Mike?"

Michael was stunned. He looked at Shaw in a puzzled way. "What are you doin', bro? These fools are coming in here and tryin' to change everything. And they can't. Are you sidin' with them now? What's it gonna be?"

Shaw threw his hands up. "Maybe I'm just tired of the bullshit, bro. You remember when Coach told us that stuff about Trayce."

"Bro, shut up! What are you doin'? We weren't supposed to talk about that."

"Why? The man is dead, Mike. You sure didn't have any problem acting on what he told us."

"You need to shut up because you were there too. Remember, guys?" I watched some of the team begin to fidget. A few of them removed their jerseys, rejoining their wives and whatnot. "You were the one who did all the smooth talkin' anyway, stud. Got her to the house and everything. *Big Man Shaw.*"

I grimaced, hearing things that had floated by my ears years gone by. Hearing it like this, was far worse.

Shaw dropped his head. "Yeah. And I've had to live with that. I'm not proud of it."

Trayce looked up from my arms as I continued to cradle her on the floor.

"I am so sorry," he said to her. For the first time, I was starting to believe him.

"Please! Stop. This isn't the place for all of this," Donna shouted. She literally ran a circle around us, waving her arms frantically. "The hotel's going to throw us out and all this will be ruined. I spent too much time to have this ruined."

"What about the lives ruined, Donna?" I asked, realizing the bleeding on Trayce's hands had stopped. "Don't you care about that? Trayce was raped and all you're worrying about is a production. It's just a stupid reunion. How sick is that?"

Donna was indignant. "It's not that. I'm just looking out for everyone that came here to have a good time, not the few that want to hurl accusations at a dead man. I worked on the school paper and never heard about this."

"But I'll bet you heard all the other rumors-Trayce and the football team and all the other bad stuff. Why is this so hard to believe?"

"Maybe I heard some of the other rumors, but they were just that . . . rumors. I'm just saying the man's not able to defend himself."

"He did do it! I'm not lying!" Trayce screamed as she hurled her tiara at Donna. "Why won't you believe me?"

Shaw commented when no one else would. "Coach Taylor doesn't deserve to be defended or honored. From just what I know, he was a horrible person."

Michael rushed Shaw. He jabbed his finger in Shaw's lapel. "How could you do this, bro? You're a fuckin' backstabber and a traitor. That man did everything for us. He made us men and took us to the State Championship. How you gonna disrespect that and throw it all away because this bitch feels like lying?"

Shaw ignored the finger poking. "We're not teenagers anymore. We're grown-ass men. Bro, do you really think she's lying? Look at her."

"She's psycho, that's all. *You* look at her. She should be on Dr. Phil or sumthin'."

"She's not a liar and not crazy either, you dumb mother-fucker," I responded.

"Shut up before I beat your little no-name ass again!"

I went after Michael, knowing what the outcome might be, but frankly not caring. Shaw grabbed me by the collar to hold me back. Michael hit me in the gut with a cheap shot causing me to wince in pain. Shaw retaliated and leveled Michael before he could even gloat. Some of their teammates ran over. The crowd, too stunned to speak before, erupted in chatter as they witnessed The Crew fracturing right before their eyes.

Shaw balled his fists, letting Michael get back to his feet. I pushed Trayce behind me and prepared to help Shaw as best I could. If not for the circumstances, I would've laughed.

"Stop!" someone amongst the bystanders uttered. "Trayce's telling the truth."

The woman who dared speak up approached Trayce and me. We were equally stunned.

"Now why you gonna say something like that?" Michael asked, more upset that she was interrupting the pent-up aggression he held toward Shaw.

She turned and looked Michael dead in his eye. "Because Coach Taylor raped me too."

76 Janet

Naomi stood before Trayce and Solomon, dropping the bombshell of the night. She stared at the ruined picture of Coach Taylor for the longest as if involved in some silent communication. A hush fell over the ballroom. Even Shaw and Mike had lowered their fists.

"I didn't know he'd raped you too," she said to Trayce. "I thought . . . I thought I was the only one. Coach used to say I was so pretty. He said he'd never do anything to hurt me. I guess I never told anybody because they wouldn't believe me." She let out a nervous laugh. "I was kinda loose in those days, but I still didn't want . . . didn't want him to . . . I mean . . ."

"I know," Trayce said. "It's alright." She embraced Naomi as the two of them, polar opposites united in tragedy, wept openly.

Donna stood dumbfounded. If she didn't believe Trayce before she sure did now. The deejay looked toward her for instructions and she motioned to him to wrap things up. Poor thing had no idea what she was getting into when she gathered us together. No one could ever say it was boring.

When I returned, utter chaos was not what I expected. I didn't expect to see Trayce on the floor smashing Coach Taylor's picture. I was relieved that the near brawl between Shaw and Mike had nothing to do with me this time. I took some solace in that. But this rape thing . . . damn.

It shamed me that Coach had preyed on two of my classmates with nothing being done about it. I shuddered, wondering how many other Marion students had fallen victim to him. I wasn't very religious, I was a follower of the almighty green, but I prayed Coach was in a right proper hell.

Both Naomi and Trayce were being consoled. Solomon stood at the ready like a baby pit bull ready to pounce, but acknowledged me with a faint smile. I placed a hand on his shoulder as I walked by.

"Here." I handed Trayce's crown to him. It had almost been trampled on. "I think this belongs to your woman."

"Thanks."

"You've won me over, little man. That's hard to do. Maybe I should've gotten with *you* back in the day," I joked.

"You didn't know me."

"True." I smirked.

"Janet."

"Yeah?"

"No offense, but you're not my type anyway. Too skinny."

I let him get away with the last jab. Told you he won me over. "You the man, Solomon. Keep being strong for her," I said as I continued on.

Naomi shouted as she saw me walk up. I gave both her and Trayce hugs and offered my support.

"Have . . . have you seen, Shauna?" Naomi murmured. "I need to tell her."

My last image of Shauna popped into my head. "No, haven't seen her."

"I hope she's okay," Naomi responded, seemingly forgetting her own state. "She just disappeared."

"Don't worry about, Shauna. She'll turn up. Is there anyone you want to call?"

"No. I don't think so."

After telling her shadow Solomon that she'd be okay, Trayce accompanied me out of the ballroom to take Naomi to her room. Naomi was still asking for Shauna. I began regretting what I'd instigated as my tension headache reminded me.

I glimpsed Shaw darting out one of the side doors.

"Trayce, will you be alright taking Naomi to her room? I'm going to track Shauna down for her."

Trayce agreed. I waited for them to get on the elevator before following Shaw.

I'd never heard him cry until tonight. Not even when his father died during our sophomore year. He didn't hear me as I let the door close shut. In the field nearby, crickets carried on with their insane noise.

"I saw what you did back there." Shaw was startled and quickly wiped his eyes on his sleeves. I continued. "I'm not forgetting our differences, but that was really big of you tonight."

He blinked twice to clear his eyes and sighed. I knew he was sick of seeing me. "Didn't do it for the recognition, Janet. It's just that there are a lot of things I would change if I could."

I came closer and looked into those swollen, puffy eyes. "Like us?"

He opened his mouth to speak, but was too choked up.

He tried again, but gave in to the emotion. I felt him his arms around me as he lowered his head on my shoulder and cried like a newborn. "It's just too much," he whispered over and over. "I'm just so tired."

"Tired of what?"

"Yeah, Shaw. Tired of *what*?"

I turned toward the sound of the voice that mimicked me. "Can I help you?"

It was our classmate, Cameron, the drum major. He staggered out of the shadows and came toward us. The hate I saw in his eyes made me back up. "What are you doing with this bitch? Last time I looked, she wasn't Andrea."

It was as if Shaw had been hit with a jolt of electricity. "Cam, you've been drinking . . ."

"Cam? You're friends with him?" I asked. "What's he got to do with that girl?"

"Nothing, Janet. Go back inside."

"Nah, nah. Fuck that," Cameron spat. "She doesn't have to go anywhere. While it's 'confession night,' let's get it all out. I'm tired of all this heartache and pain you've put me through. I've stood by way too long enduring this humiliation. And I am sick of it!"

For reasons unknown, Cameron ran at me, but Shaw jumped in front. He wrapped up Cameron, who squirmed to free himself.

"Let me go, mother fucker! I ain't going back to the way things were!"

I was thoroughly confused about why Cameron wanted to fight me. I smelled the liquor as far away as I was. *Maybe he's hallucinating*, I thought. He'd mentioned that girl Shaw was with, Andrea. That was no hallucination. Maybe there was a love triangle going on. I felt uncomfortable.

"Are both of you fucking that girl Andrea?" I asked,

trying to get their attention. Shaw still had Cameron in a bear hug. "If so, I'll leave so y'all can talk it out."

Laughter. We had company. A fourth person had been sitting on a rock nearby. The short man spoke.

"Janet, don't you get it?" Solomon came toward me. "It's not about them and Andrea. It's just about *them*."

I didn't understand Solomon and looked at Shaw. His arms were still around Cameron, but something about it began to disturb me. I turned back to Solomon. "Solomon, I ain't got time for fuckin' riddles. Spit it out."

"Janet, Shaw's gay. Cameron's his lover."

77 Karim

"Do you think he's still out there?" I allowed Shauna to shower while she waited for the coast to clear. She'd put her black dress back on and was looking at herself in the mirror, trying to freshen her appearance.

"Don't have a clue," I said as I fumbled with the TV remote. The batteries were low so I was rolling them back and forth. I got it working and switched the channel to HBO. The final season of The Wire was starting.

"You're being quiet."

"A sore dick, *and not in a good way*, and a sore jaw will get you that."

She sat down on the bed, blocking my view of the TV. Aggravating to no end. "Thank you for not telling my husband I was here."

"You're welcome. Just don't let this lesson go to waste. I don't know why I did this. I don't know what to make of you."

"I'm just a simple country girl," she said as she flashed her teeth. "Nothing else to know."

"Yeah, and I'm Al Sharpton." I put the TV on mute.

"What's up, ma? Why would you put your husband through this? Talk. It's just you, me and the walls."

"Maybe some of it is payback. Maybe some of it is getting caught up with this reunion and trying to relive the past."

"Hubby cheated on you?"

Shauna chuckled. "Twice that I'm aware of. Don't get me wrong. I love my daughter to death, but I was too young when Ronnie got me pregnant. I was still a kid myself. That was when he first cheated on me. Like most good little wives, I eventually forgave him. Not much to do around here when you're a single mother."

"So you have a little girl?"

"Two," she corrected me. "I got pregnant again. And he cheated on me again." A lump formed in her throat. "He gave me a little STD. That's how I found out."

She noticed my eyes twitch when she said 'STD'.

"Relax. It was cleared up. Permanently. I wouldn't do that to you. I'm not as selfish and self-centered as Janet."

"What's your beef with her? Correct me if I'm wrong, but aren't you supposed to be her best friend?"

"We women can be complicated. I guess her coming back made me remember how much I hated her."

"Damn. Hate? That's pretty harsh coming from someone in the popular crowd. And I thought I had problems."

"If popular is defined by always getting Janet's leftovers or always getting passed over for Janet, then I guess I was the most popular girl at Marion. I smiled and just took it. I figured second best was all I could ever get. Even when Shaw dumped her and left, Janet still won. She abandoned us high and dry back here. I was the one with dreams of leaving this place, not her." Shauna pounded her fist on the bed. I allowed her to continue.

"She just wanted to marry Shaw and have babies.

Janet was dumb as a rock in school and you know it. I at least had half a brain. She shows up here looking all fabulous and wealthy and it reminds me that I never amounted to anything. Hell, now Trayce's knocked me out of second place. That's how I know life really sucks."

"C'mon. Stop feeling sorry for yourself. It's not that bad."

"Isn't it though? Look at you, Karim. The only reason you came to this reunion is because of Janet. The only reason I'm in this room with you is because you're mad at Janet. You gave me no play before that, no matter how hard I tried. The only reason you let things go as far as they did was because of Janet. I just don't get it."

"We all find ourselves doing stupid shit, Shauna. And mostly for the wrong reasons. I think that's the one thing I'll take away from this shit. You've gotta move on."

I don't have a logical explanation for it, but I hugged Shauna. I was closer to this woman now in an innocent embrace than I was with her pussy plastered across my face. Call it an epiphany or whatever. I've had moments of clarity when racking my brains over music video concepts, but this was different. You don't often get retakes in real life.

In chasing the perfect scene, that fairytale ending with Janet, I'd left a lot of my life on the cutting room floor.

"Thank you."

"For what?"

"For the talk."

"But I did most of the talking."

"I needed to do some listening anyway," I said as I pointed toward my chest, more specifically my heart.

She looked toward the room door. "Do you think Ronnie's gone?"

"Probably."

She took a deep breath and stood up. "Time for me to go then."

I walked her to the door. I unlocked it then peered out to make sure the coast was clear.

We shook hands and said our goodbyes. Before she left, she gave me a bit of parting knowledge.

"For what it's worth, most of that awful stuff Janet said about you was due to me."

I simply nodded my head, accepting the apology hidden within.

"So maybe I'll see you at our twenty-year reunion."

"Maybe," I answered, both of us knowing the true answer. "You going back to the party?" I asked.

"No," she said with a smile. "Home. I have things to work out. And I'm going to do just that. Finally. You really should come back in ten years to see."

78 Trayce

"Where's Shauna?" she asked again, like a little kid begging.

"Relax. Janet went to look for her. They should be back any minute now." I sat on the bed opposite Naomi, watching her and praying she wouldn't melt down.

"How did you get through it, Trayce?" Naomi lay on her side, dazed from the memories that had come bubbling up. It was surreal watching a woman who had disrespected me at every turn now acting so docile and childlike.

"The Lord is what kept me from slitting my wrists or something. There's this quote from scripture . . . 'Greater is He that is in me, than he that is in the world.' I just kept repeating it over and over. Whenever *those* thoughts got too loud. Lots of prayers and a whole bunch of therapy didn't hurt either. I'm still not right as you can tell." I sighed. "Hmph. How can you ever be 'right'?"

"What did your mother say when you told her?"

"I didn't. I couldn't bear to do that to her. My mother thought everything was splendid during my four years."

"I told mine."

"What did she say?"

Naomi's lip curled. "She said to keep my legs closed and to stop being a dirty little whore. Then she told my father."

"He didn't contact the school?"

"No. He told me to keep my legs closed too. Then he beat me with the belt. They didn't believe me when I said Coach raped me. They didn't want to hear it. I guess that's why I came forward tonight. I know how it is when people don't believe you. Until now, I thought I was the only one."

"But you had friends. You never confided in them?"

"No. They wouldn't want to hear about stuff like that. I just ignored it except when Coach was around. He'd smile and I'd almost pee on myself."

I looked at the Band-Aids on my hand that Solomon had located for me. The release I'd felt from smashing Coach's portrait was fresh in my memory.

"Are you hands going to be okay?" she asked.

"Just some minor cuts. It'll give me a break from typing," I joked.

"Y'know, you're really a nice person."

"You're saying it like I was supposed to be an ogre."

"No, but . . ."

"I know. *You're really a nice person for a fat girl,*" I said mocking her. "I was the fat kid in school and you were a skinny, popular one. For some illogical reason, you were supposed to dislike me."

"I'm sorry."

"Yeah. I know. I've been hearing a lot of that tonight. Don't worry. I disliked you too. Mo'Nique was right . . . Skinny bitches are evil."

We shared a laugh and continued to wait for Shauna. I hoped Solomon wasn't too worried about me.

79 Solomon

"Janet, Shaw's gay. Cameron's his lover."

I hated being so blunt, but poor Janet had failed to realize the obvious all these years.

It was as if she wanted to shoot back with some cocky retort, but found herself unable. Every time she'd go to speak, nothing came out.

During her silence, I mulled over how we'd come to this point.

Trayce, over my objections to stay with her, had accompanied Janet up to Naomi's room to tend to her. Michael wanted to finish what had begun with Shaw, but Shaw had turned and left with the rest of the partygoers. Donna offered her apologies, as if on an assembly line, to everyone that would listen as they filed past her. I would've stopped to offer some words of encouragement, but I had something more pressing.

I followed Cameron, worried that he might hurt himself. The drink he'd downed in one gulp was evidence that trouble was afoot. As he staggered out back, I wondered how he was still standing. I kept my distance, not wanting to piss him off anymore than he already was. He'd sat through this reunion behind a mask, nonexistent to the person who mattered most to him. I'd lived most my life being nonexistent. To regular folk, I'm sure it was unbearable.

Cameron stopped along the path to talk to himself. I paused at the same time, ducking inside the gazebo. As I waited, I thought back to the scene I'd witnessed from this very spot the previous night.

"I can't do this! Do you see how he's looking at me?"

"Andrea, please. Do this for me. I need you just for this weekend. Cameron's harmless. He's just under a lot of stress."

"What about me, Shaw? I don't appreciate your shutting me up in there either. Your ex is lucky I didn't fuck her up with her 'high-dollar hooker' looking ass. I don't know why I agreed to this."

"Because you're a good friend and because of that big shopping spree I promised you."

"There aren't enough clothes in the world, Shaw. There's way too much drama here. Baby, I'm going back to Atlanta tonight."

Cameron continued down the path as I watched from the gazebo. Unfortunately, it also brought him to Shaw and Janet.

And where we were now . . .

Shaw released Cameron, allowing him fall on the ground. "Janet, let . . . let me talk to you," he urged.

Cameron, still far from sober, stood up and dusted himself off. He smiled wickedly at her. "What are you going to tell her, Shaw?"

"Shut up, Cam!" Shaw snarled. "I mean it."

Shaw had barely turned back to focus on Janet when she hauled off and slapped him.

Crack! His head recoiled. "Yeah, Shaw. What you got to tell me?"

I resisted the urge to get involved. The time of reckoning for the three of them was at hand.

"Shaw?" she asked again, more a plea than a demand this time.

He touched his face where the sting from her hand would remain long after. Still he didn't speak.

"Tell the bitch, Shaw," Cameron slurred.

Janet, in response, ran at Cameron. Shaw snagged her dress trail almost yanking her off her feet. She kicked her legs repeatedly until one of her shoes flew at Cameron, missing his head by an inch.

"Call me a bitch again and see what happens, punkass!" she screamed. "Say sumthin'!"

Shaw had a hell of a time as he wrestled to restrain Janet and keep her separated from Cameron. Cameron, finally succumbing to the alcohol, fell to his knees and threw up.

"See what you've done, Shaw. This is all your fault," he sobbed in between heaves.

Janet watched Cameron's pitiful display then looked at Shaw again. The grip he had on her shoulders lessened as he looked visibly concerned over our drunken classmate. Janet spoke.

"Shaw, look at me. Is what Solomon said true?"

80 Janet

"Yes," he replied.

Solomon helped me along as I labored through the hotel lobby. I was beaten, spiritually and emotionally. Unlike the physical, this pain ran long and deep. People asked me what was wrong. I didn't reply. My mind kept replaying Shaw's answer.

"Yes," he'd replied.

"Don't play. I'm serious, Shaw."

"So am I."

I didn't believe him. I didn't want to believe him. I felt warm all of a sudden. A wave of nausea overcame me, but wantonly I pressed on. "How . . . ," I tried to spit out. "How long has this been going on?"

"A while."

I unloaded on Shaw like I'd wanted to do for all these years. All that time, I imagined it would be out of anger or retribution, not hurt. I'd moved beyond the hurt of being dumped with no explanation, but had suddenly found a new one to replace it. I felt foolish and humiliated. I hit him again and again. He stepped back, blocking most of my licks.

As Shaw backed off, Cameron spoke. He was a little more coherent and wasted no time masking his animosity toward me. "She wants to know how long we've been together Shaw. Tell her."

"Shut up, Cam. I'm trying to speak to my—"

"I know you weren't going to say 'woman.' She was never that . . . never could be. Both you and I know that. And now she does too."

"When we were together, you were with *him*?"

Shaw fumbled around. "Look . . . Janet. Things are complicated."

"Complicated? I'm just finding out you're gay. You could've given me something, you selfish bastard!"

Cameron laughed hysterically. "Stupid, how's he gonna give something to you?"

All those nights of Shaw ignoring my advances and invitations, always an excuse on his lips. I believed he was saving himself for marriage and like a silly little idiot I played along. I glared at Shaw. "He knows?"

" 'Course I do. I know everything about you. I know everything he did and didn't do."

Somehow I found the strength to resist Cameron's taunts. "How could you do this to me?"

"*To you*?" Shaw responded incredulously. "You always were so selfish. There were so many times I wanted to say that."

"But you didn't. You punked out and ran to your little boyfriend instead. I don't know why I didn't see it."

"Because you were too caught up in yourself, Janet. In all honesty, there were times I wanted to come clean."

"Boy, don't you dare talk about honesty! You held me. You told me you loved me."

"I thought I did. I figured that if I told myself often

enough that things might work. You don't know how hard it is living a double life."

"I think I know a thing or two about that," I remarked. I'd taken my own hint. Without so much as another curse word or punch thrown, I turned and walked away. Shaw be damned. The war was over without another shot being fired.

Back inside the hotel, Solomon saw me about to faint and caught me.

"Thank you."

"You're welcome. I'm just here to make sure you get to your room." I made him uncomfortable, but he toughed it out. He loosened his grip once he saw I was okay.

"How long have you known?"

He danced around with the thought. "Long enough," he replied.

"Shit, you coulda told a sister."

"Would you have believed me . . . or even listened?"

I smirked at the funny little man. He didn't say much, but when he did, it made sense. "No."

"Exactly," he said as he smirked back.

"Damn. You look like shit, Janet." It was Mike's oafish ass, coming back for more. Didn't this clown know when to go home? I did look like shit though. I held my head high, trying to put the image of Cameron in Shaw's arms out of my head.

It was Solomon's turn to show emotion as Mike blocked our path. I was too weary to go around. "Move," was all he said to Mike, but he looked ready to go a few rounds. Mike ignored him and took another look at me. The sash holding my dress closed was dangling, my curls had all fallen, I smelled of sweat and dirt. I don't even want to comment on my makeup.

"What you been doin' out there, Janet? Giving lap dances? Dragging the bottom of the barrel for tips, ain'tcha?

I know Solomon ain't got no money on him. Look at his clothes." Solomon didn't get what Mike was referring to. "She's a stripper, bro," Mike said, clueing him in.

I'd had enough abuse to last a thousand lifetimes. I raised my knee up with all my might and nailed Mike right in the family jewels. He howled like a wounded bear before slowly, painfully crumbling at our feet. Tae-Bo was a mother. I was still dizzy, so Solomon helped me cross over him. We'd gotten two steps when I went back to get something off my chest.

"I'm not a stripper, you worthless slob. I'm an exotic dancer. I look better than you, could get more pussy than you, make *hella* more money, and have more class in my clit than you have in your entire body. And if I ever see you in Vegas, I guarantee you'll be parking in handi-capped spots the rest of your miserable life."

Solomon seemed amused by the entire thing. I walked back to his side and let him take my arm. I adjusted my dress and smoothed my weave.

"Now we can go."

81 Karim

Iwas sleeping peacefully until the tapping started. I turned on the lamp beside the bed and shuffled to the door. I looked through the peephole, but no one was there. The tapping kept coming. The door that connected my room to the adjoining one was where it came from.

"So much for getting some sleep around here," I muttered.

The lights were off in her room, casting her in shadows. She stayed on her side.

"Is Shauna still here?"

"No. You took care of that."

"Figured that out all on your own?"

"Yep. Sure did. You could've gotten us killed."

"You look okay."

I chuckled. "You just don't know. Look, I got a flight out in the morning and I really need to get some sleep."

"I get the brush off now. Down by that tree, I was the only thing on your lips. Shauna rocked your world that hard?"

"I'm not going to stand here and take your shit. I ain't Shaw."

"Thank God for that."

She crossed the imaginary line dividing our rooms to where I could see her. I smelled the sweat on her first. Her eyes were puffy and swollen. Her clothes looked like they'd been dragged through the dirt.

"What happened to you?"

"Life. Things have been really weird tonight. Trayce wins Ms. Marion, then we find out Coach Taylor raped her. And Naomi too. To top it off, I find out my old boy-friend was gay the entire time."

"No way. I missed all that?" She'd blown my mind with all that stuff, but I didn't know whether to believe her.

"Yep, but you were busy."

She paced around the room. I was fed up with people inspecting my *quarters*. "I told you she was gone."

"How was she? Better than me?"

"I didn't have her. Well . . . at least not like that. And I barely had you."

"Shauna's husband interrupted your party?"

"No. I stopped things before they went that far."

"Didn't look that way to me."

"It doesn't matter how it looked. It shouldn't have been going down. She was a convenient piece of ass at the wrong time. I just wanted to get back at you."

"I never did anything to you."

I looked at her like she'd OD-ed on a bottle of stupid pills.

"Something you want to say?"

"Nope. Tonight, you said enough for the both of us."

"I didn't come to argue."

"So what are you here for then? 'A *little* fun?' " I asked as I made mock quotation marks in the air. "I mean, that's what you told Shauna and Naomi I was. What was it exactly? *'When this reunion is over, so is he.'* "

She wrung her hands "I didn't mean it. I was making all that up."

"I know. You're no better than the rest of them. All the fronting and pretending."

"Like you weren't stuntin' too. Boy, please. You really like to cast judgment on people."

"Don't try to analyze me. You don't know me that well, ma."

"I do, Karim," she said. "I do because I do the same thing. You judge women by what they can do for you. I judge men by what they can do for me."

"Got something to say? Get it out."

"I'm not a show coordinator. I'm a dancer."

"In one of the shows? That's not so bad. It's a livin'."

"No. I take off my clothes for men and they pay me."

"I'll be damned. You strip." I didn't plan on it coming out like that, but I was tired and sleepy. "I didn't mean it like that."

She walked back to the door. It was mere inches, but could've been as far away as the frigid tundra of Alaska. The darkness consumed all but her legs. "I can see it in your eyes. I don't want your pity or anything. I ain't ashamed of what I do. I just needed to make things clear, Karim. I've had it with lies."

She grabbed her door to close it.

"Janet?"

"Yeah?"

"Think maybe it coulda been?"

I couldn't see her face, but imagined her smiling. "Yeah. Maybe it coulda been."

"One last question."

"Shoot."

"Do you love him?"

"Shaw?"

"No. That guy Gerald."

Silence. Long, deafening silence. No denials or questions about how I knew about him. "Maybe," she replied. "Maybe."

I closed my door after hers and waited for a few minutes before returning to bed.

I guess it was fitting. All those awful paintings of Janet I'd made, and I was never in any of them.

Heartache to heartache we stand . . .

"Hello. Anybody in here?"

Like I was really going to answer. Before they'd come in the bathroom, I was taking a good after-lunch dump. I left in the middle of my algebra test, figuring I'd get some peace and quiet. The school's cornbread always did this to me, but I loved the extra honey butter. I tried to quietly control my bowels while hoping whoever was in here with me would do their business and leave.

"Dang, somebody dropped a bomb in here," the other voice said. I listened to the two of them laugh.

The first voice I recognized as Shaw's. He was the typical jock and Marion's most popular student. He had the looks, the girl, and the physical tools to make him a lot of money after college. He ran with a group that called themselves "The Crew," a group of idiots who worshipped him and loathed everyone else.

I didn't hear anything, so I began to wonder what was going on. I listened harder for sounds of someone peeing in a urinal or something, but only heard our principal on the hallway intercom.

They must be smoking weed, I thought. I leaned over to peer through the crack in my stall door. It wasn't Michael with Shaw. Michael was way louder.

"Where were you last night? I waited at the park over an hour for your ass."

"Things came up, man." Shaw sighed. "Had to put in quality time. Janet's still pissed about that shit with Trayce."

"I am too."

"Don't start. You sound just like Janet."

"Nobody made you fuck that girl. Y'all some assholes for runnin' that train on her."

"Man, you don't know how it is being me. People be puttin' pressure on a brother. I'm there with my boys 'n' shit."

"I thought I was your boy."

"Not like that. Nigga, you know what I mean. What do you expect me to do? You'd understand if you were—"

"Popular? What does that shit get you? Nothin' but headaches. Then you want to come to me complainin'. Popularity don't make you feel like I do."

"Yeah, but it's gonna help me get up outta here. Some boosters from Clemson called the house yesterday."

"I'm going to Georgia Tech," the other speaker said as if pouting.

"Don't start. I hate when you do that shit, man."

I still couldn't see who Shaw was talking to. His back was blocking my view. I leaned over a little more . . . and slipped off the toilet. I banged into the stall door and tumbled onto the nasty floor. Two sets of feet scrambled out of the bathroom before I could get my pants up.

I made it out of the bathroom right behind them, not knowing what or who I'd see. I saw Shaw as he rounded the corner down the hall, but didn't see anyone with him. I looked down the hall in the opposite direction.

The only person there was Cameron, who was calmly digging in his wall locker. Whoever Shaw had been talking to was gone. Nobody talked to me, and they wouldn't have believed me if I told them anyway. I looked at my watch and hurried back to algebra class.

83 Trayce

Shauna never returned to their room, but Naomi's family showed after calling them. Now that Naomi's ordeal was public, the same mother she had told me about was threatening to sue a school that no longer existed. Sad as it appeared she was only interested in monetary gain rather than her daughter's fragile mental state. I left Naomi my number and took my leave.

When I made it back to my room, I found Solomon in the chair about to drift off to sleep.

I gently pushed the door shut. "Hey."

He rubbed his eyes. "You were with Naomi this entire time?" he whispered. Justine had crawled beneath the covers on my bed. She slept like a little angel with my tiara atop her head. I smiled.

"I hope you don't mind. She wanted to try it on."

"Please. She can keep it. It makes her look like the little princess she is."

He nodded. "I agree. I'm just glad the queen has returned." He arose from his chair and stretched. Jordan, who had fallen asleep on the floor at the foot of the bed, stirred. The video game controller was still in his hand. He gave one of those stares as if sleepwalking, then closed his eyes again. "We talked for a little while before they fell asleep. This was the best night they've had in a long time. I guess I should be getting them home now."

"Stay. Please. I insist. It's too late to take those kids out."

He glanced at them asleep then gave in. I watched him strain to lug his son off the floor and into the bed. After that he came over and kissed me. "How are your hands?" he asked as he inspected them.

"Better. I just want to get out of these clothes, take a nice hot bath and get some rest. I'm going see my mother after I check out and don't want her to see these crop circles under my eyes."

He grinned. "I've got just what you need then." Solomon had me take a seat on the sofa. He planted another, more sensual kiss on me, then made sure his kids were asleep before running in the bathroom. "Stay out here until I come get you."

I let my shoes fall to the carpet and stretched my toes out. I liked heels, but not for as long as I'd worn them. Sounds of things clanking together piqued my curiosity. Under the bathroom door, I saw the light dim.

"What are you doing in there?"

"Come in and find out," he taunted.

I kneaded the soreness out of my calves, then pulled myself off the sofa. I turned the knob and pushed the door open. The flicker of candlelight and sweet smell of jasmine jarred my senses to attention. The bath overflowed with bubbles and tiny candles littered the vanity. He was pouring a bottle of wine into two glasses.

"Congratulations, Ms. Marion."

"Solomon, this is so beautiful," I gushed. I'd never had a man make me feel so special. "How?"

"First off, I owe Justine another bottle of her foaming body wash. At least Linda packed something worthwhile. And I kind of 'borrowed' the candles and wine from the ballroom tonight," he admitted. "They won't miss them. Your night was messed up so I wanted to make things up to you. I was going to do this out there in the room, but the kids . . ."

"I know. This is much more intimate and romantic anyway."

He shrugged. "Besides, this is where everything started. Our one-day anniversary."

"You're really trying to make me fall in love with you."

Solomon said in one of his deep, serious tones, "Lock the door."

He gave me my glass of wine and then slowly, caringly removed my clothes. He took my hand and led me to the bathtub. I closed my eyes and sipped my wine, letting the bubbles soothe and relieve me.

"Are you getting in?" I asked.

"We'll have time for that," he answered. "But tonight this is for you."

Solomon tugged a washcloth free from the towel rack. With his glass of wine in his other hand, he proceeded to bath me. From the tip of my toes to the top of my neck, I was pampered like no other. It took all my control, as well as respect for his children on the other side of the door, to keep me from pulling him into the water with me. It was then that I figured out why Linda unloaded Justine and Jordan tonight. She still had feelings for Solomon, but would never admit it to him. It's something a woman would know. He may have been broke and not up to her expectations, but he was rich with love. *You don't know what you miss until it's gone*, I lazily repeated inside my head with each stroke of Solomon's hand. The wine was really good.

I spent the rest of the night on the sofa sleeper in Solomon's arms. The kids slept soundly in the bed nearby. As I drifted to sleep, I shed a tear wondering what my own children would be like . . . if I could have them.

84 Janet

"*Room service.*"

"I didn't order any damn room service. Send it back." At 3 A.M. I was not in the mood.

"Ma'am," the guy said with the most annoying twang I'd ever heard. "It has your room number and your name on the order. I can send it back, but I need you to sign something so I don't get in trouble. I got four mouths to feed and can't afford to have this taken outta my check."

I decided to get up and answer it, thinking somebody like Shauna had pulled a prank to get back at me. I wasn't going to get any sleep anyway. When daylight hit, I'd be on my way back to Vegas. I was never looking back again. It was crazy that I'd squandered my relationship with Gerald. With the buzz of this weekend wearing off, I was realizing how much I missed him. I at least hoped he was happy now that I'd set him free.

"Ma'am?" the hick at the door called out.

"Hold the fuck up!"

I put on my robe and hurried to the door. Management was going to hear about this.

I looked at the door that connected my room to Karim's and a thought hit me. I waited.

"Ma'am, are you still there? I really need to get back downstairs."

I smiled upon realizing the voice was phony. Maybe Karim had reconsidered things and had come up with another crazy scheme to win me over. That would be just like him, I thought. Was there another limo waiting? I wouldn't know unless I opened the door.

"This better be good."

An older white man in a tuxedo greeted me. The Bloody Mary in his hand was almost empty and it didn't look like he needed a refill.

"What the fuck do you want?"

"Eeew, you got a mouth on you, missy. He was right, though. You sho' is pretty."

I pulled my robe closed out of disgust. "What are you talking about?"

"He's talking about his drinking buddy," said the figure that was hiding on the side. "Me."

He hadn't shaved in days. I liked him like that. An olive-colored shirt with cut-off sleeves exposed those sinewy arms. He wore those damn camouflage pants he'd promised he had thrown away. I smiled.

"You gonna be okay, buddy?"

"Yeah, I think I got this, Ennis."

"If what you told me about you and this gal here is true, you got yourself a great country song. Think about it." Gerald's new best friend gave him some dap then wandered off in search of a new drinking buddy.

"What did you tell him about us? And what are you doing here?"

"Besides having a few drinks with him down at the bar . . . Looking for you."

"Wait. Wait," I said. I put my hands up to keep him from advancing. "I didn't tell you where I was."

"Yeah, *thanks*. Luckily, I remembered some of the invitation. Do you know how many calls I had to make to find this place?"

I felt faint from the strain of everything catching up with me. I caught myself in the doorway so he wouldn't notice. "You came all the way out here for me? The way I treated you?"

He flashed those pretty teeth. "What's wrong? You look disappointed."

"Maybe in myself. I'm just a little shocked, 's all."

"Don't be."

He came closer. I turned my head away from his kiss. He tried to enter my room, but I kept my arm barred. With his path blocked, he looked at me.

"Do you have company?"

"No. Nobody would want to be with me."

"That's not the beautiful, confident woman I know."

"You're right. It isn't. I'm feeling a little ugly right now."

"Let me help you find your prettiness."

I laughed. My arm came down from the doorway. "I've been so awful to you, Gerald."

"And I still came back."

He took his thumb and wiped the single tear by my eye. Must've been allergies. I leaned my head on his shoulder and we rocked back and forth.

"I came back for some clothes and got your message."

"I didn't say anything."

"You said enough to make me want to try one more time."

"But you didn't call back. I thought . . ."

"I'm an artist, Janet. I needed to see you face to face, like this. A phone's too easy to hide behind. I love you. I hate your job, but I love you. And I don't think it would be living without you."

We retreated inside my suite and closed the door. I would echo his sentiments several times before the sun came up.

I weaved through the slow country traffic Sunday morning and floored my XLR back to the hotel.

"I hate when you drive like this," Gerald remarked as he stiff-armed himself in place.

"I just need to drop this off then we can go, baby."

I ran inside past the concierge who was assisting my classmates with their departures. I carefully placed my package on the counter. The front desk clerk's smile faded when I gave him my instructions.

Gerald was fumbling with the radio controls when I came out.

"Done?"

I swatted his fingers away and put on my Whitney again. "How Will I Know?" began playing and I turned it up. I turned to Gerald and adjusted my sunglasses. "Yep. Now we can go."

I smiled as I put the car in drive and spun out.

85 Karim

I tried not to listen, but I heard. I turned up my music, but couldn't turn off my imagination. And I was gifted with a really vivid, visual one. If I'd had a car, I would've driven off a cliff. If I'd had a rope, I might've hung myself. Instead, I stuck around, bearing the sound of another man putting it to Janet. More painful were the words she said . . . no, screamed. I took some solace that I could've still had her, but I knew it would never be how I'd imagined or wanted for so long.

I fell asleep when the sounds ended, letting my delirious mind process all of the weekend's events. I was taking Janet's hand and cursing her at the same time. I was under the tree again, simultaneously experiencing the pleasure of Janet against me and tasting the pain of Shauna's teeth raking across my dick. The harsh ring of the phone jolted me out of the last disturbing image.

It was the front desk. I'd overslept, but was smart enough to set up a wake-up call. The limo was going to be downstairs shortly for the long drive back to Charlotte airport.

After a quick rejuvenating shower, I hurriedly grabbed my bags and rushed downstairs. As I waited in the lobby checkout line, I saw Trayce and Solomon as they left the hotel. I caught their attention and gave them a wave. There were two kids in between them, each holding a hand. Naomi then came over to Trayce and gave her a parting hug.

"What the hell did I miss last night?" I wondered aloud as I was called next in line.

The clerk did his normal routine, asking me how was my stay, blah, blah, blah. I put on my courtesy smile and answered in kind. As he pulled my name up on his monitor, he hesitated. I knew my credit card was good and was about to start a stink. He excused himself and went in back. I was checking my watch when he returned. The scent hit my nose first, causing me to break into a smile. I looked around before my eyes came to rest on the box he held in his hand.

"A woman left this for you, sir. A very pretty woman." He winked. "She said I better not touch it or she would come back and 'slap me silly'."

I took the box of piping hot Krispy Kreme donuts from him and burst out laughing. In pen, she'd hastily written,

Sweets for the sweet. Thanks for kickin' it with me.
Love you, carrot top.— J.

"You're still my angel," I mumbled, all the while smiling.

We'd left Gaffney and were passing near familiar sites. I asked the driver if he knew the area then gave him another set of directions.

"Stop right here," I instructed.

This was my first time seeing Marion High in the light

of day since leaving all those years ago. Its walls were weathered; grass was growing wild in the few spots unclaimed by concrete. The Mighty Eagle sign was worn, faded and barely discernible. I looked at the chain link fence I'd scaled with Janet only two nights ago and smiled.

I got out of the limo for a better look. I reached into my pocket and retrieved my phone. I went back to the message I'd saved from my non-VIP number and listened. I hit the button to return the call. A flock of birds flew in formation overhead, casting shadows before the morning sun.

It rang as if no one would answer, then somebody picked up.

"Jaquel? Hey, it's me. Karim."

"I'm fine. Look, sorry I left you hanging. I'm in South Carolina."

"No. No video." I laughed. "Just taking care of some business. Uh huh. Uh huh."

"Look . . . would you like to go out when I get home?"

I blushed at her response. I reached down for a quick equipment check and felt my still wounded dick. I chuckled. "No. Just talk. *Furreal*. Y'know, get to know each other. Maybe a carriage ride through Central Park or something. Maybe I'll try to cook for you."

She laughed, but commented on how sweet I sounded.

"Yeah, I want to take it slow, ma. Get to know ya. And let you get to know me."

I hung up the phone and told the limo driver to go. As we turned back onto the highway, I left behind the crumbling high school, knowing it would be leveled soon. I gulped down another one of my donuts and licked the glaze off my fingers.

86 Solomon

Linda had called for Jordan and Justine. Trayce calmed me down, telling me not to put my children through a big argument with their mother. She followed me in her rental car, but parked down the street while I went inside.

Trayce had a few days before she was to return to Chicago, but needed to talk to her mother. She followed me over to my place, then I caught a ride to the retirement home with her. Just as at the reunion, I promised to be by her side.

She turned the car off. I rubbed her shoulders, trying to lift her spirits. "You sure you're ready for this?"

"No. But after everything that's happened, I have to tell her. It'll break her heart, but I can't lie to her anymore. I can't. My therapist told me this day would come and that I'd know when the time was right."

"I got your back."

"I know," she commented, her head resting on the steering wheel. She sighed. Her eyes remained closed. Then she spoke again. "Where do you want this to go, Solomon?"

"I know that I want a future with you, if that's what you're asking."

She raised an eyebrow and looked at me. "I need you to be as honest as possible with me because I'm going to be as honest as possible with you."

"I mean what I say."

Her voice trailed off, almost a whisper. I watched her bottom lip quiver. "I can't have kids."

I was speechless and she could tell.

"Not even my therapist knows about this. I had a miscarriage in high school."

"Coach Taylor?"

"No," she sobbed. "It was after . . . that party. Shaw 'n'em. I didn't know I was pregnant until I went to the hospital for bleeding. Things weren't right. There were problems. In all honesty, I didn't know who the father was. I lied and told my mother it was Shaw's. I thought it would be easier saying that than what really happened at the party. I was so embarrassed. My mother was devastated. I begged her on hands and knees not to confront him. I said he didn't know and had his future . . . our future ahead of us. I lied again. I pretended . . . he liked me. Just recited the same junk he said to get me to the party that night. I couldn't stand for there to be another scene. I couldn't take it."

"I don't know what to say."

"There's nothing to say. Just be here for me when I come back." She unfastened her seatbelt and opened the car door. I did the same.

"No, stay in the car. I'll be right back."

I exited then went around. "I've stood by too much of my life on the outside, Trayce. Let me in."

The elderly woman with brownish hair was setting up

a chess board in the courtyard when we found her. She hadn't noticed her daughter yet. Trayce looked at me as I put my hand on her shoulder. I nodded. We walked over together.

Her mother clapped her hands with excitement when she saw Trayce. Her daughter was back. She was home and they were reunited. They embraced for a long time, tears flowing down both their faces.

"Baby, oh it's so good to see you," she proclaimed. "Did you have a good time at your reunion?"

Trayce looked like she was wavering, skating on that edge, not sure of what to do. I could've stood around and watched. I came closer and took her hand instead.

"Momma, I have something to tell you," she said.

Sticks & Stones

Discussion Questions

1. What are your thoughts of Trayce's ordeal? Would you have returned to your class reunion?

2. Which of the four main characters did you empathize with the most?

3. Was there another character with whom you felt you had more in common?

4. How did Solomon's character strike you? If in his predicament, would you have gone about things differently? How?

5. What was your favorite scene?

6. What do you feel were key turning points in the story with regards to each of the four?

7. What do you think of some of the other classmates such as Shauna, Naomi, Cameron, or Michael?

8. Did you ever figure out where the reunion took place?

9. Do you feel Janet should have stayed with Gerald? Why or why not?

10. Were you surprised by Shaw's secret?

11. What are your thoughts about Shaw's role in Trayce's torment?

12. How do you feel this story compares to previous works by the author?

13. What lessons did you take from *Sticks & Stones*?

14. How do you feel the title, *Sticks & Stones*, fits the story?

15. Which character do you feel emerged different or changed the most at the end?

16. What the most shocking incident from your class reunion?